LOVE UNBROKEN

A DIAMOND CREEK, ALASKA NOVEL

J.H. CROIX

DEDICATION

My beloved dogs who put up with one-handed petting when I'm writing. Drumroll yet again for my husband who makes me laugh more than anyone.

Sign up for my newsletter for information on new releases & get a FREE copy of one of my books!

http://jhcroixauthor.com/subscribe/

Follow me!
jhcroix@jhcroix.com
https://amazon.com/author/jhcroix
https://www.bookbub.com/authors/j-h-croix
https://www.facebook.com/jhcroix

CHAPTER 1

*E*mma closed the back of her truck after putting a cooler inside and leaned against the side. It was just past five in the morning, and she was waiting for her friend Susie to meet her. She glanced at her tiny cabin for a long moment. Just looking at it made her smile. It was tiny and whimsical – a cedar sided A-frame with a bright green roof and purple trim, complete with a purple star at the point of the A-frame. It sat in a small open area amongst spruce and alder. The hill tumbled down behind it, offering a wide-open view of Kachemak Bay. She'd been in Diamond Creek, Alaska for almost three years.

The sun was rising behind the mountains across the bay, streaks of gold and pink reaching into the sky and filtering through the wispy clouds that sat above the mountains this morning. The air was cool and crisp, typical for an Alaskan summer morning. When the sun was high, the chill would dissipate. A faded blue Subaru pulled into the driveway. Susie climbed out of her car, grabbed some fishing gear and walked to Emma's truck.

"Morning! Sorry I'm late," Susie said. Emma reached over and took a fishing rod out of Susie's hands.

Susie was her sister's best friend and had become a dear friend to Emma. Emma couldn't help but smile at Susie. She was a petite bundle of energy and enthusiasm. Susie's head almost reached Emma's shoulder as she barely topped five feet, and Emma was just shy of six feet. Susie had warm brown eyes and unruly brown curls, which were pulled back into a ponytail this morning.

Emma lifted the window to the back of her truck and placed Susie's gear in the back. "You're not late. We said sometime before five fifteen. How's it going?" Emma asked.

Susie tossed her bag in the truck and looked over with a grin. "I'm ready to catch some fish! Promise we can get coffee at Red Truck on the way by though."

Emma nodded. "Of course. How could we not?"

* * *

"OKAY, so why are we going to Homer to fish when we could just as easily fish in Diamond Creek?" Emma asked from the backseat. She and Susie had met her sister Hannah at the harbor parking lot for the drive to Homer. Emma took a sip of her coffee, savoring the rich flavor.

"Because Homer has the Fishing Hole," Susie said as if that explained everything.

"What's the big deal with the Fishing Hole?" Emma asked in return.

Hannah turned to look over her shoulder from the passenger seat. "It's a man-made fishing hole that's stocked with kings, pinks and silvers. It's a fishing dream if you want to stock up on salmon. That's why we're going. It's not quite as fun as dipnetting, but it's close."

Emma nodded, thinking for a moment. She'd quickly learned that the words king, pink, red and silver related primarily to salmon in Alaska. Though she'd been in Alaska several years now, she'd yet to enjoy every possible fishing or outdoor activity because the options were extensive. "So how come every town doesn't have a fishing hole?"

Susie and Hannah shrugged in unison. "Who knows? Maybe because Homer has an ideal spot. The Homer Spit is an easy place to do what they did. It sticks so far out into the bay. There's nothing like it anywhere else in Alaska. So when we want to get a jumpstart on salmon, we go to Homer. Dipnetting fills the rest of the freezer after that."

As Susie drove and kept chatting with Hannah, Emma watched the landscape roll by. Homer was roughly an hour south of Diamond Creek. Homer was another tourist draw in Alaska, dubbed the Halibut Capital of the World. Emma was accustomed to the jaw-dropping views in Alaska, but had yet to lose her amazement. The highway hugged the coastline with view after view of mountains, a few glaciers and beautiful ocean vistas. Occasionally, an eagle or moose would make an appearance. Today, they'd already driven by a mother moose and her calf nibbling on alders by the road.

Not much later, Emma lugged a cooler in one hand with a fishing pole in the other. While she'd become proficient at fishing, she was by no means an expert. She hadn't even had to buy her own equipment because Hannah's husband and his two brothers ran a guide business. They geared her up the first summer she arrived. The Fishing Hole on the Homer Spit was a sight to behold. For starters, the Homer Spit was a narrow 'spit' of land that jutted four and a half miles into Kachemak Bay. The road on the Homer Spit was the longest road into ocean waters in the world. Driving out onto the Spit felt like driving on a bridge, except that it was a narrow expanse of land. Arriving at the Fishing Hole, Emma was startled at how busy it was. Parking was a competitive sport. Every inch of shoreline that surrounded the Fishing Hole was filled with people.

Emma had no idea how they'd manage to find a place to fish, but she gamely followed Susie and Hannah. As they approached the shoreline, Emma discovered that space was to be had among the constant shifting of the crowd. In minutes, she geared up in her waders and dropped a lure in the water. The next hour passed in a blur. According to Susie and Hannah, silver salmon were their goal for today and between them, they caught two apiece in short order.

Emma lifted her fishing rod to cast again and felt a tug on the line. She froze.

"Hey! That's my hat!"

Emma turned, scanning the cluster nearby to find the source of the voice. Her eyes landed on a small boy with stick straight brown hair, holding a baseball hat that appeared to be attached to her fishing lure. She was relieved to see that he was laughing and looking up at a man beside him, so she assumed he wasn't hurt. She walked over, carrying her fishing pole.

"Hey there, I think I may be the one that caught your hat," Emma said with a smile.

The little boy tilted his head back to look up at her. Emma looked down into his eyes, a rich brown with gold flecks.

"Dad, she caught my hat!" the boy said, almost gleefully. He seemed overjoyed at the accident. Emma was just relieved he hadn't been hurt.

The man the boy spoke to had his back to them when Emma walked over. He turned, and Emma's heart leapt. The boy's father was tall with dark hair flecked with silver and had the same chocolate brown eyes as his son. When he looked down at his son, a grin flashed across his face. When he saw Emma, his gaze shifted quickly to a more serious, almost austere look. His features were strong and sharp, his eyes intelligent and probing. Emma wished for his smile to return. With those eyes and that smile, all she felt was a primal pull. Her stomach fluttering and pulse skittering, she didn't speak.

Befuddled, it took Emma a moment to realize that she was staring and hadn't said a word. The man, whose mere presence had reached into the center of her and grabbed hold, walked closer and held out his hand. "Hello there, I'm Trey."

Emma's hand moved of its own accord. She thought for sure anyone nearby would see the sparks that struck when he clasped her hand, but no one appeared to notice. "I'm Emma," she replied.

Trey gave her hand a firm shake, holding on perhaps a moment too long, his eyes questioning.

"Looks like you caught Stuart's hat," he said when she didn't say anything else.

Emma finally brought her attention to the moment though her heart was beating so hard she worried he might be able to hear it. "I guess I did. I'm sorry. I was trying to cast carefully."

Stuart looked up from fiddling with the fishing hook caught in his baseball hat. "There's way lots of people!"

Trey's smile returned. Emma realized she finally understood what it meant to swoon because she feared she might just do that. She had to pull herself together and *now*.

Trey glanced down at Stuart. "How about you hand me that hat? Don't want you catching your fingers on the hook," he said.

Stuart handed the hat over, immediately looking back up at Emma. "Have you ever caught a hat before?" he asked, his smile made more endearing by the missing tooth in front.

"Not that I know of. I'm just glad your hat is all I caught."

"No harm done. I'd bet something that's not a fish gets hooked here every day. It's so crowded," Trey said. He glanced up as he finished working the hook out of the hat. "There you go," he said, handing the lure back to Emma.

His fingers brushed hers, the barest touch eliciting another jolt within Emma. She felt hot all over, a blush heating her as it bloomed on her neck and face.

She didn't want to walk away and had no idea what to say. For a second, she thought she saw an answering flare in Trey's eyes, but he shuttered it quickly, that serious look returning.

"Thank you," Emma finally said.

Silence lengthened between them, broken by Stuart's enthusiastic voice. "Dad, can I catch one more fish before we go?" he asked. He walked to the small cooler nearby and peered into it.

Trey held Emma's gaze for another moment before finally breaking away, glancing over his shoulder toward Stuart. "One more and that's it," he replied.

Turning back to Emma, his lips quirked in an almost smile. "Stuart loves to fish. He'd stay here all day every day if I let him."

Emma nodded politely, the wheels of her mind turning, wondering who Stuart's mother was, wanting desperately to know more about Trey and realizing she needed to get a grip. She looked back up into Trey's eyes. Her blush just wouldn't quit. She forced herself to speak. "Well, nice to meet you. Glad Stuart's hat is okay." Lifting her hand in a polite wave, she started to walk away.

Trey's voice halted her steps. "Nice to meet you too."

Emma turned back, that flare she thought she'd seen in Trey's eyes definitely there this time, his eyes darker and brighter. Flustered, her words stumbled. "Oh...okay." She turned away, almost running back to where Susie and Hannah were fishing.

Her face still flushed, Emma quickly got her line back in the water, appreciating the bustle around her.

"So you hooked Stuart Holden's hat, huh?" Susie asked. Susie was situated on the shore between Emma and Hannah.

"Sure did. It was an accident—obviously," Emma replied.

"Stuart's dad is one of the best pilots around. He runs a wilderness flightseeing business and also has a law practice on the side," Susie said with a wink.

"Oh god, no. He's a lawyer?"

Susie gave her an odd look. "Yeah, not sure why that's a bad thing. They moved to Diamond Creek about a year after you did. I don't know Trey well, just as an acquaintance. Even though they've lived in Diamond Creek for a while now, he's not out and about much."

"I'm glad my hook only landed in Stuart's hat," Emma said, her blush returning just thinking about Trey.

Emma felt Susie look toward her. She hoped Susie didn't notice how flushed she was.

"Wow, you are blushing. What does that mean?" Susie asked slyly.

Emma tried and failed to un-blush, which only flustered her more.

"I think you might have noticed that Trey's a bit handsome. Trust me, you're not the only one. He's widowed and has his share of women drooling over him. I mean, he's hot, he's a pilot, and he's prime marrying age at forty. Rumor is that he moved to Diamond Creek to start his flightseeing tours because he's a single dad now and needed more time with his son. I guess he used to be pretty busy doing the lawyer thing in Anchorage. The only reason you haven't heard about him is that he's not seen in public enough to blip on the gossip radar," Susie said with a chuckle.

Emma heard only that Trey was widowed and her mind was off to the races, prodded by the undeniable pull she felt toward him. She didn't even notice she hadn't bothered to respond to Susie.

"Hannah, your sister's gone gaga over Trey Holden," Susie said, leaning in front of Emma to catch Hannah's attention.

Hannah was busy reeling in another silver salmon and glanced over with a wide smile. "You don't say?"

"Oh my god, Susie. I met the man for maybe three minutes. I will admit he's handsome, but I'm not gaga," Emma retorted.

"Coulda fooled me. As soon as I told you he was widowed, you were in fantasyland over there."

Emma's blush deepened. After a moment, she gave in and laughed. "Think whatever you want," she remarked.

Susie's curls shook with her laughter. Hannah glanced over to Emma as she placed the silver salmon she'd caught in their cooler. "Good luck. Once Susie's on the scent, she's hard to shake. If you want her to stay out of your business, you'd better play your cards close."

Emma shrugged. "It's okay. I can deal with nosy friends. Just don't go and embarrass me in front of him," she warned.

"Fat chance of that. Like I said, he's not around much. If you do have the hots for him, you have your work cut out for you," Susie replied. Her gaze sobered. "I don't think I've ever seen Trey without Stuart at his side. I don't know for sure, but I heard his wife died from some heart problem. He doesn't seem too interested in a relationship."

Emma absorbed the information Susie provided and looked over to where Trey and Stuart were standing. He was bending over to help Stuart untangle his fishing line. Susie let her off the hook from further teasing, and Emma found herself strangely disappointed because she didn't get to hear more about Trey.

Within the hour, they were jostling for space at the cleaning tables. Before they headed home to Diamond Creek, she got one more view of Trey when she saw him walking with Stuart, Stuart's small hand clasped in one of his hands and a cooler in the other. The sparks he elicited were so strong she couldn't ignore them. She wondered if she'd completely lost her mind. At thirty-four, she'd written off any chance of a relationship after her first marriage ended, which had been nothing short of a disaster. She hadn't counted on anyone making her second guess herself.

Emma gestured for Susie to walk into the cabin first. Susie had persuaded her to take some of her mother's extra zucchini and insisted she needed to get it out of her car today. Emma's cat, Sula, whom she had gotten from the local shelter, slipped in the door with them, sashaying around their feet and rubbing against Emma's legs. Sula was a small, but feisty cat. She was black and white, her fur soft and luxurious. Susie plunked the zucchini on the counter and gave Sula a quick pet while Emma shifted items around in her freezer to fit today's salmon catch. The inside of the cabin was open and bright. The downstairs consisted of an open living room and kitchen area with a bathroom to the back. The front wall was nothing but windows, a great feature in the long Alaskan winters. A spiral staircase led upstairs, which included a loft area that was furnished with a desk, two reading chairs, and built-in bookshelves lining the walls. A door upstairs led to the single bedroom. A small deck overlooked the bay in the back.

"So you said you had a plan for all this?" Emma asked, gesturing to the zucchini Susie was already washing in the sink.

"You get to choose. We shred it in a food processor, or we just slice it up. Either way, we freeze it. What's your preference?"

Emma shrugged. Sula leapt softly onto one of the stools by the counter between the kitchen and living room and looked solemnly at Emma before she began cleaning her feet.

Susie's ponytail came loose when she tilted her head to the side, rolling her eyes. "You have to have an opinion. Come to think of it, you hardly ever seem to have an opinion. Have I mentioned that before?" Susie asked with a knowing smile.

Emma returned Susie's eye roll. "You have, in fact, pointed that out. I would argue I do have opinions, but I'm just not as outspoken as you. I mean, you're...you."

"Well, duh. Of course, I'm me. And I know most people would consider me outspoken. I'm just saying that unless someone prods you into it, you don't offer your opinion." Susie said with a shrug.

Susie was right, and Emma knew it. What she didn't want to get into was that she'd developed the habit of keeping her thoughts and opinions to herself when she'd been married. It was just easier that way. Rather than getting into that with Susie, Emma thought for a moment about what she wanted to do with the zucchini.

"Shred it," she said firmly. "My mom used to make casseroles with it like that."

"And I can give you my mom's awesome zucchini bread recipe. Where's your food processor?" Susie asked, immediately on task.

A few hours later, Emma sat on her back deck and watched the sun set over Kachemak Bay. Susie had helped her get the zucchini shredded and ready to freeze before taking off. The sun was falling in the long, slow slide of summer sunsets in Alaska. It was going on nine at night and the light was just beginning to fade. The mountains across the bay were darkening as the pink orb of the sun slid behind them —lavender, pink and gold rays arced into the sky. Diamond Creek was a small town in Southcentral Alaska on the Kenai Peninsula. The town was situated on the shores of Kachemak Bay, one of Alaska's most treasured coastal areas. It was famous for its breathtaking beauty, which included ocean views, mountains on all sides, glaciers, and volcanoes in the distance. Mount Augustine was the lone volcano that sat beyond the entrance to Kachemak Bay in Cook Inlet, the long inlet that stretched inland from the Pacific Ocean to Anchorage.

Along with its beauty, Kachemak Bay and Diamond Creek offered world-class fishing and hunting, which drew tourists from all over the world. What could have been a quiet, middle of nowhere town had phenomenal restaurants, art galleries and a busy social life. Year-round residents were tight-knit. Emma had been welcomed into the community of Diamond Creek, her acceptance eased by her connection to Hannah who'd grown up here.

Emma took a last look at the view. She was still

adjusting to the joy of not feeling tied up in knots inside, which is how she'd felt for most of her marriage—the marriage that had thankfully ended before she moved to Alaska. The sense of home and freedom she felt here was such a blessing it over-whelmed her at times. When she walked the spiral staircase into the loft, Sula was seated on the railing and leapt down to follow her into the bedroom.

CHAPTER 2

hree years prior

No one ever told you that you could make stupid decisions when your mind and heart were screaming at you every step of the way. That's what Emma thought as she stood with her back to the locked bathroom door, flinching with each strike of a fist against the door.

"Stupid bitch! Open the damn door, or I'll break it down!"

Miracle of all miracles, the bathroom door was fairly sturdy and had a decent lock. Despite Greg pounding on the door for a solid five minutes and trying to wrench it open, the door held its ground. He gave up and left the apartment, slamming the front door on his way out. Emma crept to the window, remaining in the shadows, and cautiously looked out to the parking lot.

She watched Greg shift from the person he was inside the privacy of their home to his public persona as he offered to help a neighbor carry groceries inside. Nausea welled. She was disgusted with his façade and more disgusted with herself for staying with him as long as she had. She waited, her breath quiet and slow, barely moving, until he got into his car and drove away. He was most likely headed to one of his preferred bars where he would drink and send a series of texts to her. The texts would start angry and attacking, shift to apologetic and then syrupy sweet. He'd come home drunk and fall into bed. She would lie on the far side of the bed and wish herself away, wondering night after night just how she ended up here.

Tonight was different though. After Emma was certain Greg was gone, she slipped out of the bathroom, moving quickly and quietly. Within minutes, she walked outside with a small duffel bag that contained all that she could carry with her from this life. The drive to the Boston airport was several hours away. She and Greg lived in western Connecticut, but she'd decided on Boston because Greg wasn't that creative. If he tried to find her trail, he'd start at Bradley International Airport in Hartford and then perhaps New York. Pushing further north would hopefully throw him off. Roughly two hours into her drive, she exited off of the highway in Massachusetts and turned into the used car dealership she'd visited last week. They'd already drawn up the paperwork to purchase her car.

Emma had to give the dealership points for efficiency. Inside of another fifteen minutes, she was walking outside, her old car no longer hers. With a car rental place another block away, she drove away in a rental car, trying and failing to push thoughts of Greg out of her mind. When they'd met, she'd fallen for the charming, solicitous man he'd seemed. The first few months of their relationship had been marred by a few of his explosive episodes of anger, though he never touched her. It was only after she moved in with him that he became violent. She'd become the master at hiding bruises. Although, and this is the part that she hated to contemplate, Greg was adept at *not* hitting her in obvious places. He never struck her face.

Emma had been married to Greg for over two years now. She'd never imagined that she could feel so isolated from her family, but the unease her parents gave off when they visited was strong and pushed her further into herself. Greg had family in Connecticut, so she'd moved with him, too far away from her parents in North Carolina. Prior to her relationship with Greg, Emma had been close to her parents. No matter how hard she tried to stop it, Greg managed to chip away at her connection to them. There was always one reason after another why it wasn't a good time to visit. He interrupted her calls with them, usually for innocuous reasons.

Emma had always felt lucky when it came to parents. She had known for as long as she could remember that she was adopted and knew this made her special. She had no recollection of how her parents originally told her she was adopted, but she'd turned it into a fairy tale—that she'd been chosen by them. And they'd been amazing parents, always supportive. Until Greg. Now she felt anxious calling them, worried they judged her, worried they knew what was really happening with Greg. She also knew that Greg would likely try to find her if she went to them just now, so going there wasn't an option.

Out of the blue, she'd finally dug up the information on her biological family that her parents had given her years ago and posted on an online forum. A few weeks ago, she'd gotten a response from a woman named Hannah who might be her biological sister—in Alaska of all places. This possible link from so far away was a doorway out of her situation. Hope blossomed in the barren soil of her heart. Though she wondered every other minute if she was crazy and if she could pull it off, she booked the ticket to Alaska. As the plane lifted into the sky, Emma felt free in a way she hadn't in years.

CHAPTER 3

*E*mma quickly typed up a note from her last session. She was a therapist at a local community mental health program, Kachemak Bay Counseling. When she'd decided to move to Diamond Creek, she'd worried about how she'd find work in her field. She had a graduate degree in social work and had worked in various positions as a clinical therapist. Her training made her experience with Greg even more shameful for her. She should have known better, or that's what she told herself over and over.

She was finally reaching a place of acceptance that her personal experience wasn't unusual and wasn't her fault. Domestic violence had bedeviled researchers, treatment providers, courts and law enforcement for years because it crossed every imaginable social boundary. Being an educated woman with actual training around domestic violence didn't help her when she became a victim. She was merely another statistic. Rich, poor, middle class, every color of skin, every culture, every religion, every city, town, state, country, continent and more had victims, over-whelmingly women. Despite the massive social problem domestic violence was, society still didn't have a reliable way to prevent it, to effectively support victims and keep them safe, or to effectively prevent perpetrators from repeating the pattern. A history of domestic violence often traversed through multiple generations of families—perpetrators and victims.

Emma abruptly stood from her desk, wondering if she'd ever stop reciting statistics about domestic violence to herself. She often told herself to treat herself the same way she'd treat a client. She'd tell them it wasn't their fault, that this was how domestic violence happened, it slipped into one's life before they saw it coming, the hints were only obvious after the fact, and most of all, they shouldn't blame themselves because it wasn't their fault they gave someone the benefit of the doubt.

Once again, she forced her thoughts back to this moment. Just in time because her phone beeped, the receptionist letting her know her client had arrived. Moments later, a teenage girl named Stella Walsh slouched in the corner of the small couch in Emma's office. Emma sat across from her in a chair, a coffee table between them. Stella had been coming to see her for about six months now. She was a bit like a cactus at first, all bristle and prickle. If Emma touched on something too close for comfort, Stella would lash out. These days, Stella was only cranky for a few minutes, the façade a coat she needed a few minutes to shed. After that, it was all Emma could do to get a word in edgewise. Like so many troubled adolescents, Stella desperately needed to feel like someone was listening to her, like what she had to say mattered.

With the hubbub around evidence-based treatments, Emma found time and again that the power of listening without judgment could be immensely healing and was often the most powerful thing she could offer clients.

"So do you think I should try out for that recital?" Stella asked, an abrupt shift in topic. A moment ago, she'd been a solid few minutes into a rant about how horrible boys were, particularly when they thought they were 'like men or something.'

"Catch me up here. What recital are we talking about?" Emma asked. She mentally riffled through the recent sessions she'd had with Stella and couldn't think of any recital mentioned.

Stella sighed dramatically and started chewing on her nails. She tended to go for a combo outdoorsy goth look. Today, she wore practical hiking boots paired with black leggings and a denim mini skirt. A scarf of black fabric patterned with skulls hung haphazardly around her shoulders atop a practical raincoat. She never wore makeup and had creamy skin with rosy cheeks. Her dark brown hair and eyes stood out against her complexion. Much as Stella was loath to admit it, she was a beautiful girl. She'd once said, "No one would think I was cute if they knew where I grew up. It was the dump of all dumps."

Stella had been in foster care for two years. She'd been removed after years of reports and investigations about drug abuse by her parents and concerns about the condition of the home. Her mother had died of an accidental overdose, and her father didn't fight the removal. He'd drifted in and out of jail. She'd flat refused to attend therapy until she had a brush with the wrong crowd and almost gotten nailed for dealing drugs at school. Not because she was dealing them, but because someone had decided her locker would be a good place to hide them. The only thing that got her off the hook was the cop who noticed the gap in the surveillance recording from the hallway. Turned out that the vice-principal's son happened to be the one that put the drugs in Stella's locker. Diamond Creek might be rural, but it was pretty high tech. All of the school surveillance recordings were backed up to an off-site server.

Once the investigator got the backups, Stella didn't have to worry about legal problems. But she was in a world of social hurt. She'd spent most of her childhood as a social outcast—the kid who came to school dirty, sometimes smelly and who *never* had the right clothes. Bringing friends home was out of the question. When she'd finally been placed in foster care, she'd gotten a bit lucky, if there was such a thing in that situation. She'd been placed with a single foster mother, Janie, who was experienced at dealing with troubled teens, completely imperturbable and the perfect combination of blunt and warm. Stella respected and cared about Janie and had slowly started to bloom there. But her social naiveté made her vulnerable.

After the incident at school, Janie had dragged Stella into counseling. Stella paused from chewing her nails and tilted her head to the side.

"Well?" Stella asked again.

Emma pursed her lips. "I don't think you mentioned this recital to me. What do you think my answer would be?"

Stella sighed dramatically again, rolling her eyes for good measure this time. "Usually you say something about how you're not here to tell me what to do." Stella couldn't hide her smile.

"That sounds like something I would say," Emma replied, returning Stella's smile. "What do *you* think about the recital?"

Stella sighed and this time it wasn't for effect. The sigh sounded tired and vulnerable. After a long silence, she spoke, her voice small. "I want to try out for the piano part. Mrs. Cooper—she's my music teacher—says I'm really good. Janie signed me up for lessons all summer, and Mrs. Cooper says I keep getting better. It's the fall recital, so they have tryouts this summer so we can start practicing. But I'm scared. I've never done anything like it. Not even close. And who will come to see me if I get in?"

Emma waited a beat before responding. "If you want to try out then you should try out."

"Brilliant," Stella said. "That's genius. How come someone can't give me instructions? I'd like instructions for life."

Emma smiled ruefully. "Because there aren't any. And when I tell you that I'm not here to tell you what to do, it's because I'm not. Aside from pointing out the obvious, I don't think you'd listen to me if I told you what to do. Back to the recital, it sounds like it might matter to you. Feeling nervous about something like that is pretty common. It'd be weirder if you weren't nervous. And to answer at least one of your questions, Janie would be there, along with everyone in her family. And you have to admit, her family is huge. They think of you as part of their family and would be heartbroken if you thought they wouldn't come to your recital."

Stella sat up a little straighter, the barest sheen of

tears in her eyes. "Janie would come. Grannie too. And lots more…" she paused and took a breath. "Guess I have to just blow through this. What if I get stage fright?"

"Well, you won't know if you'll get stage fright unless you try."

Stella wrinkled her nose, chewed her nails, but didn't slouch again. She finally made eye contact with Emma again. "K…I'm gonna try out. It's next week before my appointment with you. Can I call you to tell you if I don't get in? That way, if the news sucks, I can get it over with."

Emma nodded. "Of course you can. I'll send good vibes. Plus, if your music teacher thinks you're really good at piano, you're probably really good."

Their conversation moved on. Emma considered bringing up the issue of Janie's family again, but decided against it for today. Emma thought a sense of belonging would be incredibly healing for Stella. At sixteen, Stella had to consent to her own adoption. With her mother deceased and her father long gone, his parental rights had been terminated, so there weren't many legal hoops to jump through for an adoption. So far, Stella had resisted the idea. She claimed it was stupid for sixteen year olds to get adopted. Janie had told Emma many times she'd love to adopt Stella, and she made sure to tell Stella that even though Stella brushed it off.

Stella had come a long way in six months, so Emma had high hopes Stella might take a few more steps that could help her. At the end of their session, Stella skipped down the hall, turning for a last wave to Emma just before she pushed through the door to the waiting area. Emma loved working with adolescents. They lived in that odd mix of child and adult, the tug of war between those parts of the self.

* * *

STOPPING by the grocery store on the way home, Emma was perusing the fruit section when she heard her name. Turning, she was startled to see Trey. Instantly, her heart jumped. *Don't be an idiot, Emma. There's no way he's into you.*

She promptly dropped the apple she held. "Oh!"

She leaned over to pick it up, only to have her purse swing as she moved and bang into the edge of the produce shelf. Apples and oranges rolled off the shelf, hitting the floor in a series of thumps.

Emma stood, the lone apple she'd originally dropped back in her hand. Blushing furiously, she glanced up at Trey.

Trey bit his lip to keep from laughing, but a laugh burst forth. "Sorry. Not your fault, just one of those things." He looked around, apples and oranges surrounding them in a messy circle.

Emma shook her head and smiled ruefully. "Guess it's better to laugh. Not much else to do."

"Dad!"

Emma followed the sound of Stuart's voice to see him on the other side of the produce display.

"I found the grapefruit!" Stuart exclaimed, holding a grapefruit high above his head, a proud smile on his face.

"Good job," Trey replied.

Stuart noticed Emma and turned his wide smile on her. "You're the lady who caught my hat!" He paused, wrinkling his forehead. "I can't 'member your name."

"That's okay. I have a hard time with names too. Remind me what yours is."

"Stuart," he said with a firm nod. He started to walk around to where they were, still holding the grapefruit aloft.

"My name's Emma. Maybe we'll remember the next time we see each other."

"Hey Stu, careful with the grapefruit," Trey said just as Stuart came around and saw the fruit scattered on the ground. He came to a quick stop, his arm finally dropping to his side. He kept a good hold on the grapefruit, cradling it in both hands now. Eyes wide, he looked around, his eyes questioning when he looked up to Trey.

Trey smiled. "Minor accident here. How about you stay put while Emma and I clean these up?"

Stuart nodded with alacrity, politely remaining in place. "What happened?"

"My purse ran into the apples. Once they started falling, the oranges came along for the ride," Emma said. She set her purse on the ground and carefully began collecting the fruit. Trey waved a store employee over and worked quickly and methodically, placing the fruit in his grocery basket. He gestured for Emma to do the same. Once the employee arrived, Trey succinctly explained he wasn't sure if they wanted the fruit back on the display until it was cleaned. The appreciative employee relieved them of the basket piled with fruit, and the mess Emma had made was gone.

She couldn't help but admire how practical Trey was. Oddly enough, that only made him more attractive to her. Just thinking about how much she enjoyed watching him clean up her mess made her hot inside. She fought her blush, but could feel her face flaming. Stuart conveniently distracted her.

Stepping to her side, he smiled up at her, one side of his brown bangs sticking up. His missing front tooth brought a twinge to her heart. Knowing the mother of this sweet boy died just wasn't fair.

"All cleaned up," Stuart said. He started to gesture with his hands, and Trey deftly grabbed the grapefruit from Stuart.

"I wasn't gonna drop it," Stuart said.

"Just being safe," Trey replied.

Stuart looked up at Emma, his brown eyes so bright. "My dad's good at cleaning up," he said proudly.

"He sure is," Emma said. She turned to Trey. "Thank you for helping me with that."

Trey nodded firmly. Emma noticed Stuart's nods were a semblance of his father's. With Stuart, they were endearing as he appeared to be trying to look decisive. On Trey, they were sexy. That level of clarity just layered onto everything else drew Emma to him. It was absolutely ridiculous she was so gaga over Trey she got turned on by him cleaning up fruit and nodding.

Just as Emma was wondering what to say next because what did one say in this situation, Stuart spoke.

"Dad, can we have Emma over tonight? I can show her Tootsie and Neon."

Emma was startled at Stuart's question, although Trey looked unperturbed. He tilted his head, a small smile gracing his face when he looked at Stuart. Shifting his gaze to Emma, his smile faded.

"Stuart would like more people to meet Tootsie and Neon," Trey paused and smiled wryly. "Tootsie is our cat, and Neon is his fish."

Emma wasn't sure what to say. She wanted to please Stuart and say she'd come over, while she also desperately wanted Trey to *want* her to come over for reasons that had nothing to do with Tootsie and Neon. She was simultaneously mortified because she knew she could *not* contemplate her feelings for Trey. Even if, and it was a big *if*, Trey was interested in a relationship, if he knew her history, he wouldn't want anything to do with her.

She focused on her last thought when she responded. "Stuart, that's very nice of you to want me to come over. But I can't come today. Thank you for asking me though." Emma hoped keeping her response polite and vague would allow her to bow out gracefully and avoid an awkward moment with Trey.

Stuart looked disappointed, but he nodded politely. "Maybe another time?" he asked hopefully.

"Maybe," Emma said with a smile.

She glanced toward Trey and for a split second, his eyes darkened. Almost as quickly, Trey's expression shifted into a polite, serious façade.

"Maybe we'll find a time Emma can meet Tootsie and Neon. For now, we need to finish shopping," Trey said, placing his hand on Stuart shoulder. He nodded to Emma, his smile bland, his eyes shuttered. "Nice to see you again."

Emma's heart hammered, but she merely nodded, pasting a polite smile on her face. "You too. Have a good evening." She turned away quickly and finished her shopping, her mind only half paying attention.

When she pulled up in her driveway a little later, her whimsical cabin was bathed in soft pink light. The sun was just beginning its slide down the horizon. The mountains were dusted with gold and pink, the dark green of the spruce trees covering the mountainside haloed in the shafts of light.

Once she put away the groceries, she curled up on the couch and absentmindedly flipped through television channels. Sula curled up beside her. Emma couldn't keep her thoughts away from all the reasons someone like Trey would never even consider her. Her marriage to Greg felt like an anchor that she couldn't shake loose. For a while after she'd gotten the courage to leave and moved to Diamond Creek, she'd felt so free, the world wide-open again. She'd even managed to successfully divorce Greg, which had been terrifying for her. After finally leaving, she feared the court process would offer him an avenue to find her, or worse, an avenue to shame her. With her parents help, she used her father's business address for all court filings. As far as Greg knew, she resided at a post office box in North Carolina. The fight she expected from him hadn't happened. The relief she felt when she received the finalized divorce papers was immense. She immediately had her maiden name restored and savored every time she signed Emma Davis rather than Emma Neals.

Trey was the first man Emma had even the slightest attraction to since her marriage ended. She thought it would never happen again, and frankly, that had been just fine with her. But why oh why did this attraction have to be so potent? And why did it have to be to a man she could never consider? He was just way too together. Single father, pilot and lawyer…and sexy as hell. Definitely not in her league. If Trey knew her history and how she should have known better, he'd question her sanity.

CHAPTER 4

Trey stood on the beach, watching Stuart valiantly hold a kite in the brisk wind. The kite in question was bright orange, in honor of Neon, Stuart's beloved goldfish. Flying kites was Stuart's favorite activity. They spent many a weekend afternoon down on the shore. Trey had moved to Diamond Creek because he loved this part of the coastline, and he thought it was a perfect spot for flight tours. The wind skidded across Kachemak Bay today, stirring up white caps. Clouds hovered around Mount Augustine, but otherwise the sky was clear. The bright orange kite stood out against the blue sky.

When it became obvious Stuart's small arms were getting worn out despite his protests, Trey helped him bring the kite down. Stuart was about as well behaved as a six-year old could be. Even when he protested, it was never tinged with defiance, just hope. Trey held Stuart's hand as they walked along the beach back to the parking lot. Thoughts of Helen ran through his mind.

Trey credited Helen with everything good about Stuart. While he'd been an okay dad before Helen died, he hadn't been around too much. He'd worked grueling hours as a prosecutor in Anchorage. Helen had cut her legal practice in half once they had Stuart. She had been an amazing mother. The afternoon two years ago when she collapsed was seared into his memory. He'd been working at the kitchen table. She'd been in the laundry room. Trey heard a loud thump. Stuart had mercifully been napping upstairs in his bedroom. The moment Trey saw her, he knew with certainty that she was gone. But he'd pushed the thought away and held her in his arms while calling 911, pleading with them to hurry.

Helen had died from an undiagnosed congenital heart defect. Since her death, Trey tried to become a father that might be half as good as Helen had been as a mother. Stuart made it easy. He'd grieved his mother's death, still did. But he was such a good-hearted boy. Stuart seemed to realize Trey was trying and frequently bragged about him to others—such as his comment to Emma that his dad was good at cleaning up. Trey smiled to himself recalling that moment.

"Dad, can we go fishing again soon?" Stuart asked, his question breaking into Trey's thoughts.

Trey glanced down, absently smoothing his hand across Stuart's hair, which was prone to have tufts sticking up. "Of course we can. How about we go next weekend?"

Stuart nodded enthusiastically. "Can we invite Emma to go with us?"

Trey was thrown off guard by Stuart's question. Stuart seemed unusually interested in her. Trey couldn't help but wonder if Stuart picked up on his own attraction to Emma. Trey found himself thinking of her again and again ever since they'd first met her at the Homer Fishing Hole. Their encounter at the grocery store only heightened his interest. He wasn't sure what to do about his interest and experienced twinges of guilt—over how trying to bring someone into his life might affect Stuart and that it represented he'd truly moved on from Helen.

"Dad, can we ask her to go?" Stuart asked again.

Trey forced his thoughts to the moment at hand. "Uh...I don't know about that Stuart."

Stuart wasn't dissuaded. "She's nice! I like her. And that's how you make friends. 'Member? That's what you said. To make friends, I ask them to do things so I can get to know them. You need lady friends, like Dave said."

Trey chuckled and wished Stuart didn't have such good hearing. Dave, one of Trey's friends from Anchorage, had been on him recently to move on from his self-imposed isolation from women since Helen had died. Stuart must have overheard Dave when he was over the other day.

"So you've decided Emma should be a lady friend?" Trey asked.

Stuart looked up at him, eyes wide and innocent as they approached Trey's car, a dark green Subaru hatchback. Stuart nodded.

"I'll think about asking her to go fishing with us. How's that?"

Stuart's return smile was so hopeful it almost broke Trey's heart. He knew Stuart needed a mother figure. Trey just didn't know if he was ready to try dating anyone. Before meeting Helen, he'd dated his share of women, but work had always been his focus.

He'd kept relationships casual. If he hadn't met Helen through work, he wasn't so sure they'd have ended up together. They'd been thrown together by their shared commitment to work, which had allowed love to bloom. When Trey tried to imagine letting someone into his life and heart that way now, it seemed too complicated. He had to consider Stuart first.

Trey shook those thoughts away and helped Stuart carefully stow the kite in the back of the car. A few minutes later, he saw a faded red Toyota truck pulled over along the highway, a form kneeling beside the truck, checking the tire. He immediately slowed, pulling over to park behind the truck.

"Stuart, I need you to stay put, okay? The road's pretty busy. I just want to see if they need any help." Trey reached into his pocket and handed Stuart his iPhone. "You can play Angry Birds if you want." Stuart rarely got to play games like that, so it was a guarantee that he would stay right where he was. He immediately grabbed the phone, tapping it open to start playing.

Trey quickly stepped out of the car and walked around to the passenger side of the truck parked in front of them. A pair of long feminine legs in jeans and cowboy boots greeted him. Whoever had been kneeling by the tire was now on the ground, looking under the truck.

"Need any help?" he asked.

Trey heard a thump and then a muffled "Ow!" before the person started shifting to slide out from under the truck.

"You okay?" Didn't meant to startle you," he said.

Emma's face came into view just by his feet. He automatically reached down to offer his hand. She shook her hair out of her eyes and placed her hand in his, immediately sending a jolt through him. With a steady tug, he helped her up. As she came to standing beside him, he took in the sight of her. She was almost as tall as he was, somehow curvy and willowy at once. She had dark brown hair that fell to her shoulders, straight with just a touch of curl at the ends, long bangs framing her face. Her eyes were bright blue, her cheeks flushed. Her lips were lush and full. At the moment, her hair was in disarray. Paired with the faded jeans and cowboy boots, she wore an open red blouse over a fitted white tank top. He had to force himself not to stare at her breasts, taut against the thin cotton of her tank top.

Trey stood frozen for a moment until he realized he hadn't released her hand. He was a man that was *always* in control. With Emma, he seemed to forget how. For God's sake, he'd met her twice. The mere act of holding her hand to help her up kick started his pulse. He slowly released her hand, immediately missing the warmth of it in his.

Emma looked back at him, her blue eyes wide with a hint of something he couldn't quite read. She brushed her bangs out of her eyes and straightened her shirt.

"Flat tire," she said matter-of-factly. "When I checked around the tire, I thought I felt a nail sticking out on the inside. I crawled under to see."

Trey realized too late that he was staring. Emma's already flushed cheeks became another shade darker. She twisted a ring on her hand and fiddled with a simple silver chain around her neck.

Trey silently swore and forced himself to focus. "So was there a nail?"

Emma nodded. "I was going to change to my spare, but it's flat too. I haven't checked it in a while." She paused and sighed.

Before Trey could think, he spoke. "We can give you a ride if you need it."

Emma looked as taken aback as he was by his offer.

"Oh. Um…are you sure?"

Trey nodded. "Of course. I can drop you off somewhere if you need me to." His mind spun, as he realized the moment Emma got in the car, Stuart would ask him again if they could invite her over. Trey decided to go with the flow. So what if he was so attracted to this woman that he couldn't think straight? It wouldn't hurt to be decent.

Emma appeared to be thinking, her eyes distant. "Okay. You can drop me off at my friend's office. That way, I can call someone about the tire and wait nearby."

"Sure. Need anything from your truck before we go?"

Emma quickly got her purse out, following Trey to his car. Stuart's head was down, focused on the game. Trey opened the backseat passenger door for Emma, his eyes automatically tracing her motions as she seated herself in the car. Stuart lifted his head at the sound of the door opening. "Hey Emma!" Stuart exclaimed, his smile so filled with joy, Trey couldn't help but smile in return.

He glanced to Emma. "Stuart thinks you're a nice lady. Be prepared for him to ask you over again." Trey silently added that he wished she would say yes and then wondered what the hell he was thinking.

Emma nodded, a small smile gracing her face, and turned to Stuart.

"Hey Stuart, how's it going? Your dad is giving me a ride to my friend's office because I got a flat tire."

Stuart immediately jumped to asking Emma if she'd ever played Angry Birds.

Trey shut the car door. As he walked around the car, he swore under his breath, "Get a grip."

LATE THAT NIGHT, well after Stuart's bedtime, Trey sat at the kitchen table and ran his hands through his hair with a sigh. His laptop sat idle on the table in front of him. He wasn't sure how it had happened, but he'd promised Stuart they'd take Emma fishing with them next weekend. He'd even let Stuart ask her, and she'd said yes. He told himself to stay logical, to think clearly. Instead, his thoughts kept summoning the sight of her full mouth and her wide blue eyes. Much as he had loved Helen, he'd never felt anything close to the sparks that flew between him and Emma.

With a shake of his head, he focused his eyes on the computer in front of him. He was prepping some documents for a client who needed to update their will. After Helen died, he'd decided a career shift was in order. Though he'd enjoyed his work as a prosecutor, the hours were long and the work high stress. He wanted flexibility, so he could be more available for Stuart. He also missed flying. He'd enlisted in the Air Force straight out of high school and loved every minute of flying. He'd gotten his law degree and moved on from the Air Force, flying recreationally whenever he could. Looking for a career change, he decided to do what he wanted and started Seat of Your Pants, flightseeing tours for the hordes of tourists that descended in Alaska every summer. Diamond Creek was a great spot for his business, and he kept a small law practice. His flightseeing business kept him busy spring through fall, and his law practice supplemented his income on the side and through winters. Though his schedule was much more flexible, he usually brought paperwork home with him, working after Stuart went to bed. Trey's thoughts wandered to Emma again. He swore and logged off his computer. His thoughts were too scattered for him to usefully formulate anything else tonight.

CHAPTER 5

*E*mma sidestepped puddles on the way into the office. Rain had fallen steadily since last night, softening to a cool drizzle this morning. Diamond Creek was cocooned in a misty cloud, nothing but gray to be seen in all directions, the outline of the mountains across the bay barely visible. Emma flipped her hood back and gave her coat a shake once inside. The waiting room for the office was already full this morning. She quickly checked her calendar, noting that two emergency assessments were booked in open appointment slots. That was part of the drill at community mental health programs. She had been surprised when she first started working as a mental health clinician here—her caseload had been full within the first week, and she carried a wait list at all times. Unbeknownst to her before she moved here, Alaska had some of the highest rates of mental health and substance abuse issues per capita in the country.

While Emma didn't consider that a good thing, it

kept her busy. She couldn't remember the last time she'd had a slow day at work. After helping herself to coffee, she began seeing clients. The day flew by, barely enough time between sessions for her to complete her notes. Her last appointment of the day was with Stella. Stella slouched into the office, rainwater dripping off of her coat. She'd foregone the use of her hood, so her dark hair was damp.

"This sucks! Summer disappears the minute it starts to rain here, and it's been raining all day," Stella said, absently untangling her wet hair with her fingers.

"Want some tea?" Emma asked, gesturing to the selection of tea she kept available, along with a single cup hot water machine.

Stella smirked and then nodded. "Even if it makes me a geek, I'll take it. My hands are cold."

Emma chuckled softy and waited while Stella got her tea ready. Emma had wondered several times this week if Stella had gone through with it and tried out for the recital. She knew Stella well enough now to know it was best if she gave Stella the time to decide to talk about something than to directly address it. Stella, like most people, needed to feel like what they discussed was up to her.

After a few minutes of Stella venting about how mad she was at some girl at school who was teasing a younger student, she abruptly shifted gears.

"I did it. I'm playing the piano for the fall recital," Stella said, the words rushing out so fast, Emma barely understood.

Fortunately, Emma managed to decipher Stella's comment. If not, Stella likely would have become irritable and refused to repeat what she said.

"Awesome Stella!" Emma leaned across the coffee table and high-fived Stella.

Stella leaned back, grinning madly and twirling a piece of hair.

"Well, how did the tryout feel? I know you rocked it because you made it in the recital, but what was it like?"

Still grinning, Stella shrugged. Emma waited her out.

"Janie came with me, but I made her sit way in the back. Mrs. Cooper let me come over the day before to practice extra too. Honestly, I don't remember much. I got so nervous once I was up there, all I saw was the piano. I guess that's good or else I might have freaked."

"Sounds to me like it couldn't have gone better. How do you feel now you made it through?"

Still twirling her hair, Stella bit her lip and shrugged before replying. "Good. But now…" She paused and looked over, her eyes skittering past Emma's before coming back. "Before the audition, I thought that was the hardest part. I have practice three times a week until school starts and then we add a fourth practice. Now I'm totally freaked about the recital. I mean, the school auditorium will be full. It's not like Diamond Creek is a big deal, but this is…just a lot for me."

Emma resisted the urge to jump up and down and clap. The fact that Stella tried out for the recital, got in and was actually talking out loud about how she felt was such phenomenal progress for her that Emma was overjoyed. But Stella tended to shy away from overt praise. Instead, she nodded and waited a beat.

"Janie can't shut up about it. You'd think I was

about to be famous," Stella said, a hint of pride and disbelief in her tone.

"Janie's your personal cheerleader. We could all use one of those. And honestly..." Emma paused, gauging Stella's reaction to her words before continuing, "...it's pretty amazing. A lot of people would never even try out. You got up the nerve to do that *and* you're in the recital now. It's okay to be proud."

Stella sat quietly, still twirling her hair, but her eyes only briefly broke contact before she looked back. "It's a pretty big deal, huh?"

Emma nodded, letting her smile expand. "I'd say so."

Stella's grin returned in force. "Janie's totally stoked that I have practice so much now. You know how she's all about the activities," Stella said, using air quotes for her last word.

"I'm guessing the practice won't be so bad. From what Janie told me, music class and those piano lessons are about the only thing you don't complain about."

Stella rolled her eyes, but the grin stuck. The session moved on, Stella chattering about various topics of the typical teenage fare—friends, who hurt her feelings, who she couldn't stand, et cetera. A mere few minutes before it was time to wind up, Stella pulled one of her doorknob moves. Doorknob moves were lingo in the therapy world for a meaty topic dropped just when there wasn't enough time to deal with it, just about when they had their hand on the doorknob to leave.

"I've been thinking about that adoption thing," Stella said as she was sliding her arms back into her raincoat.

Emma willed herself to keep her expression calm. "What have you been thinking about it?"

Stella busied herself fiddling with her jacket, a moment of silence lengthening. Emma waited.

Stella kept her eyes on the floor when she answered. "I've been thinking maybe I could go for it. Janie keeps telling me that I'm her daughter in every way that matters, except legally. I don't think she's gonna shut up about it unless I let her adopt me."

Sensing that Stella could handle it, Emma shifted the focus. "I know it's important to Janie, but what about you?"

The crinkle of Stella's jacket was loud. The hair twirling commenced. When she spoke, her voice was soft. "I think maybe it would be important. Being a foster kid is like…you never get the full deal. Plus, my mom's gone and my dad might as well be."

Emma stood and stepped to Stella's side, gently placing her hand on Stella's shoulder. "I think maybe it *is* important to you and to Janie. And both of you are critical to this equation."

Stella finally lifted her eyes, uncertainty and hope battling each other. Her shoulders rose, the deep breath hissing through her teeth slowly. "Could you maybe help me talk to Janie about it?"

"Absolutely," Emma said firmly. "Next week. How about I call her and ask her to come?"

Stella nodded with alacrity.

"Same time, same place," Emma said with a smile.

Stella zipped her jacket and turned to go.

"Stella," Emma said just as Stella reached for the doorknob. Stella looked over her shoulder. "I'm really proud of you for trying out for the recital. But I'm even more proud that you're talking about how you feel about things."

For a flash, Stella's eyes widened, pride arcing across her face. She caught herself and rolled her eyes. "Okay therapist. You done good this week. Don't get too excited though."

Emma shook her head and returned Stella's eye roll. "I'm not that one that 'done good,' that was all you. Now get going before it's starts raining hard again."

* * *

EMMA RAN from her truck to the door at Sally's, the rain blowing sideways. She hurried in, immediately tossing her hood back, the warmth of the place enveloping her the moment she stepped inside. Sally's was a local favorite restaurant and bar. She strode over to the restaurant side, looking for her sister and some friends she was meeting.

"Hey there," Emma said, sliding into the only empty seat at the booth.

"Hey!" Susie said, leaning over and pecking Emma on the cheek. "You're soaked. The rain must have picked up."

"It's pouring. It might as well not be summer," Emma replied, slipping out of her rain jacket and tossing it over the back of a nearby chair.

"Hey Emma, haven't seen you since I got back," Tess said. Tess was married to Hannah's brother-in-law, Nathan Winters. She was cute and curvy with ginger eyes and honey-gold curls that fell to her shoulders. Nathan, who Emma had understood to be a party boy once upon a time, had become completely smitten with Tess when she had visited Alaska for a fishing trip with her family. They'd married this spring.

"I know," Emma said. "How was your trip to Seattle?"

"Good. I'd never been to Seattle, unless you count changing planes in the airport. It's a great city to visit. Nathan's mom gave me the tourist treatment. We went to Pike Place Market, to the glass blowing district and more restaurants than I can remember."

Hannah nodded. "The Winters make pretty good in-laws. I may be biased, but you married into a good family," she said with a wink.

Susie rolled her eyes. "Oh god, now we have to listen to two of you talk about how awesome the Winters boys are."

Hannah chuckled. "Hey, it's your fault. You're the one who played matchmaker with Luke and me. And don't even try to pretend you kept your opinions to yourself when it came to Nathan and Tess."

Susie harrumphed and took a swallow of beer. "Maybe I can see a good thing coming, but it doesn't mean the rest of us won't get tired of hearing about how amazing your husbands are."

"It bothers you because you can't keep your eyes off Jared and won't admit it to save your life," Tess said slyly.

Susie choked on her beer, grabbing a napkin to wipe her chin. Emma gave Tess an admiring nod. "You may be kinda new around here, but...wow...that took nerve."

Susie glared at Emma. Hannah bit her lip and shook her head. Susie swung her glare to Hannah.

"What?" Hannah asked, feigning innocence. "If you can dish it out, you'd better be ready to take it."

Susie straightened her shoulders and glanced around the table. "While I won't deny Jared is handsome—that whole damn family is—I can certainly keep my eyes off of him. Plus, can you imagine me with someone that uptight? That man seriously needs to loosen up."

"And maybe you're just the girl for the job," Tess said with a wink at Emma.

Susie tossed a balled up napkin at Tess. "Definitely *not* the job for me. If you want to set Jared up, good luck. I love playing matchmaker, but even I wouldn't take Jared on."

Hannah gave Emma a knowing look, lifting her eyebrows. Emma barely shook her head. They had all noticed at one point or another that Susie had some pretty strong feelings about Jared and definitely couldn't keep her eyes off of him. Emma figured Susie needed to come to that conclusion on her own.

As they ate pizza and bantered, conversation eventually rolled around to the upcoming weekend. Emma was doing her damnedest not to think about the fact that she accepted Stuart's sweet invitation to go fishing with him and his dad. Just thinking about Trey made her blush.

"So Emma, what do you think?" Tess asked.

"About what?" Emma asked, realizing she'd lost track of the conversation for the brief moment Trey entered her thoughts.

"About going to Anchorage for the weekend," Susie said.

Emma felt her flush deepen. "Um...how about next weekend? That would work better for me."

Susie, Hannah and Tess all gave her puzzled expressions.

"What? I have a few things to do this weekend," Emma said, momentarily annoyed with how impossible it was to keep anything private in Diamond Creek.

"Such as?" Tess prompted.

Emma closed her eyes and sighed, knowing they weren't going to let it go until she explained. "I'm going fishing with Trey and his son." She waited for the third degree to begin.

"By Trey, do you mean the Trey you met at the Fishing Hole? Just trying to clarify," Susie said, overly polite.

Emma slanted her eyes in Susie's direction.

Susie was all innocence. "What? I wasn't being a smartass. There's more than one Trey in town."

"Fine. Yes. By Trey, I mean that one." She threw her hands up. "I ran into him at the store and then he stopped to help me when I had a flat tire the other day…"

"Oh my god. That's who dropped you off at my office and you didn't even bother to mention it," Susie said indignantly.

Emma flattened her lips, but nodded. "His son, Stuart, is the one who invited me. I'm not so sure Trey would have, but he went along with it."

Susie looked toward Hannah. "What did I tell you?" She glanced to Tess and then Emma. "I knew you were into him. I knew it!"

"I didn't deny it. I just didn't think I'd ever see him again. You were the one who said he was never around."

"Well, he does live here, so it stands to reason that

you'd have to see him at some point," Susie replied. "And maybe his son is the one that invited you, but trust me, Trey noticed you just as much as you noticed him. Didn't he Hannah?"

Hannah nodded, holding back her smile. "We both saw him looking your way quite a few times the other day."

Just hearing that Trey may have noticed made Emma fluttery inside. She wanted to ask how often, for how long and more, but knew that would only add fuel to the teasing fire.

"Sounds like you're into Trey, who I don't seem to know. Could someone fill me in? I was only gone for a week," Tess said.

Susie grinned. "Trey Holden. You've seen him around. He runs Seat of Your Pants, a flightseeing business, and has a small law practice. He's widowed and quite sexy, or so Emma thinks," Susie said, catching Emma's eyes and winking.

Emma sighed, trying and failing to stop blushing.

Tess pursed her lips and winked at Emma. "I'm still not sure I'd know who he was if I saw him, but it's about time you showed interest in someone."

"I'm just going fishing with them. It's not like fishing with someone in Alaska is a big deal."

"Well, I may not have known you as long as Hannah and Susie, but let's see if I have this right. You haven't dated anyone since you moved here. All I know is you got divorced before you moved out here. I mean, you've never even mentioned anything about anyone. I started to wonder if you swung in a different direction," Tess paused and took a bite of pizza. "And now you've apparently got the hots for this guy and you're going fishing with him. If I were you, I'd be all worried about how I was going to keep myself looking proper and keep the fish slime to a minimum."

"You have a point there. I *am* wondering how the hell I can avoid looking like a mess. As for whether I'm into men or women, men are the flavor for me," Emma responded with a shrug.

"And Trey is the flavor that gets you going," Susie interjected with a sly grin. "I want every detail of your day with Trey..." Susie said, a heavy emphasis on Trey's name "...and don't you dare think you can hide this from us." Her eyes sobered. "Seriously though, I've worried about you. You've said so little about whatever happened with your ex, and you've practically been a nun since you moved here."

Emma stared at the table and traced the grain of the wood with her fingertip, quiet for a moment, wondering what to tell them about Greg. A quick glance around the table and she saw three pairs of concerned eyes. All teasing aside, she knew these women had her back. And yet, if they knew what her marriage had been like, what would they think? Greg was a chapter of her life that she wanted to tear out of the book. She knew though that trying to erase the past only handed it more power.

"My marriage was a living hell. Greg was abusive —emotionally, verbally, and physically. It took me two years to leave him, and that was two years too long. I don't like to talk about it..." Emma paused and shrugged "...because I wish it had never happened and it's even more embarrassing because I'm a therapist. If anyone should have seen the signs, I should have."

Glasses clinking, muted laughter and music, and the rumble of conversations around them were all

Emma heard. She released her breath slowly and glanced up. Hannah, Susie, and Tess looked stunned.

Susie's eyes filled with tears. "I'm so sorry. No one deserves that." Her words, plain and bare, held no recrimination, no judgment, just sadness tinged with anger.

Susie was seated beside Emma and reached over to hug her. Relief washed through Emma. She'd been so focused on moving on from Greg, she hadn't realized that it hurt to hide this from her friends. They may not have known her before she trekked here to find her parents and found Hannah instead, but they were her closest friends now. Much as she wished she could surgically excise her past, she couldn't.

Hannah looked across the table at Emma, her eyes so similar, holding Emma's for a moment. "I understand why you haven't said anything sooner. But I'm sorry you've had to go through that alone. Maybe you don't want to talk much about it, but we're here if you do."

Tess and Susie chimed in, echoing Hannah's comment.

Emma bit her lip. She would have imagined she might have cried, but she didn't. Oddly, she felt free, free from keeping this blot in her past a secret. "Thanks...for being there. I'm okay—really. It's been long enough now I'm in much better shape than I was before. I didn't bring it up sooner because it's not exactly fun to talk about. Even though I know in my head that I'm one of millions of women who have gone through something like that, I hate that it's a part of my past. So if you wondered why I didn't date, honestly, I didn't think I'd ever want to."

Susie, ever the tease, didn't tease now. She rubbed

Emma's shoulder. "Well, who would? I mean, what an asshole. You should be so proud of yourself for leaving," she said firmly.

Emma nodded slowly. "I am proud of that, just not so proud of ending up there in the first place. But I'm a therapist. It's not like I don't know that otherwise intelligent people end up in horrible situations." She looked to Hannah. "When you responded to the forum post about our parents, it was a lifeline for me. I wanted to find my birth family anyway, but the timing was just right. That's why I just showed up like that. I was afraid if I asked if I could visit, you might say no. Hopping on a plane to Alaska put enough distance between me and Greg that I felt safe leaving."

Hannah merely held her gaze, her blue eyes mirroring Emma's. "Well, I'm even more glad you came out here. Is that why you decided to move here too?"

Emma shook her head. "I fell in love with Diamond Creek, and I really wanted to get to know you, get to know where my parents lived. Don't get me wrong, it helped me feel safe leaving Greg for good, but I had a lot more reasons to come here."

Hannah smiled slowly and reached over to squeeze Emma's hand.

Tess started to say something just as the waitress appeared.

"Another round for everyone. It's on me. Don't ask why, but trust me when I say we all need a drink," Susie said emphatically to the waitress.

Unruffled, the waitress simply asked, "Same thing for everyone?"

When the waitress stepped away, Tess caught Emma's eyes. "All I want to say is this: we all have jerks in our past. Sounds like your ex was a doozy and then some. But whatever you do, know that you do *not* need to feel ashamed around us."

"Thanks, that means a lot. I should have told you about it sooner...but..."

When Emma paused, Susie jumped in. "There are no shoulds here."

Emma started laughing. "Coming from you? No shoulds..."

Susie widened her eyes. "Hey, maybe I'm opinionated, but for stuff like this, I'm not."

"I know, I know. You just opened that door and I couldn't resist," Emma replied.

Conversation shifted to lighter territory after that. Luke and Nathan showed up, Hannah's and Tess's husbands, respectively.

"Where's Jared?" Susie asked.

"The usual, something to do with work," Nathan replied.

"You'd think that man could learn how to relax," Susie said with a roll of her eyes.

Emma caught Tess's eyes and then Hannah's, the three of them sharing a knowing glance.

*S*unlight arced through the cab of Emma's truck as she turned onto the main road, driving toward the harbor to meet Trey and Stuart. She'd inherited her little Toyota truck from Hannah. After Hannah and Luke married, they had one too many trucks. Emma loved that it was slightly worn, its red paint faded. It gave her a sense of comfort.

The early morning sun was bright, the sky crisp blue. Trey called her yesterday morning to check that she could still meet them to fish. She had been in between appointments when she answered. He had sounded formal and polite. When he'd explained that they'd be going out on his boat, she'd inexplicably gotten more nervous. The doubts in her mind kicked at the tires of her attraction to Trey—assessing its worth, its frivolity and just how ridiculous it was that a tiny part of her wished he was as attracted to her as she to him.

Emma stopped for coffee at Red Truck Coffee, a tiny coffee shop, housed in an old red square truck, just before the turn into Otter Cove Harbor. Cammi, another friend she'd met through Hannah, owned Red Truck Coffee and had started it on a whim one summer. It was now a Diamond Creek fixture, owing to Cammi's amazing coffee and an incredibly convenient location for summer traffic.

Cammi greeted Emma with her usual warmth. Between her honey brown hair in its cute pixie cut, her soft blue eyes and ever-present sweet sentimentality, Cammi's presence was soothing. "Where are you headed today?" she asked when Emma walked up.

"The usual, fishing."

"Going with Hannah or Tess?"

Given that's who Emma almost always went fishing with, Cammi's question was innocent.

Emma hedged. "Not today, another friend."

Cammi lifted her eyebrows in question.

Emma sighed, knowing if she didn't just say who she was going fishing with, someone else would mention it and then there'd be more to explain.

"With Trey and his son, Stuart," she added.

"Oh, Trey Holden?"

At Emma's nod, Cammi beamed. "Stuart is such a sweetie! They stop by here a lot. Trey is such a good dad." Cammi paused and gave Emma an assessing look. "Not to be weird, but Trey isn't the most social guy. The only reason I've gotten to know them a little is that Trey is a serious early bird and comes by for coffee when most of the town is still asleep. How did you meet him and do I get to ask just what this little fishing jaunt is about?" Cammi had a slightly protective edge to her questions.

"It's not a huge deal. Stuart invited me. I met them kind of by accident..." Emma explained how she'd hooked Stuart's baseball hat and then ran into them twice more after that.

"That little boy wants his dad to find a 'lady friend'. I can't help but say it—if Trey went along with it, he must like you. He's protective of Stuart." Cammi wrinkled her nose and winked. "Can't wait to hear how it went."

Emma brimmed with questions and got jittery at the mere mention that Trey must like her. But she didn't want to let on how curious she was, so she swallowed her questions and shook her head. "I'm just going fishing." She took a sip of coffee. "Coffee's amazing by the way. I'll catch you later."

Someone else had just shown up, providing Emma a chance to gracefully make her exit. Moments later, she parked at the harbor and sat in the quiet for a moment, sipping her coffee. Anxiety coursed through her. What she knew to be an innocent and sweet invitation from Stuart had her nerves in knots. Her attraction to Trey discombobulated her. The cool, calm and stable self she'd tried to recapture since leaving Greg didn't involve her hankering after a sexy wilderness pilot who just happened to be a lawyer too. While Emma hadn't spent much time with Trey, she could imagine that austere, shuttered expression coming over his face if he knew anything about her marriage to Greg. With a hard shake of her head, she got out of the truck, gathered her fishing gear from the back and headed to the docks, clutching her coffee, comforted by the warmth in her palm.

She paused for a moment at the top of the dock and looked into the harbor. A salty gust caressed her face, the brisk air enervating her. Otter Cove Harbor was nestled in a small cove with hills curling around it. Spruce trees covered the hills, which gave way to a rocky shore. Beyond the cove lay Kachemak Bay and even further beyond was Cook Inlet, which led to the open Pacific Ocean. World-class fishing happened in every nook and cranny of the Alaskan coastline. Trey had explained he preferred to keep trips close when he brought Stuart with him, so they were heading not too far out in Kachemak Bay to fish for silver salmon.

Emma took a deep breath, savoring the crisp air. She'd grown to love Alaskan summers, so different from the humid, languid summers back East. She loved both and enjoyed the contrast. When the sun wasn't shining, it didn't feel much like summer in Alaska. When it was, the air was crisp, the warmth a balm. With Diamond Creek situated on the coast, there was an ever-present ocean breeze. Another gust of wind blew her bangs into her eyes. She shook them away and began walking down the dock, glancing around to find the boat slip Trey mentioned. She quickly caught sight of Trey and Stuart. Trey was leaning over the boat engine while Stuart stood atop a bench to one side of the boat. Stuart was attired in a bright orange life jacket over a bright blue fleece jacket and jeans tucked into Xtratufs, the indestructible rubber boots favored by Alaskans. He wore a blue baseball cap. Emma had been gifted a pair of Xtratufs by Susie not long after she moved here and was wearing them today. Though she wanted to feel sexy, she knew that was all but impossible when fishing. She also had enough sense to know that she'd look like a fool if she didn't dress practically for fishing. As with Stuart, she wore her boots over jeans. She'd allowed herself a small frivolity by wearing a bright red fitted button-down jersey over a gray tank top that hugged her curves. Her hair was pulled back in a loose ponytail, though wisps were already blowing free around her face.

"Hey Emma," Stuart called as she came within earshot. His face shone with a bright grin.

"Hey Stuart, how's it going?"

"Great!" he exclaimed before hopping down from the bench and tapping his father's shoulder. "Dad, Emma's here," Stuart said, tugging Trey's sleeve.

Emma reached the side of the boat and heard a muffled response before Trey lifted his head and stood. When he turned, his eyes landed right on hers, that rich brown gaze so direct she thought he must be able to see through her. While she willed her mind otherwise, butterflies swirled in her center, a wash of heat coursed through her and her face flamed. Despite knowing that it wasn't a good idea, she couldn't deny the attraction she felt for Trey. For the barest second, his eyes darkened. Before she could think, he gave his head a quick shake, his expression shifting to bland and friendly.

"Hi there. Stuart's been asking when you'd get here," Trey said, his eyes flicking from hers to smile down at Stuart. "I told you she'd be here any minute. And she's even early," he said, ruffling Stuart's hair.

Stuart beamed. "Are you ready?"

"Absolutely," she replied, returning Stuart's smile. His earnest sweetness was endearing.

Trey stepped over to the side of the boat, quickly climbing out onto the dock.

"Can I help with that?" he asked with a lift of one brow, gesturing to the bag she held.

"Sure," Emma said, handing over the small bag that held waterproof gear. Trey had explained there was no need to bring a fishing rod, as he had several on the boat. While Emma had learned that many Alaskans were quite specific about their fishing gear, she had yet to master it, so she was happy to go along with whatever was available.

Trey immediately stepped back into the boat and handed her bag to Stuart. "Got it?"

Stuart nodded firmly, holding the bag with both hands.

Trey turned and reached his hand out to Emma. Placing her hand in his, a current buzzed through her at his touch. His grip was firm and strong as he gave her a lift to step over the side of the boat. Flustered, she stumbled slightly once in the boat, her shoulder bumping against Trey's.

"Easy," he said, his voice right at her ear, his hand anchoring her.

Her feet steady again, she risked a glance. Her eyes collided with his and she couldn't look away. His guarded gaze gave way, a smoldering heat arcing from his eyes to hers. She stood close enough that she felt the deep breath he took. Her own breath caught in her throat, her heart raced. She couldn't seem to look away even though she knew she must. Trey's eyes fell to her lips before locking with hers again. He closed his eyes quickly. When he opened them again, the heat was gone. A wry smile lifted the corner of his mouth as he stepped away, releasing her hand.

Emma quickly took another step back, her legs bumping against the side of the boat. She forced herself to look away. The boat was a medium-sized motorboat. There were two cushioned chairs, one at the steering wheel and another at its side, flanking the opening to a small cabin. There was a bench on each side. Though it felt like forever when Trey's eyes had locked onto hers, Emma noticed that Stuart was just setting her bag down by the bench across from where she stood.

Stuart quickly turned back. "Dad, can we go now?"

Trey had remained in place once he stepped away from her. He looked to Stuart. "Just a few more minutes, bud. You want to show Emma around the boat while I finish getting us ready to go?"

Stuart nodded so fast it was comical. He stepped over to Emma's side and slipped his hand into hers, giving a tug. "Come on, Emma. Let's go to the cabin first."

Emma let herself be led around, Stuart's small hand in hers. His utter joy at having a visitor with them touched her. The boat cabin was small and utilitarian. A tiny cooking area, consisting of a mini refrigerator, two-burner stove, microwave and sink, was situated across from a dining nook. A v-shaped bed was tucked into the bow, barely large enough for two people. Stuart helpfully showed her the bathroom, which had precisely enough room for a stand-up shower and portable toilet. When they climbed out of the cabin onto the deck, Trey was waiting for them.

"Is the tour complete?" he asked Stuart.

"Yep. Can we go now?" came Stuart's quick response.

Trey looked to Emma. "Ready?"

The few minutes she'd walked around with Stuart had grounded her. She'd braced herself to *not* keep making a fool of herself, so she managed a nod without losing her sense of time and place.

Trey returned her nod and looked to Stuart. "Now we can go." He caught Emma's eyes again. "I'll start the boat. Do you mind holding onto the steering wheel while I hop out and get the boat untied?"

"No, not at all," she said "I've even driven a few boats if you need help driving."

"Good to know," Trey said. In the next few minutes, he started the engine, climbed onto the dock and tossed lines into the boat. Stuart appeared to know the routine and followed each line to where it landed, slowly and carefully winding the lines. His small hands fumbled with the lines, but he insisted he didn't need help.

As Trey stepped back into the boat, he looked over to Stuart. "Great job, Stuart."

Stuart stood, a tuft of brown hair sticking up from under his baseball cap, and grinned. "I told Emma I could do it myself," he said, pride threading his voice.

"And you did a great job," Trey replied, giving Stuart's shoulder a squeeze as he stepped over to the steering wheel.

Emma slid out of the way and moved to the other chair. As they drove through the opening to the harbor, Kachemak Bay unfurled in front. Mount Augustine, the sole volcano that sat outside the entrance to Kachemak Bay, rose in the distance, dark and still against the bright blue sky. The shoreline receded behind them. Gulls swooped and called. The high screech of an eagle call cut through the air. The eagle in question flew low above the water to one side of the boat, its talons extended as it swooped to the water in a splash, rising with a fish held in its grip. Every eagle she saw elicited a sense of wonder. She'd never laid eyes on one until she visited Alaska. Their presence was commanding and intense. Its wings cast a shadow across the boat as the eagle arced into the sky, heading back to the shore.

Stuart came to stand between her and Trey.

"Do you want to sit here?" Emma asked Stuart.

Stuart looked up at her, his eyes so open and sweet. "I like to stand," he said simply.

Trey looked over. "That he does. Even if you weren't here, I couldn't get him to sit down. Whenever we fish, he stands right here while I'm driving unless he's too tired. Then he falls asleep in the cabin," he said as he ruffled Stuart's hair.

Stuart looked up at her again. With a quick smile, he stepped in front of her and leaned back against her chair. Emma looked down at the top of his head, her hands falling to his shoulders. She looked over at Trey. He gave her a quick smile and a shrug.

The morning passed in a blur. Trey anchored the boat for a few hours within view of Gull Island, a tiny rock island toward the other side of the bay. Gull Island swarmed with birds—gulls, puffins, cormorants and kittiwakes clustered on the rock ledges. Emma leaned over the cooler to pour ice inside when she felt a tug and then half of her ponytail lifted straight in the air, forcing her to stand. Reaching up, she felt a fishing hook caught in her hair and turned slowly around to find Stuart giggling. Trey's back was to them while he fiddled with the reel on his fishing rod.

Emma laughed. "Well, you got me back. I caught your hat, and now you caught my hair. How do you suppose we take care of this?"

Stuart kept giggling, but managed to keep his grip on his fishing rod. Emma knew she looked ridiculous when Trey finally turned around to see her with her ponytail hovering above her head. Trey merely shook his head and laughed.

He glanced down to Stuart. "I'm hoping this was an accident," he said though he had to bite his lip to stop laughing.

Stuart giggled and nodded. "I didn't mean to. It was just like when Emma caught my hat! I went to cast and then it didn't go anywhere."

Emma shrugged. "Turnabout's fair play. Do you think you could loosen your line now?" she asked Stuart.

Still giggling, Stuart adjusted his reel and the line went slack. Emma's ponytail fell. She sifted through her hair, trying to untangle the fishing hook.

Trey took the rod from Stuart's hands and set it in a holder before coming to stand by Emma. "Let me get that," he said, reaching up and carefully extricating the hook. Having him stand this close set her pulse aquiver. Her breath became shallow and her face hot.

"There, got it," Trey said, stepping back, the hook in hand. He flashed a quick smile, which only deepened her flush.

Flustered, she nodded quickly and stepped further away. She was relieved that Stuart immediately asked Trey to help him cast his line again, taking his attention away from her. By early afternoon, they each caught their daily limit of silver salmon. Stuart's energy was unflagging until the last fish was tucked in the cooler. The enthusiasm that buoyed him throughout the day finally waned. Standing at his father's side while Trey layered ice over the fish, his eyes fluttered and he swayed.

Emma moved quickly behind him, clasping him by

the shoulders. "Hey Stuart, you're about to fall asleep," she said softly.

He shook his head forcefully. "No I'm not." His eyes gave it away as he fought to keep them open.

Trey looked over his shoulder. "Hey bud, I'm thinkin' it's time for a nap. It's been a long morning."

"But Dad, Emma's here. I want to stay awake the whole day," Stuart said, his tired voice tinged with a whine.

Trey put his hand under Stuart's chin, his touch light. "How about this? You take a nap and we can ask Emma if she'll have dinner with us tonight?"

Emma's heart leapt at the question. She'd kept her feelings under control, but the part of herself she didn't want to take the lead was begging for every moment with Trey. The more sane part of her realized Trey was wisely bargaining with Stuart.

Stuart tilted his head up to look at Emma. "Will you have dinner with us?" he asked. "You can meet Tootsie and Neon."

"If I say yes, will you take a nap?" Emma asked, forcing her eyes away from Trey to Stuart.

Stuart nodded quickly. "Uh huh."

"Then, yes. I'd love to have dinner. I'd especially love to meet Tootsie and Neon." Emma looked to Trey when she replied, gauging his reaction.

Stuart was so tired his chin had dropped to his chest. Trey quietly closed the cooler, his eyes meeting hers. Without a word, he quirked a brow and nodded, one side of his mouth tilting up. He reached for Stuart and lifted him into his arms. Stuart was asleep in seconds, his head resting against his father's shoulder.

Emma watched Trey carry Stuart into the cabin. He carefully laid Stuart on the bed, tucking a fleece blanket around him. Watching him with Stuart only strengthened the draw she felt to him. And *that* made her wonder if she'd truly lost her mind. Since she'd shaken free from Greg, for the most part, she figured she'd be perfectly fine steering clear of any relationship...ever. But when she allowed herself moments to wish for something, she knew that it would have to be uncomplicated. A way too sexy widowed pilot who also happened to be a single father was pretty much the opposite of uncomplicated. Not to mention, as she'd told herself about five hundred times today, if Trey knew even a hint of what her marriage had been like...

Trey climbed up the steps back onto the deck and quietly shut the cabin door. "He'll probably sleep all the way back. He usually wears himself out when we fish," he said as he moved to pull up the anchor. In short order, they were headed back to shore. Trey was quiet as he steered the boat. Emma couldn't help but sneak glances at him. His dark silvered hair was windblown. Every time he looked at her, his velvety chocolate gaze stoked the burn she felt.

She forced herself to look into the bay. *Keep it together. For God's sake, just looking at him turns off your brain.* It was early afternoon, the sun high and bright. She took a gulp of air, wondering just what the hell she'd been thinking when she agreed to have dinner with them. At the moment, she'd said yes for Stuart's sake, but it was becoming obvious that her attraction to Trey was more than she bargained for. Another fortifying breath of the ocean air blowing by and she faced forward again. Just as she did, the boat's engine stuttered. A few seconds of that and the engine stopped completely.

Trey was back by the engine before Emma could say a word. She followed him to the back of the boat. "Is there anything I can do?" she asked.

Glancing up, he smiled wryly. "Not sure what's wrong. Mind holding the wheel while I take a look? Even though the engine isn't running, the rudder still keeps us aimed in the right direction."

Emma nodded and returned to hold the wheel. A few more minutes of Trey checking things, and he asked her to try starting the engine. Conveniently, it started right up. When Trey returned, she tried to slip out of the way. Her boot caught on the chair leg and she stumbled right into Trey. "Sorry," she said quickly, glancing up as she did.

Her hands landed on his chest, and his face was barely an inch from hers when she looked up—straight into his mesmerizing eyes. Desire raced through her, a current striking sparks between them. Trey's eyes darkened. In what felt like suspended time, Emma noticed that one of his hands had landed on her waist when she stumbled—its warmth seared into her, blazing a trail of heat that swirled through her center. Trey's eyes fell to her mouth and flicked back to hers. Afterward she couldn't be sure if there was a question in his eyes, but whatever he saw in hers must have answered. With no preamble, he closed the space between them, his mouth coming against hers.

Trey tugged her close against him. The feel of his body against hers was a heaven Emma hadn't imagined. He stood just tall enough above her that she felt sheltered in his arms. He turned so that he could lift her onto the seat and pressed against her, standing in the cradle of her thighs. His hand tangled in her hair, slipping around to cup her face. His thumb stroked down the side of her throat, brushing across her pulse. His kiss was masterful—a patient, thorough and searing exploration. He traced the contours of her lips with his tongue, alternating with soft kisses, nips and deep strokes.

She was aflame, almost frantic at the intensity of his kiss. He was water to her parched desire. His lips traveled down her neck, shivery heat following. She gasped his name.

He paused, the moment heavy and humming with the sheer yearning between them. He lifted his head, his eyes locking with hers. All of his control, all of measured reserve had disappeared. His eyes held such bare *want,* it took her breath away. She couldn't hide what she felt. She'd never felt anything close to this kind of passion with anyone *ever,* and she was utterly in thrall to the moment.

Wordlessly, she lifted a hand and traced his lips with her fingertip. Holding her gaze, Trey tipped his head toward hers. His lips landed against hers again, her hand falling away. Their kiss went wild. Emma was awash in sensation, her heart racing, heat unfurling through her body, desire sizzling in her veins. His hand slipped under her shirt, his palm strong and sure as it slid up her back in a heated caress. He deftly unhooked her bra, his palm sliding around her ribcage and softly curling around her breast. She gasped against his lips when he lightly rolled her nipple between his fingertips.

He pushed closer, though they were already plastered together. The heat of his hard length pressed into the cradle between her legs, right against her damp heat. What little hold she had on sanity scattered—she strained against him, desperate for relief. Trey broke away from her lips, his tongue blazing a damp trail down her neck and tracing her collarbone. His breath came in deep gusts against her skin. With a quick tug, her breasts spilled out above her tank top. He paused for a long moment, cupping both breasts with his hands.

Her nipples ached, peaked with desire. In slow motion, he circled one and then another nipple with his tongue. Pulling back, he blew softly against them. His warm breath heightened the ache she felt.

"Trey...please..." she gasped.

In response, his lips closed over one nipple and then the other, drawing deep and pulling back with a soft kiss. The relief was so acute, Emma's breath came out in a sob.

"Dear God, you are beautiful," Trey whispered, his voice raspy.

He pulled back to look at her, slipping his hands up to cup her face and then trailing down her neck, his thumbs tracing along her pules, skating over her shoulders to curl around her breasts again. Emma felt...treasured and vulnerable. She was lost in the fire between them. The raw vulnerability shattered her defenses. A distant warning bell rang in her head.

Trey caught her eyes and gave the barest shake of his head. "Don't think," he said softly, his words a warm command laced with an understanding that she didn't know how he could have.

Just as she started to think, he slid a hand down her abdomen, shoving her flimsy tank top out of the way. Holding her gaze, he deliberately unbuttoned her jeans, hooking his thumb over the top and pushing her zipper down. Her eyes fell closed as his hand slipped down to cup her through the thin silk of her panties. She was dripping with moisture, which she knew he felt. Barely moving his hand, he established an incremental rhythm, stroking her through the damp silk. In moments, she was on the brink. All thought vanished. All she felt was what lay between them—an incandescent passion. Trey slipped his hand away, replacing it with the pressure of his hard cock through his jeans. He ground into her, cupping her face with one hand, holding her gaze. Just as she tumbled over into an orgasm that went on and on, he brought his mouth to hers, capturing her fractured cries in his kiss.

As she slowly stilled, the pulses of her orgasm fading, Trey gentled his kiss and pulled away. Tilting her chin up, she found herself once again looking into his intense brown eyes. Emma couldn't have guessed what she would see, but she was startled at the bare desire reflected there.

Trey held her eyes, the moment shaped by a lingering pulse of desire and uncertainty. He finally spoke.

"I didn't expect that."

Emma wordlessly shook her head.

"I take it that means you didn't either?' he asked, a smile flirting at the corners of his eyes.

"No, no I didn't," she finally said, somehow finding her words. She forced herself to look away, staring blindly out over the water.

Trey remained where he was, his warm palm resting against her cheek, his thumb caressing her jawline. She could still feel his hard length against her, the denim rough against the damp silk. She took a shaky breath, trying to gather herself. Her wits had scattered. She felt out of control in a way she hadn't ever experienced. Part of her wanted to simply revel in what just happened and perhaps allow herself to enjoy this moment with Trey—when he seemed entirely at ease, his focus on her laced with an intense passion and tenderness. And yet, now that reality was hitting her, the wheels in her mind started to turn. Aside from Greg, she hadn't been with any other man, and she'd never had an orgasm with anyone but herself. She figured that she was too uptight to relax. With Trey though, it just *happened.* And that blew her mind.

Though her body, and perhaps her heart, thought what just happened was amazing, her mind...well her mind was definitely not in agreement. Her mind ran wild with reminders of why letting a kiss with Trey get so out of hand was plain stupid. And now she had to figure out how to gracefully handle this without looking like more of an idiot than she already did. For God's sake, he just kissed her like she'd never been kissed and made her fall apart in his arms. And he didn't seem to realize that what he'd done was a huge mistake. In fact, he seemed oddly comfortable with it.

Emma finally turned back toward Trey. Not yet able to meet his eyes again, though she felt them on her, she stared at his shirt, a soft worn navy t-shirt. She wanted to cry because so much of her wanted to let this be real, but she couldn't. She was who she was with the past she had. This would have to be just what it was—a moment of time that could never happen again. She swallowed against the tightness in her throat.

"Hey," Trey said, his voice low. "I don't know what

it is you're thinking about now, but how about not worrying so much?"

Somehow, his soft question relieved the building tension inside. She took a slow breath and finally looked up at him. His eyes were still unguarded. He slipped his palm under her chin and leaned forward to press a soft kiss on her lips, lingering for a moment. When he pulled away, his eyes became serious. "Emma, I meant it when I said I didn't expect that. But I won't pretend I didn't want it. I have since the first day I saw you. I just thought..." he paused, appearing to mull something over. "My life has been pretty focused since my wife died..."

"I'm so sorry that happened," she blurted out, her words tripping over each other. Though she hadn't known Trey long, she knew simply from watching him with Stuart that he was a good man with a good heart. She knew it must have been terrible for him to lose his wife.

Trey nodded, his lips twisting into a small smile tinged with sadness. "It's okay. It's been a while now. What I was trying to say is that even though I took one look at you and wanted to kiss you, it's not something I considered because I haven't let myself consider it with anyone. Not because I'm stuck in the past, but because it's hard enough being a single dad without trying to figure out how to bring someone else into my life with Stuart."

Emma began to nod. Trey was going to make this easy for her. Of course she understood how complicated that would be for Stuart. "I understand. I didn't expect this either. You don't need to worry. I'm not expecting anything from you, and I completely understand Stuart is your priority. There's no way to make promises, so don't worry. We can just be friends and pretend like this never happened," she said quickly.

Trey gave her a long look, arching an eyebrow. "That's not where I was going with this."

Emma's heart stuttered and raced, her nerves on high idle, barely settled from what had happened a few minutes ago. "What? I don't understand…"

Trey released her chin and began stroking his hand through her hair, which had come loose from its ponytail hours ago. He carefully untangled it as he spoke. "Obviously this," he gestured between them with his free hand "between us is a lot more than either of us bargained for. But I'm not going to just ignore it. It's too amazing. I haven't felt anything close to this. I know you can't make promises and neither can I. But Stuart adores you, and you blow me away. I don't want to pretend like this never happened. If I'm going to give myself a chance to try, it might as well be with a woman that I can't seem to stop thinking about. Not to mention what you do to me," he said, his voice deepening as he pressed his hips into her again. She felt the pulse of his cock against her.

In the quiet that followed, Emma felt Trey's hand slowly caressing her hair. He'd shocked her into silence. She'd have guessed he would want to see this as an aberration, not as something to hold onto. The corner of her mind that had held so much power over her the last few years, the corner that had helped her stay sane, move cautiously and get away from Greg wanted to be heard and wanted to tell her to walk away from this before she got in too deep. But the rest of her wanted, so desperately wanted, to do just as Trey suggested—to try this.

Cautiously, she lifted her eyes to his again. Her doubts clamored for attention and yet—she knew in her heart that no matter what, he was just as vulnerable as she was, and his heart was true. Her heart shoved her mind out of the way as she nodded. "I don't think I can say it quite like you did, but whatever it is between us… I don't want to pretend it's not there. I don't know what this will look like, but…"

Trey cut her off with a kiss. It started gentle, but in seconds, she was on fire. He stroked deeply into her mouth, his tongue tangling with hers. For a brief moment, he pulled away, stared intently into her eyes and then brought his lips down hard. Several breath stealing moments later, Trey broke away. Emma wouldn't have been surprised if steam lifted off of them. He took a step back and gave his head a hard shake. "If you were wondering what you do to me, let me just say this: we have to stop, or I won't be able to stop. You have me so out of my mind, I can't think straight," he said, shaking his head wryly, a wondering edge to his words.

A laugh burst out of her. "It's a two-way street. I almost forgot where we were," she said. "We should get back," she said.

Trey nodded and stepped close again. "Just a sec," he said, reaching down to slowly pull her zipper up and tug her tank top back over her breasts, his hands lingering in a soft caress before stepping back again.

He glanced out over the water and looked back to her. "Hope you like fresh salmon because that's dinner."

"I love fresh salmon. Should I bring anything?"

Trey shrugged. "If you want. I've gotten so used to

cooking for just me and Stuart, I usually have all the bases covered. What would you want to bring?"

Emma thought for a moment. "I could bring a salad. I make a great strawberry vinaigrette salad that kids usually like."

Trey smiled slowly as he nodded. "That would be perfect."

Emma thought she might just melt. Those smiles of his, which until their kiss had been like tiny surprise gifts, were so special she wanted to squeal. Instead, she kept it together and nodded. She finally slipped off of the chair behind the steering wheel, straightened her blouse and climbed onto the other chair. "Time to get going. I need to get back, so I have time to change and get what I need for the salad."

Trey shifted the boat into gear and flashed a quick smile in her direction.

 rey checked the propane tank for the grill, confirming what he already knew—there was ample propane to grill salmon tonight. It was late afternoon, and Emma would be here any minute now. After they'd returned to the docks, Trey managed to steal a quick kiss before it was time to wake Stuart. Thoughts of Emma had turned in his mind ever since he'd been unable to prevent himself from kissing her. Kiss was a weak word to describe what happened. All he knew was that any restraint he had dissolved under the sheer power of the current between them. He'd wanted to kiss her the first time he ever saw her.

But he couldn't have imagined what it would do to him. He chuckled to himself when he thought about how he'd imagined trying to start another relationship. He'd figured it would be months of dates, a careful introduction to Stuart, and then…something else. The last thing he would have guessed was that he'd get singed by the ferocity of passion that Emma elicited. He'd barely, just barely, remembered they were on a boat in the middle of the ocean with Stuart napping nearby. Oddly enough, he wasn't too bothered by how much power she held over him. He'd known passion with Helen. But he'd never experienced anything close to the fire that swirled when he touched Emma. He'd also known love with Helen. And though he'd be a fool to think he knew Emma the way he'd known Helen, his heart sensed that she rang true for his—and *that* he recognized.

He hadn't planned on this, not for a second. But he wasn't going to be so stupid to let something this amazing slip away just because he didn't anticipate it. Though he hadn't known she'd all but bring him to his knees with one kiss, he'd been interested enough before today that he'd made some careful inquiries about Emma. He had a few friends around town, including Jared Winters, a fishing guide he'd gotten to know. They often sent business to each other during tourist season and fished together when they could. One of Jared's brothers was married to Emma's sister, Hannah. Jared had bluntly pointed out he figured Trey must be asking about Emma for a reason. When Trey hadn't confirmed it, Jared merely shrugged and filled him in. That was how he'd learned Emma was a therapist, she'd moved here after finding out Hannah was her biological sister, and she was single and had been since she'd been in Diamond Creek. Jared had finished his quick summary by pointing out "...she's low drama and beautiful. Perfect for you."

His rational side politely reminded him not to move too quickly for Stuart's sake. Yet, he trusted Emma wouldn't want things to happen too quickly either. Though she'd thrown herself into their kiss with an abandonment that took his breath away, it was clear she was a cautious person, almost a touch too much.

He took a quick look around the back yard before stepping inside. He'd bought this house only months after Helen's death, needing a space that didn't echo with reminders of her. It occurred to him that he didn't think Helen had even visited Diamond Creek. He'd gone fishing here a number of times with Dave, and they'd talked of taking a day trip here with her, but it never happened. He loved the town and wanted some semblance of a fresh start for him and Stuart. The house was situated midway up the bluff that ran along the highway, which was flanked on the other side by the bay. The house faced Kachemak Bay with a wide-open view of the water and mountains across. Spruce and birch trees were scattered to one side and behind the house with a field to the other side. A stream ran through the field, which bloomed with lupine and fireweed each year. The house was a single story timber frame style, popular in Alaska. The living room had a cathedral ceiling and an entire wall of windows facing the bay. The kitchen sat to one side, the space melting into the living room, the only divider being a small island. There were three bedrooms, a bathroom and the laundry room off a hallway towards the back of the house. The master suite had its own office and bathroom. Of the other two rooms, one was Stuart's bedroom and the other a combination guest room and playroom for Stuart. With it just being him and Stuart, the house often felt larger than necessary.

Walking inside, it occurred to him that the only woman that had set foot in the house since he'd bought it was his sister, Risa. At thirty, Risa was ten years younger than he was and much bossier than he'd ever imagined a little sister could be. Even when they were little, she'd bossed him around. After Helen died, she immediately offered to stay with him and Stuart for a little while to help however she could. Her assertiveness had helped keep him afloat in that fuzzy time when he'd been shocked and grieving. When he decided to move to Diamond Creek, Risa suggested the name for his flightseeing business and accompanied him to look at houses. She was solely responsible for furnishing and decorating the house. Among other things, she was a painter. Her eye for color and warmth made the house a welcome, cheerful haven. She'd chosen a soft, comfy sectional couch of a deep wine red fabric with a matching set of reading chairs. A simple round birch table served as the dining area just past where the kitchen blended into the living room. A few of Risa's paintings hung on the walls, along with artfully placed items, including a beautiful piece of whale baleen and driftwood carvings. She'd created a reading and play corner for Stuart with a hand-painted bookshelf in bright, whimsical colors.

Looking around, Trey once again sent a thank you to Risa for making his house a home. Without her touch, Trey imagined the home would be spare and utilitarian. He quickly checked on the salmon that was marinating in a maple syrup and balsamic vinegar sauce. Nudging it with a fork, he turned the filets over.

"Hey Dad, can you come here?" Stuart asked, his voice drifting out from his room.

"Be right there," he called. He pulled a bottle of wine out of the wine rack that was built into the kitchen island, set it on the counter and headed down the hall.

Glancing in Stuart's bedroom door, he saw three t-shirts laid out on Stuart's bed.

Stuart had just finished his bath, which he'd needed after a day of fishing. He wore a pair of jeans with an elastic waistband and already had socks on, which was a miracle since Stuart had an oppositional streak when it came to socks. He claimed they made his feet feel 'tight' and generally resisted wearing them at all costs, even when it was freezing cold outside. Wet spikes of hair stood on his head, and his eyes were serious.

"What's up, Stu?" Trey asked.

Stuart waved his hand toward the shirts on his bed. "I have to pick the right shirt."

Trey looked to the shirts, which were basically the same shirt in three different colors—red, blue, and purple.

"So we need to pick the color, is that it?"

Stuart nodded emphatically. "It has to be right for Emma. Which color do you think she likes best?" he asked, his question so earnest, Trey's heart squeezed.

Trey had known for a while now that Stuart badly needed a mother figure, but it hurt to see how hard he was trying for Emma's sake.

"I bet Emma will like whatever color you pick."

"But it has to be right," Stuart said, a thread of stubbornness in his words.

"Right?" Trey asked, recognizing this was impor-tant to Stuart on a level he hadn't initially grasped.

"Uh huh. I want Emma to like you as much as you like her. And since we're a package deal like Aunt Risa says, I have to pick the right color," Stuart said, completely serious.

Trey stepped into the room and walked over to the bed. He carefully sat down in the only area that didn't have a t-shirt draped on it. "Come here," he said.

Stuart walked over and leaned against his leg. "What?"

Trey rubbed his hand up and down Stuart's back, his shoulder blades like tiny wings under his palm. "I know you want Emma to like me. And you're right that I like her," he said, pausing to consider his words. He didn't know if it was best to be open with Stuart about how he felt, but Stuart was so perceptive he knew Stuart already noticed that he liked Emma. "Stu, I know you want someone who can maybe be here for you the way Mom was. And no one will ever replace your Mom, but I bet it'd be nice for you to have somebody other than me cook dinner and lots more. I wish I could promise you I could make that happen. But it isn't that easy. Emma's a really nice lady, and maybe she and I will get to know each other better. But here's the hard part, even grown ups don't know how things will turn out. So while I can't promise you that if you wear the right color, everything you want to happen will happen, I can promise you that I'll be honest with you. And I know, I really know, Emma will like whatever color you wear. Actually, part of why I like her is I'm pretty sure we don't need to worry about her liking us based on the colors we wear. You know?"

Stuart's head was down and he stayed quiet for a moment. "I know. That's why I like her so much. 'Cause she's nice. But how come it's not that easy? The part you said."

Trey realized Stuart was asking how come it wasn't easy that if two people liked each other, they ended up together. Because he knew that's what Stuart wanted—a woman who could somehow fill the hole that had been left when his mother died. It almost took his breath away how simple it sounded. In a way, Stuart was so right. If two people like each other, how come it wasn't easy? Much as Trey wanted to assure him it would be, if there was one thing he knew to be true, it was that human beings were complex and each person was shaped by so many factors beyond their control that what should be simple often wasn't.

"That's a really good question I wish I could answer. All I can say is maybe it should be easy, but it often isn't. For now though, how about you put on the purple shirt because purple is *your* favorite color? Then you can tell Emma all about why you love purple so much. She's gonna be here soon, and unless you want to be half-dressed, you'd better get moving."

Stuart lifted his head sharply. "Oh!" he exclaimed, racing to tug on his purple t-shirt. Trey gathered up the other shirts and folded them before returning them to the shelf in the closet.

He turned to find Stuart carefully tying his tennis shoes and sat on the bed to wait until he was ready. When Stuart was ready, they walked down the hall together. While Trey knew the second he saw Emma, the fire that never died around her would crackle and hiss, he also knew he had to be careful for Stuart's sake and to remember whose heart was the most important.

Walking into the living room, Trey saw Emma's truck turn into the driveway. Stuart ran into the kitchen and whipped through the side door onto the deck. Trey followed at a much slower pace, trying and failing to keep his heart from pounding in anticipation. As he stepped through the door, Stuart was already by Emma's truck and chattering away. He grabbed her hand and tugged her to the house. She gamely followed his lead.

She wore fitted jeans and cowboy boots with a gauzy purple blouse that hugged her curves and tied with a bow at the juncture of her breasts—those luscious breasts Trey just couldn't get enough of earlier today. Her long dark hair was tied in a loose knot, wispy curls and bangs framing her face. As she followed Stuart up the steps, her blue eyes were bright, her lips and cheeks rosy. Forget Trey's heart pounding, it would take most of his control to keep his cock from staying hard all night. This was a new problem. He'd never had to worry about being appropriate around Stuart. No one, not even Helen, had brought him this close to the edge. He figured Stuart would be the ideal chaperone. If anything could pour a bucket of cold water on desire, a six-year old could.

"Dad, Emma's here," Stuart announced once they were all on the deck.

"Really? I didn't notice," Trey replied with a smile.

Stuart nodded and giggled. Trey caught Emma's eyes. "In case you didn't notice, Stuart's pretty excited you're here. And if he hasn't mentioned it, you happen to be wearing his favorite color," he said with a smile.

Stuart clapped. "I told her purple's my favorite!"

Emma chuckled. "He made sure I knew that right away. Nice to see you both again." She held a bag in her free hand. "I've got all the salad fixings ready to go. I forgot to bring a salad bowl though. I like to wait until right before we eat to toss it together. The strawberries are better that way."

Trey reached for the bag, taking a quick glance at Stuart who'd yet to let go of Emma's other hand. "I'll get that. We definitely have a few salad bowls, so don't worry about that." He was relieved to have something small to do to keep his mind off the fact that all he wanted to do was tug her close and kiss her until she was breathless again. Stuart rescued his sanity by insisting on giving Emma a tour, starting with his bedroom where Neon, the beloved goldfish, resided in a small rectangular fish tank elaborately decorated with various rocks and items.

Though Trey could barely keep his eyes off of Emma, dinner went off without a hitch. While Stuart gave Emma the house tour, Trey got busy grilling salmon. When Emma came in to assemble and toss the salad, there were a few moments where he had to work to keep his desire in check. Having her that close gave his body all kinds of ideas. It also made him realize how much he could get used to having her around. The mundane tasks of getting the table set and cleaning up in the kitchen with her made his heart clench. Though he'd surprised himself today by so readily accepting that what lay between them was worth giving a shot, the comfort he felt with her presence startled him.

Just after dinner, Stuart went onto the deck to call for Tootsie, his cat. Emma was putting dishes in the dishwasher. When she straightened from leaning over, the bow on her blouse caught on the dishwasher rack, immediately unraveling. Trey happened to be turning toward her, his eyes falling to the soft flesh exposed between her breasts. In a flash, the air between them became heavy. Trey forced his eyes up and they collided with her bright blue eyes. Her lips were parted, her gaze zeroed in on his. If it weren't for the sound of Stuart earnestly calling Tootsie, Trey knew without a doubt he'd have dragged her to him and kissed her senseless and then some. He saw her chest rise and fall in rapid breaths, mirroring his own. He gave his head a quick shake. Emma's eyes fell away. She looked down and quickly tied the bow on her blouse.

It was just enough to break the electric spell that flared between them. A few more moments of quietly cleaning up and Stuart returned to the kitchen holding Tootsie in his arms. Tootsie was a gorgeous orange striped cat. Risa had gotten him for Stuart shortly after Helen died. Though Tootsie, like most cats, was all but impossible to train, he'd slept with Stuart every night since they'd gotten him and usually came when Stuart called him.

Stuart walked into the living room, politely asking Emma to follow. Trey watched from the kitchen while he finished cleaning up. Emma was amazing with Stuart, which Trey would have guessed since she was a therapist. She was easy-going and patient, and Stuart soaked up her attention. He'd seated himself in the corner of the sectional with Tootsie on his lap. Tootsie was the ideal child's cat as he tolerated being carted around and would happily drape himself on Stuart's lap. A few minutes of Stuart showing Emma how Tootsie liked to be petted and his voice faded. Trey glanced over to see Stuart's hand mid-stroke on Tootsie's back and his chin on his chest. Emma caught his eyes and shrugged.

After drying his hands, Trey walked over, sitting

down on the couch at an angle across from Emma and Stuart. "I wondered how long he'd manage to stay awake," he said, looking down at his watch. "It's close to his bedtime, but between fishing and then having you over, he's about worn out."

Emma glanced down at Stuart and smiled softly. "He's such a good boy."

Trey nodded. "That he is. I have to give his mom a lot of credit for that. She did most of the work when he was younger."

Emma's eyes sobered. "I'm sorry about your wife. That must have been hard."

He paused to gauge his own reaction. In the first year after Helen had died, every time someone offered condolences, he would experience a stab of pain, the loss reverberating. That had gradually faded to a small twinge. The loss had woven itself into the fabric of his feelings. Time made a difference, if anything because it allowed him to adjust to her absence. He nodded. "It was. I didn't expect it, no one did. She had an undiagnosed heart defect, a faulty valve. Once it happened, that was it." He took a slow breath. "Afterward, I worried more about Stuart than myself. He'd just turned four. Helen had cut back on her hours after he was born while I worked too much. So she's definitely the one who laid the groundwork for the good boy he is now."

Emma nodded, her expression measured, but kind. "Well, Stuart seems to be doing okay, which I'm thinking is probably because of you."

Trey nodded. "I've done what I could to make up for his mom being gone. His Aunt Risa, my sister, has helped a lot too. She stayed with us for a few months after Helen died. She was always close to Stuart, but she's gone out of her way since then. She decorated the house, along with helping us with just about everything. She lives up in Anchorage, but she still comes down at least once a month if we don't make it up there for a visit."

"It's nice to have family like that," Emma replied. She started to say something else when Stuart shifted and Tootsie slid off his lap into the side of Emma's leg.

Trey stood. "I'd better get him to bed. He's out for the night once he falls asleep." He leaned over and gathered Stuart into his arms, carrying him to his bedroom. Stuart was deep enough into his sleep that he didn't budge when Trey changed him out of jeans into pajama bottoms. Tootsie silently leapt onto the bed beside Stuart once Trey tucked the blanket around him.

Returning to the living room, he found Emma standing by the front windows looking at the view. He walked to stand beside her. "Amazing, isn't it? I never get tired of the view here."

"It's beautiful, and you've got a nice spot here." She remained still for a moment and then moved toward the kitchen. "I should help you finish cleaning up."

Trey sensed tension in her, but he elected to ignore it for now. Trailing her into the kitchen, he leaned his hips against the counter, bemused when she picked up a lone fork by the sink and transferred it to the dishwasher. "Not much left to do," he said when she turned around.

She smiled and twisted a ring on her hand. She bit her bottom lip and glanced away from him. Trey pushed away from the counter and closed the distance between them. Part of him recognized he'd thrown caution to the wind when it came to Emma, but at the moment, he didn't give a damn. He paused directly in front of her and reached for her hands. She stilled in his clasp, her hands warm in his. He stroked his thumb across the back of one of her hands, turning the other up and placing a kiss in the center of her palm.

At the sharp intake of her breath, his pulse kicked into gear. He lifted his head, his eyes meeting hers. The desire he'd kept on a low simmer all afternoon since they'd kissed roared to life, her mere presence oxygen to the fire between them. The moment their lips met, he was lost...*again.* Emma felt like a living flame in his arms. She opened to his kiss, her tongue dancing with his. She pressed her full-length against him, almost matching him in height in her boots. He cupped her bottom with one hand, holding her hips tight against his throbbing cock, while his other hand tangled in her hair. He licked, stroked, sucked, and nipped at her lips.

Trey's entire body pulsed with the throb of desire, but he didn't want to rush this. He scrambled for control, ruthlessly slowing their kiss and creating a pocket of space between them. He pulled back to look into the blue of her eyes. He'd never seen eyes quite like hers—the color of the sky on those days when the blue was a shade deeper. Untangling his fingers from her hair, he caressed her ear, relishing her responsive shiver. He traced her jawline, his lips leading the way down the side of her neck, pausing for a soft kiss over the pulse that beat in her throat. He trailed his fingers along her collarbone, finding his way to the silky bow that held together her blouse. Her blouse had been teasing him all evening, it's gauzy fabric revealing shadowed glimpses of her curves. When he untied the bow, the fabric fell away, revealing the tops of her breasts. He leaned forward and rained kisses across the soft skin.

Emma gasped his name, arching into him. Trey lifted his head and almost lost control just looking at her. Her hair had come undone, falling in loose waves on her shoulders. Her lips were swollen and full, her eyes bright with passion. Her tongue darted out as she licked her lips. Trey forced himself to breathe. He tried to tell himself he meant to take his time, but his mind had little say in the matter. When Emma unbuttoned a tiny button and her blouse fell apart to reveal a tiny scrap of lace covering each breast, what little control he had shattered.

The dusky pink of her nipples was visible through the thin white lace. He shifted forward and sucked a nipple through the lace. Emma's voice broke when she gasped his name again. He turned his attention to the other nipple, pulling back just long enough to unhook her bra and push her blouse off of her shoulders. Her nipples pebbled in the cool air.

"Trey?" Emma asked, her voice breaking into the fog of passion that had enveloped him.

He looked into her eyes, a question within them.

"Yes?"

"I know we said we wanted to see what happened, but this..." she paused for a breath "...is happening pretty fast..."

Trey held still, forcing himself to think. He knew that on any other day with any other woman, he'd have wholeheartedly agreed. But this was now, this was Emma. All he knew was it didn't feel like anything between them was anything other than right.

He held her eyes for a long moment. "I suppose, rationally speaking, we may be moving a little too fast."

He forced himself to step back. Seeing as they were plastered against each other, creating even inches of space felt like an effort.

Emma chewed her bottom lip. "I don't want to slow down, but…" she finally said with a small laugh.

Trey closed his eyes and took a measured breath. It didn't do much to help. "Look, I get anywhere near you and all I want is you. But the last thing I want is to push you too far, too fast."

He saw something flash through Emma's eyes. Whatever it was held pain, but it was gone as quickly as he saw it.

"I just don't want you to regret this," she said.

Though it was only a blink, the pain he witnessed in Emma's eyes gave him pause. Not because it lessened what he felt, but because she already meant too much to him, and he couldn't ignore what he saw. He took another breath, attempting to slow the beat of lust pounding through him.

Emma remained quiet. Trey finally took another step back, reaching to help assemble her clothing again, carefully slipping the scraps of lace over her breasts. He had to close his eyes for a moment to keep from kissing her again. After she'd buttoned her blouse again, Trey reached over to tie the flimsy bow. When he was finished, he glanced up to find Emma watching him, her eyes vulnerable and guarded at once. Though his body had a different opinion, he knew it was right he'd managed to stop. Emma needed to know this wasn't just a fling for him.

He leaned forward and placed a soft kiss on her lips, which were plump from the ravishing he'd given them a few moments ago. "I won't regret this, but perhaps a little pacing would help."

Emma laughed softly and nodded. Hard as it was with her closeness a magnet, desire lingering in the air around them, Trey took another few steps back, leaning against the counter across from where Emma stood. Her chest rose and fell in a deep breath. Though the flash of pain in her eyes hadn't reappeared, Trey felt her worrying over something. He wanted to ask what, but he sensed now wasn't the time.

"Thank you for today and tonight. I enjoyed everything," Emma said, her voice cutting into the quiet.

"I should be the one thanking you. You made Stuart's day—and mine," he said with a wry smile.

"Tell Stuart I said thank you when he gets up tomorrow. And...you pretty much made my day too," she said with a blush. "I should get going."

Trey pushed away from the counter. "Before you go, when can I see you again?"

Emma shrugged. "Whenever you want. I'm not the busiest person around. Oh, except I'm going to Anchorage next weekend with some friends."

"How about dinner sometime this week? Stuart would love it, but we have to eat early enough he's in bed by eight o'clock."

"That'll work. What time do you want me to come over?"

"Is six too early?"

Emma shook her head. "That's perfect." She pushed away from the counter and looked around for her purse. He savored a long look, her hair in tousled disarray, her lips still swollen and her eyes bright.

Trey followed her outside, walking her to her truck. When he automatically reached to open the door for her, Emma threw him an incredulous glance.

"What?" he asked.

"I'm just trying to remember the last time a man opened the door for me. I didn't know anyone did that anymore."

"Maybe not, but I was raised to have some manners," he said, holding the door while she climbed into her truck.

Before closing the door, he leaned forward, sliding his hand under her chin and pulling her close for a long kiss. In a flicker, the intense yearning he felt for her roared back to life. Her mouth opened under his and he groaned in relief, stroking his tongue deeply inside. Emma gasped when he slipped his hand up into her hair and trailed his lips down her neck. He forced himself to stop, although it took all of his discipline. Gentling their kiss, he slowly pulled away. In the soft evening light, he held onto the promise of the feeling he saw in her eyes—desire and hope.

CHAPTER 8

*E*mma looked across the small coffee table in her office. Stella was slouched into the corner of the couch, furiously twirling her hair around her index finger. Waves of hurt pulsed from Stella, and it was painful to sit with it.

"I hate recital practice," Stella said, her eyes trained on the wall.

Emma waited quietly. Stella had been here several minutes and aside from choking out a hello, this was the first sentence she'd spoken.

After a few more quiet moments, Stella switched from twirling her hair to chewing her nails. "So I was hoping this recital thing would be fun. And the music part is fun. But one of the jerks who's friends with asshole of the year is in the recital too. Mrs. Cooper didn't tell me he'd be there."

"Okay, just so I keep things straight. If I recall, asshole of the year is the vice-principal's son, right?"

Stella nodded vigorously. "Yeah, Byron Landers.

And his dumb friend is in the recital. Parker Schmidt," Stella said emphatically.

"So what do we know about Parker other than who one of his friends is and that he's in the recital?"

Stella shrugged. "That's it."

"What instrument does he play?"

Stella rolled her eyes. "Okay, you got me. He plays drums."

Emma chuckled. "I wasn't trying to get you there, I was curious. So tell me more. Has he done or said something to you?"

Stella pursed her lips and shook her head.

"So he's a jerk because of his friend?"

Stella nodded. "That's all it takes. Byron was ready to let me get charged just because he hid his drugs in my locker. And I used to see him and Parker together all the time at school."

"Okay, I get why you'd be angry with Byron. And maybe Parker is a jerk. But even if he is, are you going to let him ruin the whole recital for you?"

Stella dropped her hands to her lap and finally made eye contact, her dark brown eyes tinged with shades of bravado and vulnerability. "No, no, I don't want him to ruin it. It's just that ever since that whole thing went down last year, half the school pretends like I'm not there. I just had the wrong locker. Byron's popular. I'm not. I'm worried Parker's going to make the whole thing not fun for me."

Emma's heart clenched at the pain she heard in Stella's voice. She'd yet to work with, or even know, a teenager who didn't share some variation of what Stella felt—different, alone, and desperate for the approval of their peers. But she knew telling Stella that wouldn't change how she felt. For Stella, her journey up to this point had involved climbing up and over one obstacle after another. Though Janie was doing her best to create a foundation for Stella, she was doing so from the ground up.

"I can see why you wouldn't feel good about Byron's friend being in the recital with you. What if you just try—and I know it won't be easy—to play it by ear? You're saying Parker hasn't done or said anything to you, so what would it hurt to try to not worry about it until he does something you might need to worry about?"

Stella started chewing her nails again, but only for a few seconds, before she looked back over at Emma. "It wouldn't hurt, but it won't be easy."

"Did I say it would be easy?"

Stella rolled her eyes and abruptly changed topic. "Janie couldn't come today."

Emma had been waiting for Stella to mention Janie. After last week, Emma had called Janie to ask her to come for the appointment to support Stella to talk with Janie about being adopted. Earlier today, Janie had called to let Emma know that Stella had demanded she agree not to come today. Janie had thought it best they let Stella call the shots on this, which Emma readily agreed with.

"Yeah, Janie called to let me know she wouldn't be coming today. Do you want to talk about that?"

Stella shrugged. "I'm still thinking about it. I told you before that getting adopted when you're sixteen is weird."

"You did. It's your decision," Emma replied, knowing in the end, no matter how much she thought it might help heal a part of Stella's heart for her to be adopted, it had to be Stella's decision. Though her heart wanted Stella to belong somewhere, she knew it had to be on Stella's terms.

Stella gave her a skeptical look. "You keep saying that."

"Well, it's true. It *is* your decision. You know Janie wants to adopt you, but she's not going to force it on you."

Stella started to twirl her hair again. "I think maybe it's too much to try to do this recital and decide about that. I barely have time to think these days because I'm at practice so much. Just like I said, Janie's in heaven. What is it with her and the activities?" Stella asked, air quoting her last word.

Emma chuckled. "I think you know the answer to that."

Stella rolled her eyes, letting go of her hair again. "Yeah, she thinks I'll make friends and that music is healing. You don't see that side of her much, but she gets all spiritual about stuff like music. I keep telling her I just like to play piano," Stella said with a laugh.

* * *

WHEN EMMA GOT HOME, Sula greeted her by twining around her ankles and purring madly. After she filled Sula's food bowl and gave her fresh water, Emma served herself from the pizza she'd picked up at Glacier Pizza on the way home and settled in for a quiet night of television. Aside from outings with her sister and friends, her evenings were quiet, which she savored. The peace of solitude was such a marked contrast to the tension and anxiety she lived with during her years with Greg. Quiet was often the precursor to an explosion, or to hours of simmering tension.

It was Tuesday, which meant she'd get to see Trey tomorrow. The only reason she hadn't thought about Trey non-stop was work tended to keep her so busy she rarely had time to think of anything. After she got home Saturday night, she'd lain awake for hours, replaying the moments on the boat with him when she had the first orgasm she ever had with anyone other than herself. Leaving Saturday night had taken all of her willpower. She'd wanted to curl into him and stay.

Before Greg, she had a few semi-serious relationships, but none lasted long enough for her to get comfortable. With Greg, relaxing enough to find her own pleasure had been impossible. That was why she'd been so stunned by what happened with Trey. When they touched, all apprehension dissolved. The comfort and intimacy between them didn't make sense rationally, but it felt so right and true. She tried thinking about it from her therapist mind, but it was hard to be objective about herself.

As she nibbled on a slice of pizza, her cell phone rang. After she said hello, there was a long silence.

"Hello?"

Emma stomach clenched, a cold chill racing through her. The silence lengthened. Though she wanted to believe there was no one on the other end of the line, she could hear faint breathing. She didn't wait any longer and quickly hung up. Checking her phone, she saw that the call was listed as private. After setting the phone back on the coffee table, it rang again. She stared at the screen, the word 'Private' flashing with each ring.

Emma ignored it. She tried to eat, but her appetite had fled. Ever since she left Greg, even a full three years later, she still got random calls like this every few months. She changed her number a few times, but it didn't stop the calls. No matter how she tried to talk herself out of it, she was convinced it was Greg. All the way through the divorce, she figured he let it happen because he didn't like anything that happened publicly. Court was public, so he had to lie low. He also nursed grudges. During the time they were together, she heard repeatedly about former girl-friends and friends he believed had wronged him. She knew beyond doubt she was high on his list of grudges. Though she was clear across the country, she didn't know if she'd ever stop worrying about whether he might force himself back into her life.

Having thoughts of Greg collide with her fantasies about Trey made her tired. This was why she'd known from the start that she needed to steer clear of Trey. Her past would keep intruding. The passion and longing she felt for Trey had caught her off guard. She had to find a way to gracefully back out. She could imagine the look in his eyes if he knew about Greg and how long she stayed. He needed someone without that kind of baggage, especially because of Stuart.

A tear slid down her cheek, cool on her skin. Sula silently leapt onto the couch and nuzzled her hand. Emma stroked her absently and tried to collect herself. She'd been silly, thinking she could explore what lay between her and Trey. She just hadn't real-ized how much it would hurt to shut the door on it. The other day and night had been so...*good*. Not just the intimate moments between them, but the comfort of being with him and Stuart, of being a part of something. As much as she loved Diamond Creek, loved her sister and her other friends, she always felt slightly apart. It wasn't being in a new place, it was how she felt ever since she'd moved in with Greg and then just allowed herself to be boxed in. Even before she and Greg had moved to Connecticut, he created a wedge between her and her parents. Her shame about staying with him amplified her emotional isolation.

The other day with Trey and Stuart had been a balm. Stuart was so earnest, so pleased to have her around. And Trey, well the electricity between them was one thing, but his tenderness and silent under-standing after they kissed had reached into her heart and grabbed hold. For the first time in far too long, she felt like she belonged. And now, she had to remember why it wouldn't, couldn't work.

Her phone rang again, this time Trey's name flashed on the screen. Her hand appeared to have a mind of its own, reaching to pick up the phone even as she tried to tell herself now wasn't the best time to talk to him.

"Hey there," Trey said, his voice threaded with warmth. Emma could see his eyes in her mind, crinkling at the corners.

"Hey," she replied, her heart lifting to hear him.

"I know we planned for dinner tomorrow, but I just wanted to call anyway."

Emma felt conflicted. The part of her that so desperately craved the possibilities Trey offered was ecstatic. The realistic part of her reminded her there were many things she could change, but her past wasn't one of them. *But you can change how you think about your past,* her therapist voice said, a hint of mocking to the tone. Emma shook her head and forced herself to focus on Trey.

"I'm glad you called," she replied, the bald truth coming out before she could think of anything else.

Trey chuckled softly. "Well, that's good. Perhaps I should have called sooner, seeing as I've wanted to every day."

Emma's heart stuttered and leapt. She couldn't hold back a smile. He wanted to call her...*every day.* "Really?"

"Really," he said bluntly. "Stuart finally gave me a reason. Before I forget, he asked me to ask you to bring Sula over. He tells me Sula is your cat, and he wants her to meet Tootsie. Just so you know, I explained to him cats don't always get along and some cats don't even like riding in the car. But I promised him I'd ask you."

Emma laughed and glanced down at Sula. "I told him about Sula when he was giving me the house tour. As for bringing her over, she's actually pretty friendly with other cats, but she hates being put in her kitty kennel for car rides. Can you tell him we'll have to pass on that, but maybe he can come over here to meet her sometime?"

"You got it. Now that we got that out of the way, how have you been?"

Emma couldn't stop the warmth that stole over her. Despite her worries about Greg and how she knew she couldn't let this keep going, she couldn't stop herself from savoring the joy of Trey calling her and asking how her day went. Despite the fact that the call lasted maybe five minutes, her pulse was racing and she was hot all over when she hung up. Trey said he needed to get dinner ready for Stuart.

And then… "Before I go, let me just say this: I haven't forgotten where we left off the other night," he said, his voice low.

Emma flushed head to toe at his words. "I haven't either," she whispered, her belly fluttering. She was so undone by his words she didn't remember saying goodbye. Falling asleep later, it occurred to her that instead of her night being ruined by one of those random silent calls, Trey's call had taken her mind off of them.

THE NEXT DAY dawned gray and rainy. Emma left for work early to stop at Misty Mountain Café for coffee. The café was housed in an old Quonset hut, one of many leftover from World War II when the United States used Alaska for strategic purposes due to its geographic proximity to Asia and Russia. Quonset huts were half circles of corrugated steel, open and airy inside. The owners of Misty Mountain had modernized this one with finished walls and decorative timber beams across the ceiling. The café was decorated with bright colors and local artwork. Summers were relentlessly busy with tourists, and this morning was no exception. Emma found herself in a crowd when she entered. Waiting in line, she felt a tap on her shoulder and turned to find Susie.

"Hey!" Susie exclaimed, pulling her close for a quick hug. "Do you have time to sit down? I have a table over in the corner."

"Of course. Just let me get my coffee."

Emma grabbed a savory roll once her coffee was ready and joined Susie in the corner.

Susie grinned madly once Emma sat down. "So?"

"So, what?"

Susie sighed dramatically and took a sip of coffee. "You know exactly what I'm asking about. But since you're being obtuse, how was your fishing trip with Trey and Stuart? I've been dying to know but work's been crazy, so I didn't have time to call you. You just missed Hannah here, and she said you hadn't even called her."

Susie said all of this as if Emma was supposed to know she should have called them both with updates immediately. Emma laughed and shook her head.

"My fishing trip was great. They invited me to dinner after," she said, wondering how much to share with Susie.

"And you didn't call to tell us! So what happened at dinner?"

"We had dinner. I met Stuart's cat and his fish."

"And?"

"Susie, there's not a whole lot to tell," Emma said, not sure yet that she wanted to share that Trey had kissed her senseless and then some.

"Oh yes there is. If that's all there was to it, you wouldn't be so evasive. Trey doesn't just invite women over for dinner. He's lived in town for almost two years now, and I would know if he had. So *that* is a big deal. Spill it," Susie demanded.

Emma decided she could use a little advice. Even if Susie was pushy, she was the kind of friend who told it to you straight, and she was as loyal as they came.

"Okay, aside from fishing and dinner, I discovered Trey is an incredibly good kisser."

Susie squealed, and Emma glared at her. "Keep it

down, would you? That's the good part. Next is the part where I could use some advice."

"My advice is to go for it. He's a good guy. According to Jared, that is. Jared may drive me batty with how uptight he is, but he's a pretty good judge of character."

Emma tilted her head. "So how come you didn't mention what you know sooner?"

"Because I just started asking around about Trey. When you told us he invited you to go fishing, I figured I'd better do some reconnaissance and find out what I could. The guy plays his cards close, so I didn't know much. It's lucky Jared did. Apparently they got to know each other after so many run-ins at the harbor. Jared says Trey's clean as a whistle – gossip-wise, that is – that his family lives in Anchorage, he's close to his sister, his wife died from a heart defect, and he hasn't dated anyone since she died." Susie spoke rapidly, dumping the information out.

Emma couldn't help but laugh and then almost wanted to cry. Much as she'd grown to feel like she was a part of the community here, realizing Susie decided she needed to essentially run a social background check on Trey made her feel like she truly belonged.

Susie must have sensed Emma's turmoil. "Hey, I hope it's okay I asked around. I just wanted to..."

Emma held a hand up, tears in her eyes. "It's absolutely okay. Sometimes it just overwhelms me to have friends like you. It's awesome," she said with a smile, the tears disappearing.

"Oh good. You're pretty awesome too," Susie replied with a wink. She gave Emma an assessing look. "Okay, so now that I spilled my goods, what else?"

Emma sighed. "So he kissed me, maybe a few times, and it was amazing. He invited me over for dinner again tonight. Stuart's adorable, and Trey is so good with him. He says all the right things. And I'm totally freaked out that I'm being stupid. I can't help but worry if Trey hears a whiff of what happened with Greg, he'll run from me. And even though I finally told y'all about what happened with Greg, I didn't mention I still get these random silent calls. I'm pretty sure it's Greg and I don't know what to do about it." Emma's words tumbled out.

Susie's eyes narrowed and her brow furrowed, her gaze sharp with concern. "Okay, we'll get back to the Trey bit, but why the hell didn't you mention to us you're worried about these calls?"

Emma sighed and took a fortifying sip of coffee. "Because I finally told you what a nightmare my marriage was. It's not like I was purposefully hiding the whole thing. It's just when I came out here to find my parents and found Hannah, I was so focused on that and finally getting away from Greg I didn't want to dwell on what happened. I wanted to focus on the future. Not to mention, my plate was pretty full with moving, learning that my bio parents had died, getting to know the sister I never knew I had, and so on. I don't get these calls much, maybe every few months and sometimes a few weeks in a row." Emma paused and looked over at Susie whose eyes were dark. "Susie, don't be mad at me. If you'd ever been in a relationship like the one I had with Greg, you'd understand why I never wanted to talk about it. I just wanted to put it behind me."

Susie's eyes softened. "I'm not mad at you. I'm mad at Greg. We don't even know if it's him with these calls, but it's damn likely. I hate you had to go through it. Maybe I haven't had a relationship like that, but I can see how once you were out, you'd want to just forget it ever happened. So whatever you think, don't go thinking I'm pissed at you. I'm just worried and wish you'd mentioned something sooner. You do *not* deserve this. I don't have an answer just yet, but we'll figure it out. Jared's buddies with Darren Thomas, one of the cops. I'll see if he can get some help from him."

Susie gave her a considering look and reached over to squeeze Emma's hand. "I won't tell you not to worry, but you know me, I'll find a way to do something. This is obvious, but have you tried changing your number?"

Emma nodded, anxiety fluttering in her chest. That's the part that bothered her the most. She had changed her number, more than once. Each time, it wasn't too long and she'd get another call with only the sound of someone breathing. "Three times. Don't you remember bitching at me about it? Doesn't matter. The calls keep happening. I got one last night."

"Ahh, so that's what's got you thinking Trey would run if he knew about Greg. You know, I'm not going to pretend I know Trey all that well because I'd be lying. But I don't think he would. I may barely know him, but he doesn't give me the jerk vibe and Jared swears he's solid. And Jared's so damn uptight that if he's willing to vouch for someone, it means something. Jared hates bullshit, and he thinks pretty highly of Trey. Honestly, if he would run from you because you ended up in a bad marriage, well then he's not worth it," Susie said emphatically.

Emma shook her head and wondered why she hadn't talked to her friends about Greg sooner. Susie made it all seem less horrifying. "Agree with you there. But it's kind of hard not to worry about what he might do when he finds out."

"Well get it over with then. I'm all about just spilling it," Susie said, slapping her hand on the table.

"Susie, I can't dump this on him. 'By the way, I know we just met but I thought you should know I used to be married to a wife beater.' Are you serious?"

"I think you should find a different way to say it," Susie began with a smile "...but yes, I'm serious. Here you are, after one day of fishing and dinner about to see him again, and you've got yourself worked up he'd run away if he knew about Greg. If you don't tell him, you'll keep worrying about it. You're a therapist, you know this."

Emma sighed. She knew Susie was right. The therapist in her, who was generally annoying when focused on herself, knew it was best to get this out in the open. Not just for her own sanity, but if she was going to let things go anywhere between her and Trey, it was better if he knew. Just thinking about it tied her stomach in knots.

Susie reached over and squeezed her hand again. "I can't tell you when, but as into Trey as you are, and you *are* into him, you can't let this go much further without getting this out of the way for your own sake. You're the kind of person that wouldn't want to be serious with someone if you were keeping secrets."

Emma threaded her hands through her hair and took a deep breath. "I know. Ugh. It's so shitty when it's me. I know if someone were asking me about this, I'd tell them pretty much what you're telling me. It's just so embarrassing on this side."

"I get it, but anybody with a brain realizes it's not like guys who beat their girlfriends start out by hauling off and hitting them at the beginning. They start out nice and charming. I'm not an expert, but I've seen this type of thing play out. All you have to do is read the local paper and you see that Diamond Creek, our tourist mecca with its friendly vibe, has more arrests for domestic violence than anything else. There's a reason Alaska is all about domestic violence prevention. You may have gotten away from your own situation, but you landed in the state with the worst stats in the nation. I didn't have to go out of my way to find this out. It's in the news all the time. You're a member of one of the least exclusive clubs in the world. Don't be embarrassed." Susie nodded firmly when she finished.

Emma's throat tightened, and she couldn't shake the anxiety she felt. Intellectually, she knew Susie was right. Emotionally, it wasn't that simple. Shame welled inside at the thought of telling Trey about Greg. She knew all the reasons why getting involved with Trey wasn't a good idea. And now he mattered, which made it even more complicated. That damn call last night had stirred her up.

"Could I call you whenever I need a friendly reminder about this?" Emma asked wryly.

"Absolutely," Susie replied with no hesitation.

Emma looked over at Susie's warm and determined brown eyes. Hope bloomed in her heart. Maybe, just maybe Susie was right about Trey, or rather Jared was right about Trey. It wouldn't make it any easier to talk to him about Greg now, but Susie was definitely right that she'd simply worry over it until she did.

Emma glanced at the clock on the wall. "Okay, I need to get to the office." She took a long look at Susie. "I can't tell you how glad I am I happened to run into you this morning. You were the perfect person for me to talk to. I could use a little of your mojo, so I'll try to channel you later when I talk to Trey."

Susie smiled warmly, reaching over for both of Emma's hands this time. "I don't get called perfect very often, maybe never, so you made my day. You call me if you need to. In the meantime, promise you'll let me know if you get any more of those calls. I'm assuming it's okay if I ask Jared to check with Darren."

Emma nodded. "Oh yeah. I've spilled the beans now, might as well see if I can get some help." She gave Susie's hands a squeeze and grabbed her purse and coffee.

* * *

EMMA SAT beside Stuart on the floor in the living room, waiting while he selected a book from his reading corner. She stroked Tootsie who'd positioned himself between them.

"What about the Farmer's Almanac?" Stuart asked, pulling out the latest version.

Emma was surprised at his choice and looked over to the small bookshelf, painted bright red with blue starfish scattered on the sides, to see there was an entire row filled with Farmer's Almanacs.

"Stuart loves those. His grandfather gave him one last year, and he's hooked. Not sure if you've ever read one, but they're filled with information, pictures included," Trey said from the living room couch.

Stuart looked to Emma and nodded vigorously. "They have everything. There's weather, stuff about animals and plants, and the tide. Haven't you ever read one?" Stuart asked, his eyes wide with disbelief.

"I promise I've read one," Emma said solemnly. "My sister has this year's, and I saw it just the other day. If you'd like to read that tonight, sounds like a plan."

They had finished cleaning up after dinner. Trey had made a salmon casserole with salad. Emma was quickly discovering Trey was quite the cook though he insisted it was only by accident. She thoroughly enjoyed dinner. The more time she spent with Trey, the more she wanted more time with him. The physical attraction between them was an electric force, just a mere brush of his hand on her arm was enough to set her pulse off and liquid heat to pool in her center. There was that, and then so much more. Trey was so steady with Stuart, patient with his questions, and yet firm when he needed to be. He and Stuart included her in talk about Stuart's day at a summer nature school, and then led the conversation into questions about her life. The only mar in the evening was what lay in the back of Emma's mind—she promised herself she'd let Trey know about what happened with Greg. The mere thought of it caused anxiety to bloom and her chest to tighten.

Stuart nudged her on the shoulder, bringing her thoughts back to the moment. "See, they have a part about plants. Dad says I can have a garden next year, so I want to read about it," Stuart said.

A small bookmark with a picture of a walrus on it slid onto the floor. Emma picked it up and handed it to Stuart. "Don't lose your spot," she said, giving Tootsie one last stroke before standing and holding her hand out.

Stuart's bedtime was at hand, and Emma wanted to make sure her presence didn't interfere. Trey had explained that Stuart preferred to read himself, but liked to have Trey sit with him for a few minutes. Stuart had politely asked if she'd help him select his book for the night before he went to bed. When they reached the couch, Stuart leaned against his father's leg.

"Dad, can I stay up since Emma's here?"

Trey smiled and slipped his hand around Stuart's back, rubbing slowly up and down. "Remember what we talked about earlier?"

Stuart nodded. "You said Emma would know I needed to get my rest, so she'd want me to go to bed on time," Stuart said slowly. He glanced up at Emma hopefully.

"Your dad was absolutely right," Emma said, looking down at Stuart. "Bedtime is important and so is sleep. Give me a quick hug before you go." She squatted down and hugged him close. Stuart squeezed her and gave her a smacking kiss on the cheek.

Trey gave her a quick grateful smile and then stood to walk Stuart to his room. "*Be back*," he mouthed silently over his shoulder. Stuart gave her a last wave when they reached the hall.

Emma sat down on the couch with a sigh, looking out the front windows. The sun was in its slow slide, nowhere near its final bow behind the mountains. She still marveled at the long summer days. Dusk wasn't the brief window of time here like it was back East. Dusk lasted for hours, the light fading in increments as the sun inched its way out of sight. The mountains were shadowed with the sun low behind them. Soft pink and gold suffused the sky. The birch trees glowed white amongst the spruce in the faded light. The field to the side was dusted with the soft light, the purple lupine in the tall grass radiant.

Emma heard the low murmur of Trey's voice. She steeled herself to talk to him as soon as he returned. A few minutes later, she heard the bedroom door close, and Trey returned to the living room, sitting down beside her. Her pulse immediately started racing, heat swirled in her center and spiraled outward. Turning to look at him, her eyes collided with his—that rich brown, deep and intent. She couldn't catch her breath at the wave of desire that swept through her.

Trey simply leaned forward and kissed her. His kiss began gently, a soft, thorough exploration. Once Emma slid her hand around his neck, Trey cupped her face in both hands and just devoured her mouth. His tongue wound and tangled with hers. She was lost in the passion that twined around them.

He broke free from her lips to dust kisses across her face, nibbling her earlobe and tracing his way down her neck with his tongue. Heat built inside of her, her skin flushed all over. She gasped when Trey slid his hand down and flicked the buttons free at the top of her blouse. He traced the tops of her breasts with his tongue, pausing to look up at her when she gasped his name.

"Yes?" he asked, his voice low and deep, just above a whisper.

Emma forced herself to try to think, but her mind was muddled with desire. All she wanted was Trey. *Now. Completely.*

The feeling was so overwhelming, it shook her. "I...can't...can't think..."

"Do you need to think right now?" Trey asked with a quirk of his lips, his fingertips trailing across her breasts.

Emma closed her eyes against the dark passion in his gaze. She tried to slow her breath, but failed. And yet, she promised herself she'd talk to Trey and letting things spiral out of control this fast wasn't conducive to talking. Opening her eyes, she braced herself. "Yes, I need to think. We have to talk... just..." Her breath hissed through her teeth when Trey lightly pinched a nipple through the lace of her bra.

"You're not being fair," she said in between gasps.

A sly smile stole over his face. "I know, but I don't want to talk," he said simply.

Emma sighed. "I don't either, but I have to."

He seemed to read into her eyes and realize she was serious. He pulled back, his hand sliding down to rest on her ribcage. He took a slow breath and glanced back at her, his eyes serious now.

"Okay. This seems important. Talk."

Emma had rehearsed what she planned to say, which was a good thing because it took enormous discipline to force the words out when she didn't want to, but only knew she had to. "This is going way faster than I expected. I just think there's something you need to know about me before we go too much further." She wanted to stop here and just tell him to forget it, or make up some random excuse.

By now though, Trey was watching her intently. When she paused, he quirked a brow. She closed her eyes and took a fortifying breath.

"I was married once before, and things didn't go well. My ex...well...he was violent and controlling. I stayed way too long. I should have known better to begin with. I mean, for God's sake, I'm a therapist. It just happened and then I was in the middle of it all alone, and I didn't know how to get out."

Emma stopped to look at Trey and couldn't read his expression. She barreled forward, aware at this point that if he was going to question his judgment about her, it was already too late. "I had to tell you because I didn't want you to find out after the fact and wonder why I didn't tell you. I totally understand if this changes how you feel about me, especially because of Stuart."

Trey was quiet for a long moment, but he didn't look away or move away.

After what felt like forever, Emma couldn't hold back. "Could you say something please?"

Trey slowly lifted a hand and brushed an errant lock of hair out of the way, tucking it behind her ear. The gentleness in his expression almost undid her. "I know we haven't known each other too long, but why would you think this would change how I might feel about you?"

Emma shrugged, feeling small inside, and looked away. "Because... I mean, not for nothing, but you are a lawyer. I'm guessing you'd steer clear of anyone like my ex. I should have known better myself. By all means, I have more understanding of what happened in my marriage than the average person. But I was an idiot, I walked right into it anyway."

Trey toyed with her hair, which was doing funny things to her belly. The feelings he elicited were so elemental she wished even more that she didn't have to have this conversation with him and that she had a less blemished past.

"Emma, why are you so hard on yourself about this? I hate knowing you went through that, but for the same reason you think you should have known better, you should know it's not easy to see these things when they're happening to you. I used to deal with this kind of stuff all the time when I was a prosecutor. I can't tell you how many times I handled cases where some upstanding guy was beating his wife. There is no stereotype for these guys. I've seen juries convict just about anyone you could imagine, including doctors and lawyers, along with the less fortunate. So hearing that this happened to you. Well, it's awful, but it's not something I'd hold against you. It makes me furious anyone would do that to you, and if I ever meet the guy, you might question my judgment," he said, his words stark and clear, anger vibrating through them.

Emma half couldn't believe his words. "What?" she asked, finally gaining the courage to look at him again, his eyes serious and concerned. She'd been prepared for judgment and there was none.

Trey held her gaze. "I'm getting the idea you thought this might be some kind of deal breaker for me," he said cautiously.

Emma's throat tightened when she nodded.

"Did I do something that led you to think I'd just

blame you for getting knocked around by your ex?" Trey asked incredulously.

"No. I just…just got worried about it. I hate that I was married to someone like that and didn't have enough sense to get out faster. And it will always be a part of my past. It's embarrassing. Plus, you have Stuart and it's important that anyone you bring into his life is good for him."

Trey leaned back a little and tilted his head. "Okay, I get the embarrassment, I get that you can't make it go away. But you actually got out of the situation. If there's one thing I learned when I was a prosecutor, that's damn near impossible sometimes. I wouldn't hold it against you if it had taken you years longer than it did, or if you never did. Two years may seem like a long time to you, and I hate that you were in what was probably a living hell for that long, but in the big picture, it's not too long. It's remarkable you got out as soon as you did. As for Stuart, sure I want the best for him. And I absolutely want to make sure that anyone I bring into his life works for us both, but who your ex was does not mean you're not good for Stuart. You're amazing with him. I don't know what's going to happen with us, but if Stuart ever learned about your ex and what happened, I would want him to know it's something people go through, and sometimes they make it out the other side."

Emma took his words in, her heart hammering against her ribcage. Relief was washing over her, but she couldn't forget to tell him what got her so worried about this. "I can't tell you how much it means that, well, that you get it. But there's one more thing. The reason I got all freaked about this is sometimes I still get calls. I think it's my ex"

Trey's eyes sharpened. "What do you mean you still get calls?"

"Every once in a while, I get these random calls. It's an unlisted number. If I answer, whoever it is doesn't say anything, but I can hear breathing. I've tried changing my number, but it doesn't matter. My ex, Greg let the divorce go through without much fuss, but I was out of state and he hates court. He wouldn't make a scene with that. But he holds grudges. I hoped he'd just find someone else. I can't stop worrying he won't just let it drop that I actually left."

Trey took a measured breath, his eyes holding hers, tinged with anger. "Have you talked to anyone about this?"

"Just Susie and now you. I didn't want to make something out of nothing and then I met you, and I got one of the calls the other night...and I finally told Susie. I don't know how well you know her, but she's pretty, um, forceful. She wants to talk to the cops. But what can they do? The number isn't showing and whoever it is doesn't say anything. It could just be random and I'm freaking out over nothing."

Trey nodded and looked out the window, quiet for a moment. "Well, it's best if we see if the cops can do anything. If you'll let them, they can probably put a trace on your line. If it's nothing, let them rule it out. But if you don't tell the cops and something happened, we'll wish you did."

Emma's heart leapt when he used 'we' and she wished he'd say it over and over.

Trey continued. "Can't say I know Susie too well, just in passing. She does the accounting for a buddy of mine, Jared Winters." He looked back to her, his eyes sharp and intent. "Promise me you'll tell me anytime you get one of these calls."

Emma nodded. "I will. You're really okay with all of this?"

"I'm not okay you had to go through that, and I'm definitely not okay you're getting these calls. Maybe it's your ex, maybe it's not. But we need to find out and deal with it. Otherwise, I'm okay with you if that's what you're asking."

Emma couldn't quite believe Trey hadn't just politely escorted her out of the house. "Really?"

Trey turned to face her more directly. "Really. I'm trying not to take it personally that you had pretty much decided I'd hold it against you."

"I wasn't worried because I thought you couldn't understand. It's just...you have it all together. I mean you're a pilot and a lawyer, you run your own business, and you're a single father. I didn't know if you'd want to consider getting involved with someone who didn't quite have it all together before and who might have a few ghosts from her past hanging around."

Trey tilted his head and quirked a brow again. "So what? Haven't you heard all the jokes about lawyers? I'm not perfect and don't know any lawyers that are. I enjoy flying a lot more, which is why I changed gears. How about we focus on what we talked about the other day? There's something, quite a bit of something, between us. I didn't expect it either, but I'm not about to walk away from something that feels this good."

Emma looked into his eyes and what she saw took her breath away—tenderness and passion focused solely on her. She was so prepared for this conversation to close the door on what had started between them that she was almost giddy with relief. The intensity in his eyes sharpened. She bit her lip and glanced away, overcome with feelings—relief, joy, and...sheer longing. For the first time ever, she just wanted to let go into something—into what danced and sizzled between her and Trey.

Her heart pounding, she lifted her eyes to his again. Trey had begun to run his fingers through her hair and slowly slid his hand around to cup the back of her head. He gave her a long look. "Did you want to talk some more?" he asked, soft and low.

Lost in his velvet brown eyes, Emma shook her head. He closed the space between them, his lips coming against hers. It felt like coming home. She opened her mouth in a sigh. What started slow spiraled rapidly into a frenzy. Trey stroked deeply into her mouth. If they hadn't been seated already, she would have collapsed in the wave of heat that raced through her.

His lips left hers and meandered in a trail of soft, moist kisses down her neck, along the line of her collarbone and dipping between her breasts. He caressed a nipple with one hand, rolling it between his thumb and forefinger while laving his tongue over the other nipple dampening the lace of her bra. Sensation fluttered in her center, moisture pooled between her legs, her panties almost instantly wet.

He turned his attention to her other breast, taking his time to nibble and nip. Amidst her gasps and pants, he pulled away, ruthlessly tugging at her blouse, buttons scattering as he pushed it off her shoulders, her bra following in quick succession. He became still for a moment, taking in the view of her. "You're so beautiful," he whispered, stroking his hands up her abdomen to curl around her breasts. Emma closed her eyes, undone by the intimacy of his gaze. She'd never felt this desired by anyone.

When she finally opened her eyes, they collided with Trey's, reflecting heat and tenderness in equal measure. He seemed to sense her vulnerability, and yet she couldn't have stood it if he said anything. And he didn't. He merely lifted a hand to her mouth, tracing her lips before leaning forward for another devouring kiss. Tumbling into the fire, she leaned up and pushed him back, tugging at his shirt, pulling it up over his head and tossing it. The polite, austere man she met weeks ago hid a delectably well-defined and muscular chest.

Emma ran her hands across his shoulders and over his chest, reveling in the feel of his skin. His breath hissed through his teeth when she curled her hand over his heated length, feeling the pulse and throb through the fabric of his jeans. A flash of lust and confidence bolted through her, and she pushed him against the couch and straddled him. The heat of his erection against her was delicious. Losing herself in sensation, she pressed down and arched her back.

"Dear God, Emma!"

He slid his hands up her back, his palms strong and warm, pulling her forward slowly until her breasts came against his chest. She rested her forehead against his. He took her lips again, one hand tangling in her hair. She was wild, lost in the inferno between them. She ground her hips down, desperately craving release.

Trey broke their kiss with an imprecation. His hands slid down to her hips where he held her still against him. "Emma," he whispered. "Look at me."

Forcing her eyes open, she met his and instantly felt vulnerable. She wanted to tell him she knew what was between them was rare, but she could only succumb to it if she could forget herself while it was happening. But she couldn't say that, not when his eyes resonated with yearning...and recognition. Somehow, he knew this was hard for her. And *that* simultaneously drew her to him and made her want to shake the feeling off.

Trey kept his hands on her hips and slowly rocked against her. Desire shimmered in the air around them, enfolding them in its spell. He paused his slow rhythm and slowly slipped his hands up, lightly caressing her breasts. In a flash, he lifted her quickly, turning her underneath him. He tore her jeans open, tugging them down. Desperate to feel his weight on her, she kicked her legs free and pulled him down, sighing with relief at the feel of his full body against hers.

Trey kissed her deeply, slipping a hand down her abdomen and into her panties, soaked with her desire. "Please..." she gasped when he dipped a finger into her slick heat. He slipped to her side, half resting on her. Leaning on his elbow, he looked down at her as he deliberately removed his hand and trailed it back across her abdomen, engaging in a leisurely exploration with his hand—tracing between her ribs, lightly pinching each nipple.

The heat inside her built.

"You have too many clothes on," she said.

"Maybe, but it's staying that way," he said with a rueful smile.

"Why?" she demanded, the ache of desire clashing with uncertainty.

"Because I don't want to stop and trust me, you won't leave before I make sure you're taken care of... but I think maybe you're not sure about this just yet. So for now, you'll just have to wait a little longer."

Indignation flared. "No," she started to say before he cut off her words with his mouth.

In seconds, she tumbled back into the oblivion he created. His hand skated across her body, the roughness of his palm flint against her desperation. He delved his fingers into her again, tracing her clit with her own moisture. She teetered on the edge of release.

"Trey...please..." she panted.

Her mind blurred with passion and intense yearning. He established a slow pattern, delving into her with one, then two fingers and pushing deep while his thumb slowly, mercilessly teased her clit with soft strokes and bursts of pressure. She ground her hips into his hand, begging, pleading with him for more. Her head tossed against the couch.

He shifted to slip his free hand behind her head, his chest coming against her breasts. He whispered her name, yet again that soft command to look at him. Just as her eyes met his, he stroked deeply into her center. Release washed over her in a burst followed with long pulses as she climaxed around his hand. He never looked away, leaning forward to kiss her once her hips relaxed.

Emma floated in the haze of her release. Trey's hand remained inside of her, moving just barely in response to the lingering pulses of her orgasm. He dusted kisses across her face while he slid his hand up, the moisture from within her traced in circles on her abdomen and breasts. His hand came to rest at the base of her neck, his thumb stroking across the beat of her pulse.

The heat of his erection pressed against her thigh. Though she just had an almost out of body experience, when he shifted his hips she wanted nothing more than to feel him inside of her. Looking at him, her heart clenched. The moment shimmered between them.

She started to speak, but couldn't. Trey carefully stroked her hair, brushing it away from her face. He looked pensive.

"Well," he said.

She waited in the quiet, finally speaking when he didn't say more. "Well, what?"

A soft laugh fell from his lips. "You take my breath away. That's all."

He shifted back onto his elbow. "So when can I see you again?" he asked.

"Perhaps you didn't notice I'm still right here," she replied.

"Oh I noticed. I just thought maybe I should make it completely clear I don't want to miss any chance to see you."

"If you want to see me so soon, how come you're still half-dressed?" she asked, vulnerability arcing inside.

His eyes became serious. "I'll be blunt. I'm ready to throw caution to the wind. But I get the sense, just here and there, you're not so sure. And after what we talked about earlier, I'm definitely not going to pressure you."

Emma leaned up on both elbows and looked at him. Though he just brought her to a mind-blowing orgasm, the mere sight of his chest stoked the embers between them. His eyes were serious though. His gaze was steady, almost burning into her.

"You're not pressuring me," she said.

Trey shifted his weight and pushed himself up. The cool air against her skin elicited a shiver.

"I don't mean pressure in the direct way. More that I can't seem to keep my hands off of you and sometimes it seems like you're worried. I want you to have time to be comfortable. I'll be the first to admit this is moving faster than I would have planned, let's just take it a day at a time."

He reached over and cupped her cheek for a moment. She closed her eyes at the intimacy. He was so sexy, he stole her breath while also compassionate and so in tune with her, it confounded her. Though she genuinely believed in the capacity of the human heart to connect, she'd come to never expect it for herself, believing against logic that what happened with Greg ruined any chance of that for her.

"Hey," he said softly. "Don't know what you're thinking, but stop it."

He stood and held a hand out to her. Placing her hand in his, she allowed herself to be pulled up. The following moments of activity helped calm her. Buttoning the last few buttons on her blouse, she felt Trey's eyes on her. Looking up, she found him smiling and couldn't stop the smile that bloomed in her heart.

"So you didn't answer my question," he said.

At her puzzled glanced, he continued. "You didn't tell me when I could see you again."

"Oh. Aside from this weekend when I'm in Anchorage, any evening works."

"In that case, how about tomorrow?" he asked promptly.

"Tomorrow?"

"You said any evening," he replied, a glint of amusement in his eyes.

"I suppose I did. In that case, tomorrow is just fine. Should I plan to come over again?"

"How about I give you a call and we'll decide?"

At Emma's nod, he reached for her hand and brought it up to place a kiss in the center of her palm. Delicious warmth stole through her. Quiet fell between them. Emma held still, her heart hammering. The comfort she felt with him was so unlike anything she'd experienced that it shook her at her core.

"I think I should go," she said softly, her words filtering into the moment.

Still holding her hand, Trey drew her to him and dropped a quick kiss on her lips. "Until tomorrow then."

CHAPTER 9

Trey headed to his law office the following morning. His work schedule flipped summer to winter. In the winter, he handled more law cases and in the summer, he rarely spent more than a day at the office each week, his time filled with flightseeing trips. He kept his flightseeing business small, but the tourists packed Diamond Creek every year, so he stayed busy. Today, he had a meeting on a divorce case, one that seemed blessedly simple. He couldn't help but wonder more about what Emma had gone through with her ex. Some of the most heart-wrenching cases he'd handled as a prosecutor involved domestic violence. Though he believed in the legal system, he knew that the current system didn't serve victims well. Prosecutors were over-loaded with cases and rarely had the time or resources to help victims navigate the system. More often than not, charges were dropped. Even when charges stuck, the penalties were minimal—a few days in jail, a piece of paper that was supposed to keep someone away, maybe an anger management class.

With a sigh, he sat down at his desk and quickly checked his email and phone messages, which included a message from Risa demanding he call her if he wanted her to babysit tonight.

"Well, that was quick," Risa said as soon as she answered.

"Hey Risa, just calling when I had the chance," Trey replied.

"So I can come down, but you're gonna have to put up with me for two nights. The drive from Anchorage is too long for one night."

"You're the best. Of course you can stay two nights. More if you want."

"Okey dokey. I'll be there before Stuart gets out of day care. Can I pick him up?"

"Where are you? You can't get here from Anchorage in time to pick Stuart up," Trey said.

"Oh, I already left," she said with a chuckle.

Trey threw back his head and laughed. "Of course you did. You didn't need me to call, you just wanted to make me."

"Damn straight I wanted you to call. What are you doing tonight that you need a babysitter on short notice? Not to mention, maybe you should find a local babysitter."

Trey sighed. "I do have a local babysitter. But she's only available on the weekend."

"Good to know. But you're avoiding my question. What's the deal tonight?"

"I have a date," he said simply.

"Well if you'd told me that in your message last night, you wouldn't have had to call. It's way past time for you to at least try to date again. Who is it and is she good enough for Stuart?"

Trey heard the smile in Risa's voice. "Her name is Emma. And since you'll figure this out pretty quick, I really like her. She's great with Stuart, and he's the one that pretty much set us up." He paused when there was a knock on his door. "Hang on."

"Come in," he called out.

His assistant, Lucy, poked her head around the door. Lucy was an older woman who'd worked as a paralegal for over twenty years and worked with him when he was a prosecutor. She and her husband, Howard, moved to Diamond Creek before he did. A few fishing trips with Howard helped Trey decide to move here. Lucy was no nonsense and practical. Her white hair was kept short, giving her a youthful look. She favored bright colors, wearing an emerald green blouse today. She handed over a sheaf of papers. "The ex's attorney sent over a suggested settlement. I think it's crap, but you might want to take a look," she said with a wry smile.

Trey gestured to his phone and mouthed that he'd be off in a few. Lucy nodded and closed his door again. "Risa, gotta go. You're the best. Of course, you can pick Stuart up. You're on the list already. I'll see you when I get home. Promise I'll tell you more about Emma when I see you."

"I'll hold you to that. See you in a bit," Risa said, disconnecting quickly.

* * *

TREY WAS WALKING BACK to his car after a quick run to the store before heading home when he heard his name. Looking up, he saw Jared Winters leaning against his truck, which was parked beside Trey's car.

"Hey there, what's up?" Trey asked, quickly stowing the groceries in the back of his car.

Jared shrugged. "Not much. Saw you coming out when I pulled up, so thought I'd wait. How are things with you?"

"Pretty good. Been getting some fishing in every week. One of these days, we ought to head out together," he said. As they chatted for a few minutes about fishing, Trey recalled that Emma's friend Susie was also a friend of Jared's. In turn, Jared was friends with Darren Thomas, one of the local cops in Diamond Creek. Though Trey liked to keep his life private, he knew Jared would keep a lid on anything he told him.

"Have a favor to ask," Trey said.

Jared quirked his mouth, his eyes amused. "You need a favor?"

Trey rolled his eyes. "Yeah, I do. But if you're gonna give me shit about it, I might not bother."

Jared barked a laugh and then sobered. "If I can help, I'm glad to. You know that."

Trey nodded. "Here's the thing, I'd appreciate it if you keep this as much to yourself as you can."

"Of course. So what's up?"

"I'll cut to the chase. I've had a few dates with Emma, you remember when I asked you about her?"

Jared didn't even try to hide his shock. "Well, that was quick. Can't wait to mention this to Dave. He's been on you to get out of your self-imposed exile." Jared shook his head and smiled. "Don't know what I was expecting, but didn't think you'd move that fast."

Trey sighed. "Didn't you just say you'd keep this to yourself?"

"Oh right. Fair enough. But Diamond Creek is tiny. Don't forget Luke's wife, Hannah, is Emma's sister. She's close to family for me. She hasn't dated anyone since she's been in Diamond Creek. Not that I'm worried about it, but you'd better treat her right or you'll hear about it from me. You haven't gotten to the favor yet, what's up?"

Trey sighed. "Should have connected the dots. I knew who her sister was. I just plain forgot that meant her sister was your sister-in-law. And as if you need to worry about me treating her right. I'm as up front as it gets. I think I may be about to tell you something you don't know, so you're going to have to keep your word for me," he said, realizing as he spoke that Emma meant far more to him than he'd have anticipated in such a short time. The situation with her ex worried him more than he wanted her to know. He knew from experience that stalkers weren't to be taken lightly, and he didn't want anything to happen to her.

Jared's eyes sharpened, a look of concern flashing across his face. "Okay," he said slowly.

Trey quickly filled him in on the background with Emma's ex and what she'd told him about the calls. "From what she told me, she mentioned the calls to her friend Susie recently. I was hoping you could ask your cop buddy, Darren Thomas, if there's anything they can do to find out where the calls are coming from."

Jared nodded slowly. "Susie left me a message yesterday, something about helping a friend. I'm guessing she's hoping I'll do the same. Darren will be glad to help. I'll give him a call today and let you know as soon as I hear from him," Jared paused and gave him an assessing look. "So you seem, uh, pretty into Emma."

Trey pictured Emma for a moment—her bright blue eyes, dark hair, and full lips. His mind traveled to who she was—intelligent, kind, so good with Stuart, and genuine. She wasn't the kind of woman who tried to create an impression. She just was who she was. And he was falling—hard. He took a breath and looked over at Jared. "Yeah, I'm pretty into her. It's safe to say that she means more to me than anyone has in a long time. I'll admit it's happened fast, but…it is what it is," he said with a shrug.

Jared held his gaze and nodded sharply. "Alright then. I'll call you as soon as I hear back from Darren." Jared pushed away from his truck.

"Thanks Jared," Trey replied. "I owe you one."

Jared began to walk toward the store. He glanced over his shoulder. "No worries. I know you'd do the same for me."

Trey raced home to check in with Risa and Stuart before heading out. He'd called Emma to let her know he wanted to take her to dinner, so he had barely enough time to get Risa's texted request for dinner supplies before heading to pick up Emma.

When he walked in the house, Stuart was standing on a small stool beside the kitchen counter, Risa at his side, holding a mixing bowl while Stuart carefully cracked an egg on the edge of the bowl.

"Hey there. What are you making?" he asked, dropping a quick kiss on Stuart's head before giving Risa a hug.

"Stuart is helping me make coffee cake for tomorrow morning," Risa said.

"Yeah, Dad, you can have some to take to work

with you tomorrow," Stuart chimed in, focused on stirring the egg into the mix.

Risa looked over with a sly smile. "So Stuart told me all about Emma."

Stuart looked up from the mixing bowl. "Aunt Risa says you're taking Emma on a date!"

Trey bit his lip to keep from smiling. "That I am. I asked Aunt Risa down tonight, so I could take Emma out. Sounds like that's okay with you."

Stuart nodded excitedly. "I told Aunt Risa all about how nice she is."

Risa winked at Trey and ruffled Stuart's hair. Though he'd get plenty of teasing from Risa, he knew she just wanted the best for him. She'd been on him for the past year to get out and try to find someone. Though she was a full decade younger than him, they'd always been close. She'd been far enough behind him when they were kids, there was none of that sibling competition. She'd been a rock for him and Stuart after Helen died. Risa kept her dark hair short, cropped close to her head with bangs that angled across her forehead. Her eyes were a rich brown and held an almost ever-present glint of humor. Just as she'd decorated his house in warm bright colors, she wore them all the time. Tonight, she wore a bright blue wrap skirt with a purple blouse. Trey figured she chose purple since she knew it was Stuart's favorite color. That was the kind of thing she did. He loved that about her and knew Stuart was lucky to have an aunt like her.

Trey set the groceries on the counter. "As requested, everything you need for a taco dinner."

"Awesome! See Stu, I told you tonight was taco

night. We'll have to decide what we do tomorrow though."

Trey glanced across Stuart's head, catching Risa's eye and tapping his watch.

"So your dad is headed out pretty quick. Did you want to show him the drawing you did today before he goes?"

After exclaiming over Stuart's drawing of a walrus, Trey hung it on the fridge and quickly changed before heading out. Risa followed him onto the deck before he left.

"So, this Emma sounds pretty special. Stuart's got his heart set on you two being together. I hope this is going to be okay," Risa said cautiously.

"I know. Stuart's wanted me to find a 'lady-friend' for a while now. I'll be honest—I didn't expect things to move this fast with anyone. But Emma *is* pretty special. I like her. A lot. And before you go lecturing me on taking my time, don't forget you've given me quite a few lectures about how important it is to find someone else since Helen died. So give me a chance to figure this one out. If you want to meet her, I can see if she can come over tomorrow."

Risa arched an eyebrow and whistled softly. "Wow. My big brother who always takes his time is *really* into this woman. Of course, I want to meet her. If it works out, I'd love it. If not, I can wait. And you're right, I've given you plenty of lectures, so I'll stand back for a little bit."

"I think I should thank you. I'll see you later," he replied with a chuckle. He gave a quick wave before sprinting to his car.

* * *

TREY FOLLOWED Emma into the parking lot, enjoying the sway of her hips as she walked. They had dinner at Diamond Creek Brewery, one of Trey's local favorites. Though tall, Emma definitely had curves, her bottom deliciously round. She wore jeans and cowboy boots with a deep green fitted blouse with the cream lace of a camisole peeking out where the blouse stretched across her breasts. The blue of her eyes was made brighter by the contrasting green. Her dark hair was loose and fell in waves around her shoulders.

Trey reached for her hand. "Let's walk over here," he said, turning toward a wooden walkway that led from the parking lot to a small viewing platform that faced a marshy field with Kachemak Bay and the mountains in the distance. Emma threw him a quick smile and followed his lead. The sky was dappled with clouds this evening with the sun slowly falling, streaks of lavender, pink and gold angling through the clouds. As with most summer evenings in Alaska, there was a chill to the air. Emma leaned her hips against the railing and looked out across the field. In the far corner, a few moose were clustered, nibbling on alder trees at the edge of the field. A raven flew by with a call that was immediately returned by another raven in the distance.

Trey paused beside Emma. He wished he could bridge the gap between what he sensed with her and what he knew of her. With her, the space between them was at once familiar and electric. And yet, she held herself at a distance in conversations. He was getting the idea what she shared with him about her ex must have been difficult, not that it wouldn't have been for anyone. She was private and offered details about herself slowly.

He leaned against the railing beside her. Emma's phone rang. She tugged it out of her pocket. As soon as he saw her face, he knew it was one of those calls. She started to turn it off, and he put his hand on her arm.

"Let me answer," he said.

Emma threw him a startled look. "Why? I know what's going to happen. Nothing."

Trey shrugged, anger rising at the hint of fear in her eyes. "What'll it hurt for me to answer?"

Emma shrugged and handed him the phone.

"Hello," he said.

For a long moment, the line was silent. Trey heard nothing but the faint sound of someone's breathing.

He repeated his greeting, followed with, "Who the hell is this?"

Emma caught his eyes and shook her head rapidly. Trey shrugged and ignored her. If her suspicions were right and this was her ex, it obviously hadn't helped for her to ignore the calls and not confront the guy about his bullshit.

He was just about to end the call when a man spoke. "Why don't you tell me who the hell you are first?"

"None of your damn business. If you're calling this number, you'd better identify yourself."

"This is Emma's number. She knows who I am," the man said. Trey could hear the sneer in his tone.

"Here's the deal. I suggest you think twice before you keep up these calls. We've notified the police and if this keeps up, you'll wish you'd had enough sense to stop. Understood?" Trey asked, a tide of anger rising through him. He rarely got angry, but watching Emma's face made him furious. She was afraid of this guy and all he'd done was call.

There was a long pause. Once again, Trey heard nothing but the sound of breathing. "Fuck you. I'll call whenever the hell I want." The line went dead.

Almost shaking with anger, Trey stared down at the phone in his hand. Just as Emma had said, the screen read 'Private.' He slowly handed the phone back to Emma, which she quickly tucked in her pocket.

"Why did you say something?" she demanded, her face flushed and eyes wide.

Trey forced himself to breathe. "Because it's been three years and you're still getting those calls. Obviously, they're not going to stop by ignoring them. I'm sorry if I upset you, but now we know who it is."

"How do we know?" Emma asked.

"He didn't give me his name, but he knows who you are and he told me he'd call whenever he wants. Besides your ex, do you know any man that would do that?" Trey asked in return, struggling to keep his frustration in check. All he wanted was to wipe the look of fear off Emma's face for good.

She shook her head slowly, twisting a ring on her hand. Trey turned to face her fully, reaching for both of her hands. "Look, I didn't mean to upset you, but I can't stand to see that look on your face. Your ex already put you through more than anyone should have to go through. I know that without even knowing all the details. I can't stand by and let him mess with you this way. I don't know how long it will take, but I'll do whatever I can to get those calls to end." He held off on mentioning to her that he'd asked

Jared to check with Darren about it. He didn't want to give her hope unless there was some.

Emma looked at him, those beautiful blue eyes holding a tired, afraid look. "It's okay. I'd kind of gotten used to it and figured it was the price I had to pay. I know you're only trying to help." She shook her head and looked away.

Trey tried to think of the right thing to say. "You already paid a price." A wave of protectiveness washed over him. He wanted nothing more than to hold her close and make sure she never looked that tired and afraid again.

Without thinking, which he seemed almost incapable of when he was close to Emma, he stepped closer. She turned back to him. Instinct driving him, he leaned forward and took her lips. What started as a gentle kiss, an apology for upsetting her, instantly morphed into a breath-stealing, heart-pounding kiss. Before he knew it, his hands had slid down to cup Emma's delectable bottom in his hands and pulled her hard against his arousal. Her hand slid up into his hair, holding him close as their tongues went wild. She was like a living flame in his arms, arching and twisting in the maelstrom between them.

His cock was so hard, he thought he might lose control. Distant voices carried from the parking lot. Trey forced himself to focus and slowly gentled their kiss, which was decidedly difficult with Emma twined around him. He could feel the heat of her through his jeans and wanted nothing more than to tear her clothes off and sink inside of her right there. He had to remind himself they were on a viewing platform in clear view of the restaurant and anyone else that happened to be nearby.

He pulled back the slightest bit. "Emma," he whispered.

Her eyes opened, unfocused and clouded with desire. "What?"

"We have to stop."

Emma's eyes fell and she shifted her hips against him. His cock pulsed at the slight pressure. She made a soft sound in her throat. He was almost undone. Hanging onto his control by the thinnest thread, he tugged her with him, walking rapidly to the car.

The ride back to her house was quiet, heavy with the weight of desire. He'd made a decision there on the walkway. He didn't give a damn how slow they needed to go. He couldn't stand by and watch her ex stir fear from miles away with nothing but a phone call. He would do whatever he needed to make her feel safe again. And he couldn't ignore that he wanted her more than he'd wanted anyone. Ever. He'd loved Helen and they'd had a fulfilling sex life. But with Emma...she was tinder to the fire between them.

When he pulled up in Emma's driveway, she turned to him, her eyes bright. He could see her pulse beat in her neck. "Do you want to come in for a few minutes?"

Trey nodded, barely keeping himself in check. The anger he'd felt over watching her when that call came fed his thirst for her. As he followed her inside, he quickly texted Risa, letting her know not to wait up for him. He'd make sure to be home before Stuart was awake, but he wanted no other interference.

When they entered her house, a black and white cat dashed through the door at the last minute. Emma reached down to stroke the cat. "This is Sula. Let me get her food and water filled," she said, quickly stepping over to a small table in the corner of the kitchen. While she filled Sula's water and got her fresh food, Sula snaked around his ankles, purring audibly.

Emma turned to him once she was finished. "Do you want something to drink?" She twisted the ring on her finger. Her breath rose and fell quickly.

Trey shook his head and simply walked over to stand in front of her. He reached a hand up to tuck a loose lock of hair behind her ear. Her lips were still swollen from their kiss earlier. "I don't want anything to drink. In fact, I don't want anything but you. If you need me to back off, now would be the time to say so."

His words fell between them. He was so close, he could feel her breath hitch. She looked at him for a long moment, desire and vulnerability clashing in them.

"I'm just a little...freaked out. I know you said it didn't matter, the stuff with my ex. But those calls keep coming. You seem to think you can make them go away, but what if you can't and something else happens? What if this affects Stuart somehow?"

Trey took a long breath, knowing he needed to answer her question, but muddled by the lust pounding through him. He shrugged. "It's not an 'I' thing, it's a 'we' thing. I don't think I can magically make that jerk stop calling you. I think the more he knows you have people in your life who will help you, the more likely it is that he'll stop. Not just me, but your friends too. People like him thrive when they think you're isolated. You're not. That's what will help. And don't go inventing problems where there aren't any. Stuart is not going to be affected by this."

She glanced away, swallowing nervously. Once again, she started to twist the ring on her hand. Trey reached for her hands and held them, willing her not to worry. With a sharp shake of her head, she turned back. Though she didn't say a word, Trey sensed she'd decided to let it go for now.

He waited, the sound of her rapid breath instantly speeding his heartbeat. When she bit her lip, he was undone.

CHAPTER 10

*E*mma bit her lip, wondering how much longer she could stand it. On the ride home, she couldn't ignore the current of desire swirling around them. Her mind said one thing and then her body just took over. She figured after the call tonight, Trey would realize he should have known better. Instead, he kissed her and almost made her lose her mind. She'd felt alone for so long when it came to Greg, she almost didn't know what to do with Trey's insistence that she wasn't alone. All she wanted was to lose herself in the feeling between them.

She heard a sharp intake of breath and glanced up quickly. Trey's lips came down on hers, hard and fast. In seconds, all thought dissolved into the vortex between them. Her skin flushed, heat built rapidly in her center. He cupped her face with one hand—alternating with kisses, sucks and nips and then delved deep with a low growl. Her blouse was held together with laces. When he accidentally got his hand tangled in the ties, he swore and pulled away.

She reached to help, but he stilled her hands. "Let me," he said, his voice rasping.

Slowly and with deliberation, he untied the laces and drew her blouse apart, pushing it off her shoulders. It fell softly to the floor. She watched him under her lashes. The silver in his dark hair glimmered in the soft light. His eyes were dark with passion. His were lips full and soft in contrast to the austere angles of his features.

She wore no bra under her silky camisole. He swore softly under his breath and leaned forward, his lips closing around a nipple through the silk. A sharp spike of desire arced through her. By the time he'd drenched the silk over both nipples, she was nearly out of her mind, awash in sensation, heat pulsing through her. When she gasped his name between pants, he paused and lifted his head. Her nipples peaked to an ache at the brush of cool air against the damp silk.

"Yes?" he asked, trailing his fingers lightly down across her breasts and abdomen. He slid a hand under her camisole, slowly pushing it up, his palm rough against her skin, sparks skittering in the trail of his touch.

"Oh God," she gasped.

She managed to open her eyes when his breath hissed through his teeth. He forcefully pushed her camisole up, tugging it over her head. She shivered as the air hit her desire-flushed skin. He looked down at her, reverently curving his hands around her breasts, lifting them together.

"You have no idea what you do to me," he said softly, his words barely audible.

Emma was frantic to feel him. She pushed his

hands away and yanked his shirt open, shoving it off his shoulders. When she met his eyes, she was lost in his velvety chocolate gaze. His voice was low and guttural. "Come here," he said, pulling her to him.

The feel of his skin against hers was so exquisite, she thought she might melt on the spot. Trey wrapped his arms around her, plastering her to him in a searing kiss. He turned them and slowly walked them to the couch, pausing to stroke deeply in her mouth before coasting kisses down her neck. Shoes were kicked off and clothes fell in a trail. They tumbled onto the couch, Emma in nothing but the thin scrap of white lace that passed for her panties, and Trey in fitted boxers, his arousal clearly outlined.

Her knees fell apart, Trey fitting between them as he stretched on top of her. The feel of his body against hers, head to toe, was so delicious, she sighed in relief. The relief was momentary as he proceeded to raise the heat inside of her with thorough attention to every inch. His lips meandered down her neck, once again nibbling and softly biting at her nipples. His tongue traced the shape of her breasts and left a searing path across her abdomen. He paused at the top edge of her panties, his tongue dipping just below the lace. He caressed her mound through the silk, soaked with the evidence of her desire.

"Look at me," he commanded. Desire thrumming through her, she managed to lift her head and meet his eyes. The moment was so intimate, she almost had to close her eyes, but he only repeated his soft words. As he held her gaze, an invisible strand of want and tenderness arcing between them, he slowly dipped his finger under her panties, sinking into her moist channel.

Biting her lip, she gasped and her head fell back, slick moisture slid down her thighs when he slowly drew his finger in and out. In seconds, she was on the brink. He pulled his hand out and pushed away just long enough to yank her panties down. She kicked them off, desperate with need.

"I need you...inside me...now..."

His dark eyes held hers again. "Not yet." Holding her eyes until the last second, he slowly leaned forward and brought his mouth against her, licking into her center.

She shrieked and fell back.

He took his time, tracing her folds with his tongue, delving in and out of her. His fingers joined his mouth, establishing a delicious rhythm. She was adrift in sensation, waves of lust crashing through her, sensation building and building as he brought her to the edge over and over. Just when she thought she couldn't stand it, he softly sucked on her clit and she tumbled into an orgasm with a low scream. He kept his mouth against her and his fingers inside her until the pulses slowed. He made his way back up her body in another slow exploration.

For a long moment, she felt bereft when Trey lifted off of her. Then she heard the tear of the condom wrapper, and he was sliding back on top of her. He laid full length, skin-to-skin, and rested on his elbows, his hands cupping her face.

Anticipating his command to look at him, she opened her eyes. Passion was heavy around them, the air weighted with it. He met her eyes. She felt wanted and cherished in a way she'd never experienced and almost had to look away at the intensity. He reached between her legs and positioned himself. He slid slowly inside, his length thick. She felt him press deeply, so full she could barely breathe. She convulsed around him. Though she'd just found her release, his slow surges began another build up.

Through the blur of her yearning, she held his eyes as he stroked in and out, pulling all the way back and pausing before plunging deep into her. The fervor built. Her hips rose to meet his. Her release exploded through her. He threw his head back in a last thrust, convulsing inside of her.

Emma drifted down. Trey fell against her, shifting his weight to one side. Their legs were tangled, skin damp. Her breath gradually slowed. He brushed her hair away from her face. Desire hung in the air, a mere glimmer of its explosive peak.

He pushed himself up and quickly tossed his condom in the kitchen trash, returning to lie down beside her, tucking her close against him and dropping a soft kiss on her lips. For a few moments, the only sound was their breathing.

* * *

TREY STAYED until the wee hours of the morning. They stumbled into her bedroom after a shower together. His arms around her, she fell into a deep slumber. She woke early to a soft kiss on the back of her neck. The sky was just becoming light—in Alaskan summer that meant it wasn't even four in the morning yet.

"Mmmm," Trey mumbled against her skin. He was spooned behind her, his bare skin emanating warmth. "Have to get going before Stuart gets up," he whispered. "Don't wanna go…"

Emma rolled in his arms, turning to face him. His hair was in a rumple. She giggled and ran a hand through it. His eyes opened inches from hers. When he saw her smile, a wicked glint entered his gaze. With no preamble, he swiftly rolled atop her and pinned her hands over her head. Though she'd have thought her lust for him would have abated after last night, in a flash she was arching against him, aching for release. Searing kisses, a blazing trail with his lips, streaking across her breasts and back up her neck. He nibbled at her earlobe, his breath causing shivers.

"Trey...now..." she gasped. She was instantly slick with desire, desperate for the feel of him inside of her.

He pulled back. "Oh no, we're not rushing," he said, his voice low.

Emma met his eyes, shifting restlessly against him. When she saw the gleam in his eyes, she moved quickly, breaking free of his grasp and shimmying out from underneath to straddle him. She leaned forward, her nipples brushing his chest. She paused when her lips were centimeters from his. "Okay, since we're not rushing..." She trailed her lips down his neck, savoring the feel of his pulse. His cock nestled against her folds, which were drenched with the evidence of her desire. As she coasted down his body with her lips, she slowly rotated her hips, sliding against his hardness. She had to force herself not to take him inside just yet. Shifting down, she paused to glance up. His chest rose and fell rapidly, his pulse visible in his neck. She slid her tongue in a slow stroke from the base of his cock upward, relishing his guttural groan. She teased him, stroking him with her tongue, wrapping him in the wet grip of her hand, and pushing him back when he tried to sit up. "Oh no...you said we weren't rushing," she said, trying desperately to keep her own desire in check.

Trey's chuckle was low and husky. "I…" he started to say when she finally brought him into her mouth. Whatever he was about to say was lost in a deep groan. Emma took her time, dragging her lips up and down his hard length, alternating with suction and strokes. His hips bucked against her mouth. Right when his cock began to pulse, she pulled away and paused to look up at him, her lips a mere inch from the tip of his shaft. He lifted his head, his chocolate gaze almost black. With a sly smile, she drew her tongue slowly up his length again. This time, he moved swiftly. In a flash, she was stretched beneath him, her hands held above her head with one of his.

He leaned across her to reach for his wallet on the nightstand. He efficiently slipped a condom on with one hand, keeping her wrists pinned with the other. He positioned himself at her entrance and paused. Meeting his eyes, she almost flinched at how exposed she felt. Vulnerability flooded her while the look in his eyes held her through it. Lost in the shimmer of his gaze, she sighed when he slowly slid inside of her.

His hands clasped hers and held on tightly. His lips met hers in a scalding kiss. He established a leisurely rhythm. When she reached her peak and started to tumble over, he thrust deeply, arching against her and capturing her cries in his mouth. They lay still for long moments, their breath rising and falling in unison.

Trey eventually roused and shifted to get up. He shook his head when she started to follow him out of bed, and she shrugged. "I'm not falling back asleep. You shower and I'll make coffee."

She wrapped a robe around her and walked downstairs to make coffee. When he followed her down after showering, he was tidy, a far cry from the man who dove into passion with her. But the glimmer in his eyes was there, a soft echo. She had a travel mug filled with coffee ready for him. A quick kiss, and he turned to leave only to turn back and pull her close for a more thorough goodbye kiss.

After he left, Emma walked onto the back porch. The sun was cresting behind the mountains. The sky above was streaked with rich rose, rays of light arcing through the clouds. The water in the bay was choppy, wind whipping across. The wind was softer up here, just a rustle in the trees. Her thoughts wandered to last night. She blushed to think about the intensity of passion she felt with Trey. She couldn't seem to summon her usual fears and rationalizations about why it wasn't a good idea for them to move too fast. Her heart clenched at the memory of when he first slid inside of her—so right. Vulnerability clashed with the hopes of her heart. She sipped her coffee and froze when she saw a pair of sandhill cranes flying into the field behind her house. The cranes summered in Alaska every year and were lovely. Their wingspan was huge and could stretch to seven feet across. The pair landed quietly and lifted their heads to look around. Tall and elegant, they moved gracefully. They were a soft gray-brown with a bright red crown on their heads. They mated for life, and pairs often returned year and year to the same places. She watched them quietly for several moments before returning to the kitchen.

Emma left for work early, planning to get ahead on some paperwork. As she approached Misty Mountain Café, she spied Hannah's truck and impulsively stopped since she had plenty of time.

"Hey," she said, coming up behind Hannah in line. Despite the early hour, the coffee shop was hopping.

Her sister turned and smiled widely when she saw her. "Hey there! What's got you here so early?"

Before Emma could answer, Susie's voice came from behind. "Hey you two, this is prefect!"

After greetings and a few moments to get coffee, they snagged a table. Susie chattered about a local fundraiser she was helping Tess with and then honed her eyes on Emma.

"So, did you tell Hannah about your date?" she asked with a sly smile.

Emma wrinkled her nose and rolled her eyes. "Seeing as this is the first time I've seen her since then, can't say that I have."

Susie's curls bounced as she glanced to Hannah. "Aren't you dying to hear about Trey? I can't believe you didn't call her already. If I hadn't seen her the other morning here, I would have called." Susie turned back to Emma. "So?"

Emma laughed. Though she hadn't quite adjusted to it, she had friends, friends who cared a lot. That sometimes meant answering nosy questions. Giving in to the inevitable, she filled them in, minus the details of just how much Trey had blown her mind.

Hannah took a thoughtful sip of her coffee. "So you've decided to go for it with Trey."

Emma blushed. "I think so," she paused wondering whether to mention her talk with him about Greg. She knew Susie wanted to know. Funny thing about Susie was she was nosy as hell, but if she thought you needed to have something on your terms, she completely respected that. Meeting Susie's eyes, Emma decided to be open with Hannah too. The secrecy around Greg, which had cloaked around her once the violence began, needed to go. Secrecy represented another layer of what a violent, controlling relationship did to a person. Secrecy was necessary for that type of relationship to flourish. It isolated the victim as they tried to avoid having anyone find out what was happening, shouldering the blame for how they ended up there.

With a deep breath, Emma told Hannah about her worries about the random calls and told them how Trey had handled learning about her marriage and what had happened. Just as Susie had, Hannah immediately started problem solving.

"You're as bad as Susie, all ready to fix this right away," Emma said with a smile, tears pricking her eyes. As long as she'd held her fears away about the phone calls, the heavier the weight became. She'd somehow convinced herself there was nothing she could do about the calls. Even though she knew better. In all her years as a therapist, if there was one thing she knew with certainty, it was that shining a light on problems, no matter how big, helped.

They talked a little more and somewhere along the way it slipped out that she'd seen Trey again last night.

"Wait a minute, you saw Trey last night too?" Susie asked.

Hannah chuckled, throwing a sympathetic glance toward Emma. "You didn't think she'd let that one by, did you?"

"Um…I saw him the last two nights actually," Emma replied, a blush warming her face.

"Well, damn," Susie said, setting her coffee down with a thud.

* * *

THAT AFTERNOON, Stella sat in Emma's office, shoved as far into the corner of the small sofa as she could possibly be. Janie sat beside her and threw a soft smile in Emma's direction. Though they were entirely unrelated, biologically speaking, Stella bore a strong resemblance to Janie. Janie also had dark brown hair with porcelain skin. Rather than brown eyes, hers were a soft hazel. Janie definitely did not share the goth look favored by Stella. Today, Janie wore jeans with hiking boots and a bright red tank top with a loose flannel shirt. While she tended to dress with practicality, she had an air of femininity with lush curves and a warm mothering energy touched with a glint of mischief.

As a foster mother, she was rock solid. She was consistent, had clear expectations and was flexible. She was also nearly impossible to rattle. When Stella had first been placed in her care, according to Janie, it had been weeks of silence interrupted by explosions when Stella rubbed against an expectation she didn't like. Having come from a childhood that had close to no structure and no expectations, Stella fought against them. After getting through that patch, Stella gradually settled in, and she and Janie had become close. Not long after Stella started therapy with Emma, Janie shared with Emma she had been willing to adopt Stella for a while, but even though her child services worker tried to talk her into it, Stella thought it was 'stupid.'

Today was the planned day for Emma to try to facilitate a discussion between Stella and Janie about this. As with most plans for therapy sessions, that one was already out the window so far. Stella had shown up cranky and skittish. After barely speaking for the first few minutes, she blurted out that she wanted to stop going to recital practice. Janie had enough sense to wait her out. Without a word passing between them, Emma was in complete agreement on the waiting part, so the three of them had been sitting in silence for several minutes. Aside from Stella's poor hair nearly being twirled off in one spot, the silence was rather uneventful.

Stella shifted on the couch. Emma glanced over. A tear slid down Stella's cheek, and Emma's heart clenched for her. She had to swallow the urge to comfort Stella. Janie caught Emma's eyes and carefully reached over to snag the box of tissues on the coffee table, handing them to Stella without a word.

"I don't really want to quit recital..." Stella started and paused with a sob. She straightened her shoulders and swiped at her tears with a tissue. "It's just I don't have any friends there and all the other kids know each other. They've been in music class together forever. I only moved to Diamond Creek when my dad went to jail. All the kids I grew up with are in Kenai. It's not like I had a lot of friends there, but at least I knew some people. It sucks moving somewhere new."

Stella grabbed another tissue and noisily blew her nose. She finally looked up, her eyes swerving immediately to Janie. Though Stella probably didn't even realize it and wouldn't dare admit it if she did, it was obvious she was seeking reassurance.

Janie calmly looked back at Stella, her lips quirking in a soft smile. She shrugged. "And so what? Lots of kids didn't grow up here. For example, that kid Parker who you're so convinced is horrible because he was friends with Byron, well he only moved to Diamond Creek the same year you did."

Stella's eyes widened. "How do you know?" she asked, her tone incredulous and annoyed at once.

"Okay, you don't have to think I know everything, but maybe you could give me a little credit for knowing who's who around town. Whether I like it or not, I grew up here, and I know just about everyone. The scoop on Parker is his family moved here from out of state when his dad got a job on the North Slope. And while we're on the subject of what I know, even if most kids won't admit it to save their lives, it's usually not cool to have been in Diamond Creek your whole life. Most of those kids can't wait to move away and think all the new kids are cool and mysterious."

Stella rolled her eyes at that. "Um, I'm pretty sure no one thinks I'm cool and mysterious." A giggle followed.

Emma gave her a wry smile. "Did you miss the part where Janie said most kids wouldn't admit that part?"

Janie laughed and Stella threw a tissue at Emma before sitting back again with a sigh. "I don't think they think that, but I know they wouldn't admit it if they did. I just wish it wasn't so hard. I really like piano, and Mrs. Cooper's my favorite teacher. Then I get there and I get all nervous and think everyone's staring at me."

The logjam broken on Stella's silence, she tolerated Janie's reassurance with only a few pushes against it. Though Emma had let go of trying to talk about the possibility of adoption in today's session, she was surprised at how easily it came up. Stella, as usual, abruptly changed topic.

"Okay, so we're here for a reason. I promised you we'd talk about this adoption thing," Stella said, her eyes guarded at once.

Janie didn't miss a beat. "You know how I feel. You're my daughter to me in every way that matters..." she tapped her heart, "...so I just want to make it official. That's about all I have to say. But I don't want you to think anything will change if you decide not to. I just wanted to make sure we actually tried to talk about it. When Emma said you were willing to talk, I didn't want to miss the chance."

Emma looked to Stella, gauging her reaction. Stella was so naturally defensive that any softening in those defenses was a sign of massive progress. Watching her now, Emma saw Stella's face go blank for a moment, all emotion shielded. That quickly morphed into a flash of irritation, followed by sadness and a flicker of hope. Emma waited, eventually electing to nudge her a little before Stella drifted into silence again, her go to defensive mode.

"Stella?" she asked.

Stella's eyes flicked to her. She gave a small nod.

"You told me you wanted to try to talk about this, so that's why we're here. There's no 'have to' though. We could start talking today and try again later," Emma said, once again holding herself back. Though this was her job, she did it because she cared. Stella had burrowed into her heart and she simply wanted her to be okay. That meant letting her get there at her own pace.

Stella looked away and twirled her hair. "I know. I just...thought maybe we could go for it." She paused and looked to Janie. "That's all I wanted to say."

Janie's eyes held tears. "You had me all ready to *talk* talk. And that's it. You want to maybe go for it? There's still a maybe in there, so *maybe* you should think about it a little more. Maybe talk to Emma when I'm not here. I really, really don't want you to do this because you think you need to. It needs to be for you." Janie glanced to Emma, a question in her eyes.

"I caught the *maybe* in there, but I think we need Stella to clarify that one," Emma said.

Stella rolled her eyes and sighed, though a smile lurked at the corners of her mouth. "Maybe is maybe, but maybe what I mean is that we should find out what needs to happen. Last time my worker talked to me, she said all kinds of stuff about court paperwork and a home study. By now, I probably have another worker who won't know what to do."

Janie chuckled. "You've had a few workers, but I just talked to Diana Reynolds the other day. She's still your worker and she hasn't forgotten what you two talked about. So if maybe means we need to talk to Diana, how about I call her tomorrow? She'll set up a time to come see you."

At Stella's agreement, Janie wisely changed the subject, circling back to recital. After some more hemming and hawing, Stella agreed she'd keep going to practices for now. Emma watched them leave, Janie tucking her hand through Stella's arm on the way down the hall. When Emma closed the door to her office, she gave the jump of joy she couldn't show to

Stella, sitting down to type her notes with a wide smile.

As Emma got ready to leave the office, she wished she could borrow some of Stella's courage. Though Stella had wrestled with feeling accepted by Janie and Janie's family, she faced it head on once she decided to do it. If only Emma could find a way to do that with Trey. Oh she knew she was to an extent, as she felt powerless against the tow of her feelings for him. What she didn't know was how to put words to what was happening. The faster it happened, the more potent the rush of passion between them, the more vulnerable she felt and the more she worried about what it all meant and where it was going. And for now, she didn't know how to say any of that to Trey.

He had called her today to invite her to dinner to meet his sister. She was barreling towards something she hadn't anticipated. The idea of meeting his sister terrified her so much she ended up texting him later to cancel, only to regret the text about a minute after she sent it.

CHAPTER 11

*L*ater that night, Emma started getting call upon call from the dreaded 'Private' number. She put the phone on silent, but found it more disconcerting to notice the screen flashing without any sound. Sula became enamored with the phone vibrating on the coffee table and batted at it with her paws. The calls came at regular intervals for roughly an hour. A familiar feeling descended upon her. By the time she was a few months into her marriage to Greg, she'd become accustomed to the feeling that washed over her and settled—knots of tension in her center that radiated outward, cold anxiety clamping down on her chest making her muscles tight and a weariness that weighed on her.

She knew she shouldn't have let Trey answer the call the other night. It would infuriate Greg to know that she spoke to anyone about him. He would be white-hot that anyone showed any interest in her. Not that Trey had indicated as such in the brief call, but just to have a man answer her phone would incense Greg.

Sula finally batted her phone to the floor. It landed with a thud. A few seconds later, it buzzed again. Emma closed her eyes and took a slow breath. All the mantras she chanted since she walked out that night over three years ago felt flimsy and insubstantial. If Greg could keep finding her number, he could find her. She tried to tell herself he wouldn't bother, that he didn't have that much motivation. Even if he knew she was in Alaska, she was a long, long way from where she'd last known him to be in Connecticut. She desperately wanted to turn her phone off entirely. But another toll from those years of explosive rages was she always needed a working phone available—*always*. Because the option to call for help was about the only thing that kept her sane on bad days.

In a moment between those calls, Emma grabbed her phone off the floor and called Hannah only to get her voice mail. She impulsively called Trey next, desperate to link with someone outside of her own mind and the spiral of worry building inside. As she waited for Trey to answer, her phone bleeped in her ear, indicating another call coming in.

"Hey there," Trey said. "Didn't expect you to call this late." His tone was light and casual. She heard a woman laugh in the background and Trey call out that he was on the phone.

"Sorry about that. Risa's getting Stuart ready for a bath, and he's trying to talk her into letting Tootsie join him. No matter how many times I tell him cats don't like baths, he thinks it's a good idea. Maybe I'll just let him try one of these days, and that'll be the end of that," Trey said with a chuckle.

Emma managed a laugh, but had to choke back a sob that rose against her will.

Somehow, Trey cued in to her. "You okay?" he asked, his tone sharp and probing.

She nodded, even though he wasn't there to see, as if by nodding she could persuade herself she was okay. She tried to answer him, but all that came out was another sob.

"Emma, tell me what's going on," Trey said softly, but firmly.

"He keeps calling. It won't stop..." Her words tumbled out, another bleep in her ear at the same time.

Trey noticed the break in the call. "You're getting another call now. Why don't you come over here? I don't want you sitting there all alone."

By this point, Emma wasn't feeling rational. All the fears she shoved away each time she got these waves of calls were smothering her now. By giving voice to what was happening, she couldn't avoid it anymore. She was terrified Greg might know where she was and might have bothered to make his way here.

Sula leapt on the sofa and sidled up to her, curling against her arm and purring. "I don't know. I can't leave Sula here." Of all the reasons to worry, that was the one she focused on for now. Leaving her cat for one night.

Trey didn't hesitate. "Well, Stuart wanted Tootsie to meet Sula. I think it's a fine time to bring her over."

There was a long pause. Her phone bleeped again. Trey swore softly.

She could feel him thinking through the phone.

"Emma..." he paused when the connection was

interrupted by another bleep. "Just come over. If you don't come here, I'm coming over there," he said flatly.

"What are we going to tell Stuart?" she asked, desperately wanting to go, but conflicted about how much she wanted the comfort of Trey's solid presence.

"That you wanted to come over. I'll be the first to say I hadn't planned to have you spend the night here quite this fast, but I don't like that you're getting these calls, and I can tell you're scared. Do the calls usually happen this fast?"

Emma sighed. "It depends. Sometimes there are no calls for weeks or months, then they just happen. Sometimes I get a few at a time. This is more than usual."

Trey was silent for a long moment. He started to speak and stopped. "So what'll it be? My place or yours? And if you're worried about meeting Risa, it'll be fine. Okay if I fill her in a little, so she isn't wondering why the sudden change in plans?"

Emma hesitated, not wanting Trey's sister to know this part of her history before she even met her.

"Emma, Risa will understand," Trey said softly, leaving her to wonder if he was telepathic.

She shifted restlessly on the couch tilting in the direction of staying home. Her phone bleeped in her ear again. She held it away briefly to see 'Private' flash on the screen. "I'll be there in a few. I just need to get my stuff for work tomorrow."

EMMA SAT on Trey's couch, Risa sitting on the other part of the sectional. Trey was in the kitchen putting dishes in the dishwasher. Emma had arrived with Sula in her carrier. She'd almost convinced herself it was perfectly fine to leave Sula for the night, but the stopper on her fears had broken free and she couldn't talk herself out of her worry. Stuart was overjoyed to meet Sula. The introduction to Tootsie had involved some hissing, hair raising and a few swipes. Alas, they'd settled their differences quickly. Tootsie was as easy going with Sula as he was with kids. Once Sula had expressed herself, he settled down for a nap and let her be.

Stuart was tucked in bed now after quickly wearing out with the excitement of both Risa and Emma being there. He fell asleep mid-sentence, and Trey carted him off to bed.

Emma glanced at Risa, wondering what to say. Risa was a combination of comforting and intimidating. Emma thought perhaps the comfort came from how much her energy resembled Susie's—a forceful burst softened with warmth. It was intriguing to observe Trey with her. They were clearly close, teasing each other in turn. The more she got to know him, the more she realized that her first impression of him had been deceptive. The man she'd thought to be reserved and too good for her was funny, charming and warm with those who knew him well.

Emma knew Risa was sizing her up and felt sorely inadequate. Of all the nights to meet her, it had to be tonight when she felt exposed, anxious and stupid. Just being in the presence of others had abated her fears, and she now felt rather silly.

Risa had a strong beauty. Dark brown hair and matching eyes with the same sharp, angular features and full lips that Trey had. She was dressed in a bright blue jersey skirt with a loose white blouse and clogs. Risa captured Emma's eyes and tilted her head. "Don't worry about me. I'm sure you think you should, but trust me, we're good. I can tell you're good for Trey and Stuart and that's all that matters to me. I won't pretend I'm not protective as hell. Trey may be my older brother, but I've got his back. If I thought there was a problem, you'd hear about it. And if you're worried about what I think about why you showed up tonight—don't. I don't expect you to tell me all about it. But it might help if you knew that one of my closest friends showed up on my doorstep one night with two black eyes. She'd been dating the guy for years by that point, and I had *no* idea what had been going on. That's how well she covered it up. No judgment from me."

Emma was so startled she sat in silence for a long moment. Finally gathering herself, she met Risa's dark brown gaze. "Thank you. I can't tell you how much that helps," she paused, tears pressing at her eyes.

Risa calmly snagged a box of tissues on a small table beside the couch and handed them over. Emma accepted them with a small smile and quickly wiped her eyes.

Taking a deep breath, she continued. "I was so nervous about meeting you and now I just feel silly. You must think I'm crazy."

Risa's eyes were steady. "I know you're not crazy. We don't need to spend all night talking about it— unless you want to—but I watched my friend avoid calls, avoid places and more. Guys like that, they're the ones who are crazy. And they know it works. All it took was one call, and my friend would be worked up for days. Trey told me about your ex. He's just another guy with the same tired moves. And don't forget, you got away. You left. If there's one thing I know, *that* takes strength."

The knot of tension in her belly that Emma had been holding for days softened, if only a little. Though she was beyond relieved and wondering at the fact that Trey hadn't just walked away when he heard about Greg, the spate of calls jacked up her nerves. Meeting Trey's sister only piled on the anxiety. Sula leapt up and nestled against her side.

"I just wish he'd stop calling." She looked to Risa and blurted out the truth. "I was so worried Trey would tell me to forget it when I told him about Greg. I know it's not exactly convenient for me to have an ex like this. I don't know how much Trey has told you about us, but neither of us really expected this or planned this. Things have moved faster than I'm maybe comfortable with…"

Risa shook her head and smiled softly, a touch of sadness to it. "I hope you've figured this out, but Trey isn't the kind of guy that would have held something like this against you. For starters, it's not your fault. My brother has a heart of gold. He doesn't let many people see it, but he's a total softie. You have no idea how happy I am to see him happy with someone. After Helen died…I worried. It hit him pretty hard and since then, he's been a single dad trying to hold the world up for Stuart. He really hasn't let himself consider the idea of dating. So as far as I'm concerned, the way it's happening with you two is exactly how it needs to. Trey needed to be knocked on his butt, and you seem to have succeeded."

Emma couldn't hold back the laugh that tumbled

out. Trey walked into the room right then. "What's so funny?" he asked.

Emma only started laughing harder. Trey sat down beside her, immediately sliding his arm across her shoulders. His simple gesture brought immense comfort and an instant current, that ever-present spark between them.

Risa smiled widely, a hint of mischief in her eyes. "I was just telling Emma how pleased I am she's knocked you off your feet. You needed that."

Trey quirked an eyebrow. "Knocked me off my feet?"

"To be specific, I said 'knocked on your butt.' You're so into her, you didn't let yourself overthink it like you usually do," Risa replied bluntly.

"Easy for you to say I overthink when I can't seem to remember the last time you dated anyone," Trey countered with a grin.

Risa glared at him and threw a couch pillow in his direction. Trey caught it and tossed it right back. With a roll of her eyes, Risa replied, "Fine. Try to turn the tables. You overthink everything. I was just saying it's a good thing to see you forget to do that for once."

He shrugged. "If that's what you think, fine with me. I'm just glad you got a chance to meet Emma."

He stroked his hand slowly across Emma's shoulder and down along her arm. Emma's tension unraveled bit by bit.

The calls had finally stopped on her phone in the last hour or so. She was tired inside and simply wanted to curl up with Trey. And she had *no* idea what to do with how natural that felt. While she was with Greg, she learned to isolate her feelings and knew the only person she could count on was herself.

In the years since she moved away, she had to call upon every ounce of strength to push through the steps she needed to take to sever her ties to Greg and move to Alaska.

This—this intense wish to lean on Trey, to accept the comfort her offered was so foreign it shook her to her core. His mere presence slashed through her defenses so fast, it was as if they'd never been there. And tonight, she was so weary that longing washed up against the shores of her heart. Emma didn't realize her head had fallen against Trey's shoulder and her eyes had closed until Risa spoke.

"It's great to meet her, and she needs to go to bed," Risa said, her tone amused.

Emma snapped her head up. "No, no I'm awake," she protested.

Risa chuckled. "You might be awake, but barely. You're exhausted. Don't worry, I'll be here a few more days."

Trey looked down at her. "Risa's right, bed for you." He gave her shoulder a brisk rub and quickly stood, grasping her hand and giving a soft tug.

Emma didn't resist, allowing Trey to tug her to her feet. Trey glanced back to Risa. "See you in the morning."

"That you will. Emma," Risa said. Emma turned her heavy eyes toward Risa. "It's really nice to meet you. Don't forget what I said—no judgment," she said with a warm smile.

Trey led her down the hall to his bedroom. Wordlessly, she slipped out of her clothes. He handed her a soft t-shirt of his to sleep in. His scent clung lightly to it. She shivered at the feel of the cool sheets when she crawled in bed. Trey stepped into the bathroom briefly. She lay in the quiet, the spool of tension coiled inside her unwound slowly. When he slid into bed, he immediately curled against her, spooning behind her. His warmth seeped into her. Nuzzling the back of her neck, he placed a soft kiss there.

"I'm glad you came over," he said, his voice husky.

Emma sighed, relieved to her bones to be here, with Trey, instead of home alone with her mind on its personal hamster wheel of thoughts and fears.

"Me too," she shifted in his arms to face him, feeling his arousal against her hips as she turned. Though weary, her need for him arced. Desire stretched and flexed within, liquid heat pooled. In the shadows of his room, the space between them hummed with a soft current. Tired as she was, the buzz of desire between them was constant, the only variation in its intensity.

He laughed softly when she shifted again, brushing against his arousal.

"What?" she asked.

"Ignore it. All you have to do is be here and I want you. But…that's not why I wanted you to come over tonight. You're exhausted. Let's just go to sleep."

She reached a hand over, sifting her fingers through his hair, slowly drawing her hand down along his cheek. "What if I don't want to?"

He chuckled and then sucked his breath in when she slowly curled her other hand around his cock, its pulsing length heavy and warm in her hand.

Emma leaned forward, closing the few inches between them to place her lips against his. She pulled away after the soft kiss. "I can't tell you how glad I am to be here…" her voice stumbled on the depth of her relief. Desire throbbed.

Trey brought his hand to her cheek, cupping it softly, holding her gaze. "Same goes for me..." he erased the space between their lips, scalding hers with a deep, thorough and relentless kiss.

They twined together, legs tangling, hands skating across each other, lips mingling in kisses, pants and gasps.

Trey paused and pulled away. "I promised myself I wouldn't do this tonight. You have to know that I wanted you here because I was worried, not because I wanted *this*. Although," he paused, another soft laugh escaping, "you do have this effect on me. You're like a weathervane and I just rotate to find you."

Emma giggled. "A weathervane?"

His smile was wry. "That was a compliment."

She sobered. "You don't have to persuade me you wanted me to come over because you were worried. I know that and we can still..." she paused to place a moist kiss right at the base of his throat "do this..."

Trey pressed his hips against hers, his hard length nestling between her legs, against her mound. She arched against him, her head tossing against the pillow. His palm slid slowly up her spine, its warmth scattering sparks. His other hand still cupped her cheek. She opened her eyes again when he caressed her cheek with his thumb. In the shadows, his eyes were dark and intense, stripping any pretense. "Just so that we're clear...I want *this*..." he shifted his hips subtly but firmly, ratcheting her desire up a notch "... and for you to know that's not all I want."

Emma had to force herself to keep her eyes open, to not shy away. She nodded wordlessly. "I know..." she whispered just before his lips met hers again. This time, she lost herself in the maelstrom that thundered between them.

Long, slow, scalding kisses. His hands everywhere, eliciting sighs of relief and longing when they moved on. His lips on her nipples, drawing deep, biting softly. His fingers tracing circles on her abdomen, teasing her folds, dipping into the moisture and drawing back out across her clit. Gasping, pleading, thrashing.

His t-shirt was torn off of her, his boxers pushed down with her feet. He fumbled in the nightstand drawer and rolled a condom on. His weight against her, the feel of his muscled chest, dusted with hair, against her breasts. His cock resting just outside her entrance, dripping with her desire. Resting on his elbows. *Look at me.* And she did, just as he slid inside, driving deep. Long thrusts—slow, then fast, then slow. She strove higher and higher, release out of reach for feverish moments, yearning built and built. A final stroke and she tumbled over the pinnacle, her legs curled around him as he arched against her, pulsing inside. He captured her cries with a kiss, his weight slowly falling and shifting to her side.

They fell asleep entwined. All she remembered was feeling cherished, wanted...and safe.

The wind whipped the kite wild in the sky. Trey reached over to steady the line Stuart gamely held. The gust passed, and Trey released the line while staying close to Stuart. The sun was high, the sky bright, and the wind coming in unpredictable gusts. This was Stuart's absolute favorite kind of day to fly a kite because he loved when the kite danced in the wind. But it made for some work trying to make sure Stuart didn't lose hold of the kite.

It was Saturday, and Emma was in Anchorage. She wouldn't be back until tomorrow night. Risa had decided to stay through the weekend, but she left Trey and Stuart to their own devices for the day while she met a friend for lunch. Emma stayed with them for two nights before insisting she had to go back to her place before she went away for the weekend. Stuart had begged to babysit Sula while Emma was gone for the weekend, so Emma dropped her off in the morning.

He thought back to the two years since Helen died and how he'd eventually adjusted to being alone. Being a single father meant he was never really alone in the literal sense of the word, but he'd chosen to be alone when it came to any consideration of a relationship. He'd been comfortable with that. At first, he'd been grieving his loss and the larger reverberations of what it meant for Stuart. But then, he'd simply let go of the idea of being with anyone romantically.

Enter Emma. In a few short weeks, he'd gone from not even considering the idea of sharing his and Stuart's lives with anyone to not being able to imagine life without her. The depth of his feelings for her shook him. The catch in her voice the other night when she'd called, her worry and fear echoing through the line made him want to do whatever he could to never hear that in her voice again.

"Dad!" Stuart exclaimed.

He turned just as Stuart stumbled and fell on the sand. Trey moved quickly, grabbing hold of the handle for the kite. Another lashing gust of wind and the kite yanked against his grip. He glanced down at Stuart. Stuart was already clambering up from the sand, reaching to take the kite back from Trey.

"Hey Stu, I know this is your favorite kind of day, but it's pretty rough right now. How about we bring the kite down and see if we can find Aunt Risa?"

Stuart's face fell. "But Dad, it's the best kind of day." He extended his arms out gesturing broadly and pointing to the kite, which danced wildly in the sky, a ribbon of orange against the bright blue.

Trey held Stuart's gaze. "Yup, it's a great day. But you've had plenty of time and it's getting windier," he said calmly as he began to methodically roll the line around the handle, the kite slowly lowering in the sky. Stuart frowned, but didn't argue.

After stowing the kite in the back of the car, they set off to rendezvous with Risa at Misty Mountain Café where she was meeting her friend for lunch. Trey texted her, asking if he could drop Stuart with her after Jared left him a message that he'd talked to Darren and he could call or swing by if he wanted to chat about it. He didn't want Stuart to hear a whiff of his concerns about Emma's ex, so leaving Stuart with Risa would give him the time to stop by Jared's place.

In short order, he left Stuart with Risa who planned to take Stuart to a local playground and was headed to meet Jared. His phone buzzed, and he tugged it out of his pocket. "Trey here," he answered.

"Hey man, can you meet me at Susie's office? You know where that is, right?" Jared asked.

Trey recalled that it was the same office where he dropped Emma off the day she had a flat tire. He was curious to see Susie and find out her thoughts on the situation with Emma's ex.

Trey pulled up a few minutes later at Susie's office. Stepping inside, he saw Jared step back quickly. Susie was standing in front of a desk, her face flushed. Jared looked rattled, which was so unusual for him, Trey had to curb his reflex to ask him if everything was okay. He strove for a casual tone, but the room was taut.

"How's it going?" Trey asked.

"Fine," Jared replied tersely.

Trey noticed Jared's breathing was quick and shallow. Glancing to Susie, she was still flushed. At this point, he was wondering why the hell Jared asked him to come by right about now.

Susie smiled tightly at him, her cheeks bright. "How are you?"

Trey nodded. "Just fine. Stopped by to talk to Jared. Not sure if it's a good time…" his words trailed off when Jared interrupted.

"Perfect timing. I, uh, just talked to Darren a bit ago," Jared began only to have Susie interject.

"You did? Please tell me he said he can do something about that asshole," she demanded and then glanced to Trey. "By the way, I know we've met before, but you should know I'll personally kick your ass if you hurt Emma."

Trey started at that. Before he could reply, Jared cut in. "For god's sake, Susie, lay off. I told you he's a stand up guy. Not to mention that he knows I think of Emma as family. He'll have me to answer to as well, but how about we lay off the threats for now?"

Susie flushed again. The brief exchange seemed to steady Jared. He turned to Trey again. "Back to my point, talked to Darren. Long story short, not a whole lot he can do unless we can put a trace on her phone for calls. Darren's happy to do it, but Emma will need to file a formal police report and give permission for them to do that. Once they trace the calls, they can issue a warning to whoever is calling. Beyond that, not much to do unless something else happens."

Trey nodded. "I think Emma will be willing to file a report, don't you?" he asked, directing his question to Susie. He and Susie hadn't discussed any of this and he didn't know her well, but he knew from Emma that Susie had encouraged her to contact the police. Though he appreciated Jared telling Susie to back off, he also appreciated Susie's protectiveness toward Emma.

Susie nodded, her brown curls bouncing. "I think so. I wish she was here, so we could have her talk to Darren today. She's in Anchorage with Hannah and Tess. I was supposed to go, but I'm up to my neck in monthly reports. Are you going to talk to her today?" she asked, catching Trey's eyes. Though he wouldn't dare comment on it, Trey was starting to find it amusing that Jared and Susie would only look at him. Even when addressing each other, they avoided making eye contact.

"Planning to call her in a bit. I'll ask her about it," Trey replied.

Susie gave a satisfied nod and then looked at Trey. "So seems like you're pretty into Emma?" she asked bluntly.

Trey glanced sideways at Jared, but Jared was staring at the wall. Meeting Susie's eyes again, they held a curious and sly gleam. "Yup, I'm pretty into her. And I'm damn worried about this ex of hers. I'd like to close the door on him."

Susie nodded approvingly. "You and me both. Sorry to be so direct, it's just how I am. Emma's a good friend. Jared swears you're solid. As long as you know she deserves nothing but the best, we're good."

Trey nodded cautiously, glancing to Jared again who finally stopped staring at the wall.

"Darren said to have Emma stop by when he's on duty. He'll take care of it. Then we wait," Jared said.

"I'll let her know when I talk to her. If I need to, I'll take her to the police station myself. Thanks for talking to Darren," Trey said.

Jared nodded. "You got it. All of us want this guy

out of her life. Even if it's just phone calls, it's not cool that it's been going on this long. Wish she'd said something sooner."

Trey thought of Emma's eyes when she first arrived at his house the other night. Shuttered and battened down, shards of fear glimmering in the blue despite her efforts to keep it hidden.

"You and me both," he said succinctly.

Susie busied herself shuffling papers on her desk. The tautness in the room had eased, but Trey didn't think he should stay. Whatever was going on between Jared and Susie didn't need his interference. He thanked them both again and said his goodbyes. As soon as the door shut behind him, he heard Susie's voice. "What the hell is wrong with you?"

Trey walked briskly to his car, which faced the office windows. When he glanced up as he put the truck in gear, he saw Susie step in front of Jared, her finger pointed at him. Jared took a step back. Trey chuckled and turned away to back up. He had his suspicions about the tension between Susie and Jared, but first Jared was going to have to face Susie's fire. Emma had described Susie as forceful, which he was thinking might have been a bit of an understatement.

RISA LEFT the following morning with Trey's assurances that he'd bring Emma to visit soon. Trey dropped Stuart off at a school friend's house for a few hours while he ran errands. Returning to his car after he got groceries, an unfamiliar man was leaning against the car beside his. Trey's gut blasted a warning. He ignored the man and loaded his groceries in the back of his car. When he closed the hatch, the man pushed away from the car, a nondescript gray rental sedan with a sticker from the rental car company from the Homer airport on the window.

Trey took in the details of the man in front of him. He was average height and build, shorter than Trey. He had light brown hair and brown eyes. His mouth was flat, his eyes cold. Anger and resentment hung in the air around him.

The man finally spoke after staring at him for a long moment. "Here's the deal. Emma's mine. You think you're slick answering her phone for her. You're not. I've known where she was ever since she left. If you don't leave her alone, I'll make sure you do."

Anger whipped through Trey. Being face to face with the man who made Emma's life a living hell for two long years and continued to keep fear lodged inside of her every day since infuriated him. He wanted to forget trying to handle this through legal channels. That was a slow, methodical process when what he wanted to do was slam the man to the ground. Trey flexed his hands and forced himself to stay calm and breath slowly. "Emma doesn't belong to anyone, certainly not you. You must be Greg."

Greg nodded. "You got it. Think you're clever? You're not. All it took was a little digging and I figured out who you were. Think you're all tough because you're a pilot and used to be a high and mighty prosecutor. Whatever. Emma only divorced me because I let her. If you want me to keep my distance from Emma, you're gonna have to keep your distance from Emma. Are we clear?"

His fury simmered. Trey didn't think and stepped close to Greg, looking down at him. "How about this? If you dare get anywhere near Emma, you'll regret it."

Trey itched to haul off and punch Greg, but the frail hold he had on his rationality was just enough to keep him in check. He stepped back. "If you're hoping I'm the only person around that will make sure Emma's okay, think again. Get the hell out of town. We've already talked to the police about you and trust me, they'll hear about your threats right away."

Trey swung away and slammed into his car. Before pulling out, he took a quick glance at the car license plate, repeating it aloud to memorize it. In seconds, he was looking at Greg in his rear view mirror. He hadn't waited to hear what else Greg had to say. He knew he needed to get out of there fast. His mind spun. He wanted to call Emma and warn her, but he knew that would send her into a panic. But she had to know Greg was nearby. Trey swore to himself thinking about the fact that she wasn't with him right now. She wouldn't be back from Anchorage until tomorrow night. Though at this very moment, Greg was here in Diamond Creek, he could leave at any time.

Trey called Jared immediately and asked for Darren's direct line. During the call, Jared repeated what Trey told him to Susie, at which point, she grabbed the phone from Jared. Trey fleetingly pondered that Jared seemed to spend a lot of time with Susie, but he didn't have time to wonder what it might mean.

"What the hell! Emma's ex is here?" Susie demanded.

"That's what I just told Jared. I want to call Darren right away, so I can make sure they have his plates. What do you think we should tell Emma? I want her to know, so she's on her guard, but I don't want to freak her out."

"She has to know. How about you call her and I'll call Hannah? That way, Hannah and Tess will know what's up and can maybe keep Emma from flipping about this."

"Got it. Tell them not to leave her alone. I don't care how she feels about it," Trey said tersely. "Can you hand the phone back to Jared?"

"Yeah?" Jared asked.

"Look, promise me you'll be on the lookout for this guy. I wish he'd done a little more than call and threaten her. Even if we can get the cops to charge him, that's nothing. We need to get him slapped with something big enough he'll be forced to get the hell out of here. If we can get felony charges on him, he'll probably take a plea deal that includes no contact with her to avoid a trial. I want Alaska to be the last place he wants to be."

"I'm with you. Talk to Darren, let me know what he says and keep me posted. I'll talk to Luke and Nathan too. Not that they can help with the charges, but that's a few more people aware to watch out for his car," Jared replied.

Trey finished the call and hung up. Fury still pulsed through him. Greg's threat crystallized something for him. No matter how fast it had happened, his heart knew what his intellect shied away from. He loved Emma. He pictured her bright blue eyes and the lingering fear in their depths no matter how hard she tried to conceal it. He would do whatever he needed to get Greg out of her life once and for all. And when she came back from Anchorage, she was staying with him.

* * *

TREY SWORE and slammed his hand on the counter. Emma had gotten upset about Greg, which he would have predicted. But she was insisting she had to deal with this alone.

"Emma, just listen to me…"

"I *am* listening. I understand that you're worried. But this is exactly why I wasn't so sure it was a good idea for us to get involved. Now Greg is looking you up and that means we have to worry about Stuart."

"Do you seriously think Greg would harm Stuart? He's focused on you, not anyone else."

Emma's breath was rapid, and it broke Trey's heart. He knew she was scared.

"I don't think he'll hurt Stuart, but how are you going to keep this from Stuart if all the sudden I'm staying with you all the time? Stuart doesn't need to be exposed to this," Emma said stubbornly.

"We'll find a way to explain. He's not a fragile kid, Emma. He's already lost his mother. He's been through far worse than learning sometimes there are bad people in the world. I just want you to be safe until we know Greg isn't a threat. That's all."

Emma sighed. "Let me handle this. I was married to him for two years. I know how to predict what he might do. I won't stay alone. Tess, Hannah and Susie have all offered to let me stay with them…"

"You don't need to stay with them. You can stay with me," Trey countered.

"Stop it. Let me do this. I did what I had to do to leave him. I can do what I have to do to make this to stop. I'll talk to the police, I'll do whatever you think might help, but I can't handle you taking over like this."

Trey wanted to keep arguing, but Emma was digging in. He dropped it for now. "Fine. I'll let you handle this, but don't shut me out. And promise me you won't stay alone."

"I promise. I'm already planning to stay at Hannah's tomorrow night. And I won't shut you out. I just need to do this myself," she said, her tone softening with weariness.

Trey closed his eyes, willing himself to accept her request to back off a little. "I hear you. I do. Just let me help however I can."

"How about you meet with me when I go talk to Darren tomorrow? I don't understand all the legal stuff and you do."

"Tell me what time. I'll be there."

* * *

"You're being ridiculous. That's all I have to say," Susie declared. Her words were followed by two loud thumps as she kicked her muddy boots against the stairs on her way up to Hannah's kitchen door.

"I'm not being ridiculous. I'm being sane," Emma replied, kicking her own shoes against the stairs.

Susie gave three quick knocks on the door and opened it without waiting for an answer. She turned to look over her shoulder and shook her head at

Emma, her curls bouncing. "You're rationalizing. You're not being sane."

Emma rolled her eyes at the back of Susie's head and followed her inside. Hannah stood at the kitchen counter slicing apples. Her toddler son, John, was seated on the floor petting their dog, Jessie.

Susie immediately swept John into her arms, eliciting giggles from him. "You look more like your daddy everyday," Susie said as she swung him up in the air and set him back down.

Emma knelt to receive a hug from John. "Hey sweetie," she said, glancing over to Hannah. "Susie's right, he's a ringer for Luke."

Hannah smiled. "I know. So how's it going?"

Susie sighed elaborately as she sat down at the kitchen table. "Emma's being ridiculous. She doesn't want to stay with Trey because she has to handle this bullshit with Greg on her terms, whatever the hell that means. Oops." Susie slapped her hand over her mouth. "Swear word! Forgot to censor for John. I'll be good now," she continued with an apologetic smile.

Emma sat across from Susie. "Why is it ridiculous to want to handle this myself? I told you from the start why I was worried about this affecting Trey and Stuart. I'm trying to minimize the spillover into his life."

Susie glared at her. "You said you were worried he wouldn't want anything to do with you if he knew about what happened with Greg. It's fine that you didn't tell us sooner. It's your business. But I think you didn't give Trey enough credit, or us. If you'd told us sooner and told us about how often Greg was calling, we could have helped you deal with this. And Jared says Trey's rock solid. When he stopped by my office the other day to talk to Jared, it's crystal clear that the last thing on his mind is thinking he needs to run away because of your past. That man is seriously into you."

Emma fought against the prickle of irritation that rose in her. She didn't know how to explain why it was important that she handle Greg herself. She couldn't have a man be the one to take over and handle it. That only served as a reminder that she couldn't handle it.

Hannah finished slicing and set the knife down. "Okay Susie, I know you're worried and you want Emma to do what you think is right, but it's not like she's not accepting our help. She's staying with us for the week." Hannah walked over and joined them at the table. John had settled back on the rug with Jessie and was alternating between petting her and rolling his toy truck around.

Emma glanced between Susie and Hannah. "Susie, I can't tell you how much I appreciate you always being there for me. I wish I had talked to y'all sooner about Greg and let you know about those damn calls. But it's not because I wasn't giving you credit. It's hard to explain how awful it feels to be in a relationship like the one I had with Greg. Once I got out, I just wanted to forget about it. As for Trey, my god, we've only been dating a few weeks. He's blown me away with how supportive he is. But you have to admit things have been moving pretty quick."

Susie looked across the table at Emma. "I get it. I'm just worried about you. Trey obviously wants to help, and I hate that you're kind of keeping him to the side."

Hannah chuckled. "In case you missed it, Susie's loves to play matchmaker. She may not have been able to set you and Trey up, but now she wants to make sure you're swept off your feet."

Emma laughed softly. "How could I forget? Trust me, Trey's doing a great job of sweeping me off my feet. I just need to deal with Greg once and for all before I can get too swept away."

"Any word from Darren?" Hannah asked.

"I met with him earlier, and I brought Trey with me," she said pointedly with a glance at Susie. "Darren and Trey did most of the talking. He's set up a trace on my line and told me to keep an eye out for Greg, as if I needed anyone to remind me of that." The knowledge that Greg was somewhere nearby had kept her stomach in knots since Trey called about his encounter with Greg. Hannah and Tess hadn't left her side for the rest of their trip in Anchorage. Tess brought her home and waited while she packed a few things for her stay with Hannah and Luke. Though she was, thus far, resisting Trey's request to stay with him, she agreed to let Sula stay there for now. Tootsie was tolerant enough to largely ignore Sula, so they seemed to be living in peace.

Emma had gone to work today and struggled to stay focused when she wasn't in session with clients. Fortunately, therapy itself honed her focus, but during paperwork and administrative meetings, her mind whirred over whether she'd run into Greg. She obsessed that he probably knew where she worked and might come by the office. She couldn't decide if she needed to tell her supervisor about it. The mere idea of doing that caused shame to wash over her in waves. She'd tried so hard to put Greg behind her. She'd never thought she could erase what happened and knew damn well she couldn't, but she had hoped against hope that the residue of her marriage wouldn't trail her to her new life.

"I know you're going to hate me for asking, but do you have any pictures of Greg?" Susie asked.

Emma looked at her, eyes wide. "No! I didn't keep any. Why would you want to see pictures of him?"

Susie and Hannah exchanged a glance. "So that we know who to keep an eye out for. Can you grab your laptop?" Susie asked Hannah. "I'm sure we can find something online. Just need you to let us know we found the right one. It's not like his name is that uncommon."

Dread curdled inside Emma, but she waited in silence while Hannah handed her laptop to Susie. She knew Susie was right to want to know what Greg looked like, but the idea of even looking at his photo made her sick. In moments, Susie turned the screen around and Emma found herself looking at the man she wished she could erase from her memory. It was a photo she'd never seen, perhaps from a work gathering. He worked in sales for an insurance company. There he was, his sandy brown hair and brown eyes, standing beside a table with platters of food on it. He wore slacks and a button-down shirt. His mouth was smiling, but his eyes distant. A spike of fear flashed through her center, followed by a chill. She had to force herself to breathe, recalling that the last time she'd seen him he started screaming at her because she forgot to get milk at the store. When he'd started walking towards her, his hands balled up at his sides, she'd fled down the hall into the bathroom. Many long moments later, he'd stormed out, and she'd put her careful plans into motion.

To this day, she was relieved he avoided court

proceedings for the divorce, but she never stopped worrying that she'd gotten lucky with that. When the calls started coming randomly after she moved to Diamond Creek, she kept hedging her bets, hoping her luck would hold. A tear rolled down her cheek as she sat there, that damn photo of Greg mocking her. He just had to push it now. She hadn't quite believed she could have Trey. He was too good for her, too special, too…everything she didn't deserve. Women like her who had been too naïve to see the danger in front of them, well if they got lucky enough to get out of an abusive relationship, that was enough. Hoping for anything more, much less hoping for love, was just asking for more than the universe could offer.

Emma started when Hannah slipped her arm around her shoulders. "Hey, whatever is going through your head, we're going to help you get through this," Hannah said softly and firmly.

Emma gave her head a hard shake and wiped at her tears. "I know, I know. In case you were wondering, that's Greg. I hate that this is happening. I thought I'd gotten away from him." She turned and looked to Hannah. "You have to know I came out here because I really wanted to find my parents. I was so happy to find you. I didn't move here just to get away from Greg. I won't lie though. I was relieved you lived so far away. But I came here because I wanted to get to know this place and you."

Hannah rubbed her shoulder. "It never occurred to me to think that! Let's focus on getting him to leave you alone once and for all."

Susie nodded her head emphatically, her curls bouncing. "We're on it. I'm hoping I run into him first.

I'll make sure he regrets showing up here," Susie said with a snarl.

Emma couldn't help but laugh. She was tired and emotionally raw, but Susie's protectiveness brought a warm glow inside. "Oh I'll vote for you to find him!"

The lighthearted moment helped her dread lift, if only a little.

*E*mma made her way quickly through the grocery store. It had been over a week since Trey called to tell her Greg was in town, and all was quiet. No phone calls either. That bothered her because she knew it meant he was purposefully laying low. The trace Darren put on her phone was useless unless Greg called. Darren assured her they were also getting her phone records and could use those, but if Greg stopped harassing her, there wasn't much they could do.

Trey called her daily and was clearly losing patience with her. Beyond the day he accompanied her to meet with the police, she hadn't seen him. The more she thought about it, the more she wanted to make sure she kept a boundary between this mess and Trey and Stuart. She could hardly bear to think about Trey right now. She knew it hadn't been smart to get involved with him, and unfortunately, her heart was in deep. When she wasn't worrying over Greg, her thoughts traveled to Trey again and again and again.

As she came around the corner of the aisle by the deli, she ran into someone and looked up, straight into Trey's face. He brought his hands up to steady her shoulders. The warmth of his palms sifted through the thin cotton blouse she wore.

"Emma," he said simply, her name weighted with feeling. His eyes stared into hers, his velvety brown gaze probing.

She cursed her body for its weakness. Mere seconds in his presence, her pulse raced, and her breath became shallow. Desire spread its wings and flew through her body. "Trey...I didn't expect to see you here..."

His shoulders rose and fell with a deep breath. She couldn't look away, literally held in place by his eyes, her heart beating like a drum, her stomach fluttering.

"Could we talk?" Trey asked abruptly.

Emma nodded wordlessly, unable to think clearly. Trey stepped back and moved his cart out of the way. A quick glance around, and he tugged her into the hallway beside the deli that led to the restrooms. He stopped once they turned a corner out of view from the main part of the store.

Emma's back was to the wall. Thoughts bounced in her mind—how to explain to Trey that they needed some space while she dealt with Greg, how to help him understand that she couldn't stand it if any of this affected Stuart, how to keep her feelings in check. But her body...oh how her body thrummed with pleasure at his nearness. Were she a cat, she'd wrap herself around him and purr.

Trey faced her, his features somber, eyes dark. "Emma..." he started and paused. He swallowed and took a measured breath. He swore softly. Bracketing her between his arms, he rested his elbows on the wall behind her and abruptly kissed her. Her mouth opened to his instantly. His tongue delved deep, and she met him stroke for stroke. She was aflame, almost feverish with need for him. She arched against him. His lips traveled in a blazing trail down her neck. He slid a palm down and curled it softly around her breast, her nipple pebbling against his hand. She gasped when he lightly bit her other nipple through her shirt. His knee slid between her thighs. She wore a soft cotton twirly skirt that fell out of the way, his knee coming against the thin silk of her panties. Slick moisture built in her core. Her hips pressed against him, she rode his thigh, sweet pleasure spiking through her. All thought was wiped from her mind. All she wanted was him...*now.*

"Trey...please..." she gasped.

"Dear God, Emma..." he growled, his lips making their way back up her neck.

Someone in the deli nearby called out an order number, breaking into Emma's consciousness. Trey pulled away. "Dammit," he said softly. He stepped back, creating a small pocket of space between them though his knee stayed where it was. She flushed, knowing he could feel the wet heat of her need against his thigh. Even though a semblance of sanity had returned, she helplessly shifted against him, pleasure spiking with each tiny thrust of her hips.

A lingering caress of her breasts and Trey brought his hands to the wall behind her, breathing heavily. Emma looked into his eyes. The intensity of yearning she witnessed there took her breath away. "I didn't mean to start this. But I miss you," he said simply.

He stealthily shifted his knee. Emma closed her

eyes against the pleasure. She was *so* close to release, she didn't even care they were feet away from someone coming around the corner and finding them like this. "I miss you too," she choked out, her hips restless against his thigh.

"Emma," Trey whispered. "Please don't shut me out."

Emma heard his words, but she couldn't focus on anything other than cresting past the point where she teetered. Trey brushed her bangs away from her eyes and brought his lips to hers. They were standing so that if someone came around the corner, it would be obvious they were kissing, but no more. This kiss started slow with soft nips, a tracing of her lips, their tongues tangling in a scalding dance. Another shift of Trey's knee, her hips pressed down hard against him, and she came in a burst, her gasps captured by his mouth.

He slowly gentled his lips, his knee shifting away once the pulses of her climax slowed. She felt the heat and pulse of his cock against her hip. Lifting her eyes, she met his again. Thoughts tumbled through her mind. How could a kiss and a few caresses turn into a bonfire inside and push her to orgasm in mere seconds? She didn't know. But that's how it was. Rationally, she knew she should be worried someone would come around the corner. The muted sounds of activity from the deli and store filtered into the hall. Trey took a slow breath and stepped a shade further away. She immediately missed his warmth.

"So what do I have to say to get you to stop avoiding me right now?" Trey asked bluntly. Assured as he usually was, Emma saw a flicker of doubt in his eyes.

She gave in to what her heart and body wanted. "How about I come over tonight?"

A smile flashed across his face, almost boyish. "Well, that was much easier than I expected."

She giggled. "I didn't realize how much I missed you until now..." her words trailed off when he lifted a hand and tucked a loose lock of hair behind her ear.

His eyes sobered. "Have you been okay? Anything from Greg?"

Emma shook her head. "Nothing. And that makes me nervous." She shifted and Trey stepped back. "Can we talk about that later?" she asked, not wanting to get into any talk of Greg now. She needed to gather her thoughts and figure out how the hell to keep her wits about her when it came to Trey.

Trey nodded. "Sure. Just tell me what time you'll be over," he said.

* * *

SHUTTING the door to her truck, Emma leaned her head back and let out a sigh. Her body hummed from her encounter with Trey. Just thinking about it flushed her again. *Get yourself together.* She'd been so distracted on the way out of the store that she'd left her groceries at the checkout line. Fortunately, the checker had caught up with her before she left completely. Her thoughts went one direction and her body another. She was still dripping with need. With a shake of her head, she fumbled for her keys.

When she started driving out of the parking lot, a quick motion caught her eyes. Glancing over, she saw a man climbing into a grey sedan. Though she couldn't get a good look, she knew it had to be Greg.

Something about the way he moved. Though she wanted to stop and confirm, she knew it wasn't a good idea. Her hands started to shake. She tried to call Trey, but he didn't answer. Forcing herself to drive, she turned off the highway onto the side road where Susie's office was. Dust rose around her truck when she came to a jarring stop.

The sun in her eyes as she walked in, she called out Susie's name. As Emma's eyes adjusted to the light, she realized Susie stood to the side of the desk in the waiting area. Jared leaned against the wall nearby. Susie's curls were in more disarray than usual and her face flushed. Jared's eyes were inscrutable, and he looked wound tight. Though Jared was Luke's brother, he'd always intimidated her. Just like his brothers, he was tall and dark. Today, he was dressed in faded black jeans and a black t-shirt. With his black hair, the only color came from his green eyes. Hannah swore he was a sweetheart, but Emma wasn't so sure. Nathan, Luke's younger brother, was much easier to be around—laidback with a half-smile almost all the time. Jared was serious and intense with a sharp intellect.

"Hey, hope it's okay I just stopped by," Emma said by way of greeting.

Susie nodded, almost too emphatically. "Of course! What's up?"

Emma hesitated for a moment, wondering if she wanted to talk in front of Jared. She barreled forward anyway, too wired from her fear to stop. "I think I saw Greg in the parking lot at the grocery store. I tried to call Trey but he didn't answer and..."

Jared quickly pulled his phone out. Before Emma could even ask what he was doing, he started talking. "Hey Darren, it's Jared. Calling because Emma says she just saw her ex in the parking lot at the grocery store." He paused while Darren said something and then moved the phone away from his mouth.

"Car description?" he asked.

Emma quickly told him what little she had. After Jared hung up, he pushed away from the wall. "Gonna head over there myself. If he hasn't left yet, I can follow him." He studied Emma for a moment. "Between Trey, Darren, me and my brothers, you can call any of us. Anytime."

Emma nodded. "I know. I just hate this."

Susie, who'd been uncharacteristically quiet, finally spoke. "We know you do, but stop worrying about accepting help. You're family to us. Listen to Jared. Call me, call any of us whenever you need to," she said firmly.

Jared started to walk to the door and turned back. "Hope you know Trey just wants to make sure you're okay. No need to keep him at arms length."

Emma's heart skipped a beat. "I...I just..." she flushed, not sure how to explain, especially not to Jared.

Jared waited a beat. "Trey's as good as they come. I can tell you mean a lot to him. It's driving him near insane that ever since he ran into Greg, he's barely seen you. Just think about that," Jared said.

He turned his intense gaze to Susie. Something flashed through his eyes. Susie flushed again and lifted her chin. "I'll have your quarterly audit to you by the end of the week." Emma could have sworn Susie's voice trembled, but she still wasn't thinking too clearly herself, so she wasn't sure. Susie continued. "Thanks for helping Emma. Will you call if you find him?" she asked softly.

Jared nodded brusquely. "Of course. Soon as I know anything, I'll call." He turned away quickly.

Several long moments of quiet elapsed after he left. Susie was subdued as she put away some files.

"You okay?" Emma asked, unsure what to say with Susie like this.

"Oh yeah. Just tired," Susie said, giving the file drawer a soft push. As the drawer whooshed shut, Susie turned back to Emma. "You shouldn't be worried about me. I'm more worried about you. Jared's got a point about Trey."

Emma sighed and rolled her head in a circle, trying to ease the tension in her neck. "I know. I knew Trey and Jared were friends. Guess I didn't realize Trey would be talking to him about me."

Susie shrugged. "Hey, guys have to talk too. Plus, between me and Trey, Jared's heard all about how worried we are about this Greg thing. And whatever I might think of Jared, he takes care of family, and you're family as far as he's concerned," Susie said matter-of-factly.

"I know he's good like that. He's so serious most of the time that he makes me nervous. And what do you mean, whatever you might think of Jared?"

Susie shrugged again. "Just that he's uptight and so detail oriented, it's enough to drive a person insane. You should try to be his accountant," she said with a roll of her eyes. "Aside from that, he's a great guy. Controlling every detail of his life takes up most of his time. It'd be nice for him to find something else to focus on."

Emma started to reply, but thought better of it.

There was an edge in Susie's words. Emma had some ideas about that, namely that Jared had a lot to do with it, but now wasn't the time. If there was one thing she knew about Susie, it was that she tended to feel things strongly—good and bad. Emma kept the topic on her own situation, though she'd rather not seeing as the distraction kept her mind off her fears. "Well, I appreciate everything Jared's done," she said, hoping Susie would forget to ask about Trey again.

No such luck.

"So, still stuck on avoiding Trey, huh?" Susie asked.

"Can't catch a break on that, huh?"

Susie shook her head and smiled. "Nope."

"I told you already, Trey has Stuart. I can't let this mess with Greg affect Stuart. I'd rather keep my distance until I know Greg's out of my life once and for all."

"That's dumb," Susie said bluntly, never one to mince words.

"It's not dumb," Emma said, feeling defensive. "I'll be the first to admit I should have told y'all about what happened with Greg and those calls long ago, and maybe I'd have cleared this up sooner. But it's not dumb to want to keep this away from Stuart."

"I'm pretty sure you and Trey can keep Stuart out of this. It's not like you're going to chat with Stuart about it. Trey wants to help, you're totally into him and according to Jared, Trey's totally into you. So messy or not, it's too late to pretend like none of that matters," Susie said.

Emma glared at her. "Well, if you must know, even though I've been trying to stay away, I told him I'd go over tonight."

A satisfied smile bloomed across Susie's face. "See, even you knew better than yourself."

Susie's phone rang and she snatched it off the desk. "Yes," she said abruptly.

Susie listened and closed her eyes. "Okay, will you call if you have any more updates from Darren?"

Emma's heart sped up, her fear flaring again. Susie set her phone down. "That was Jared. The car you saw was gone. Darren's doing a sweep around town and so is Jared. Jared said to tell you he left Trey a message too."

Emma felt cold and weary. That's how she'd ended up feeling every day towards the end of her marriage. The fear and anxiety became such a part of her daily existence that it settled like a suffocating weight over her. She wished Darren or Jared would have found Greg right away, and she could have thought that would be it. She hugged her arms around her waist and took a slow breath.

Susie stepped in front of her and pulled her into a firm hug. When she stepped back, her brown eyes were determined. "Maybe it didn't happen just now, but they will find him. Diamond Creek's not big enough to lay low for long. No matter what, in the end, it's good Greg finally tried to play his cards. Now we can flush him out."

Emma tried to smile, but her lips couldn't hold it. "I know you're right. I just want this over." She blinked back tears, her throat tight.

* * *

EMMA SAT cross-legged on the floor beside Stuart. Stuart was showing her pictures in a gardening magazine. "See, you can eat those weeds that grow every-where!" Stuart exclaimed, pointing at a picture of chickweed.

"I heard you could eat those. Haven't tried it myself yet," she replied.

"Well then, we'll have to have Stuart plan a meal where you can try them," Trey said, coming to sit on the couch nearby. "Right Stu?"

Stuart nodded, a random lock of hair that stuck straight up bouncing in rhythm. "Can we?" he asked her.

Emma glanced down into his face, so open and hopeful. "Of course. Will we just have chickweed?" she asked with a smile.

Trey chuckled. "Stuart likes to eat wild things. We've discovered chickweed works great in salad. Tastes like most greens do, on the mild side. This past spring, Stuart found us some fiddleheads after he learned about them in school. Do you want to tell Emma about those?"

Stuart looked up from the magazine. "Yeah! Fiddleheads are the curly things at the top when ferns start to grow. You have to get them when they're all curled up tight. My teacher last year, Mrs. Roberts, said to..." Stuart trailed off and looked to his father, a question in his eyes. "I don't 'member how you cooked them."

"Mrs. Roberts told us to steam them, so we did. Do you remember how we did that?" Trey asked in turn.

Stuart nodded, a tuft of hair bouncing along. "You boiled water and said the steam would cook them and it did!"

"Did you like them?" Emma asked.

"Yeah, Dad put butter on them and they were

yummy." Stuart turned to his dad again. "So when can we have salad with chickweed for Emma?"

Trey met Emma's eyes, an unspoken question in them. She wanted to tell him that all she wanted was to be here…every night. But she couldn't say that just now. Not when there was so much up in the air. Trey's eyes shuttered, and he looked toward Stuart.

"Sometime soon," Trey said vaguely before glancing at his watch. "About time for bed. You want to show Emma one more picture?"

Stuart carefully paged through the magazine, finally selecting to show her a delphinium. When he stood up to go to bed, Stuart came over and wrapped his arms around her neck. Emma held him for a moment and rubbed her hand up and down his back. She felt him take a deep breath and closed her eyes. "Night Emma," he mumbled against her shoulder before pulling away.

"Good night, Stuart," she started to say she'd see him in the morning, but hesitated when her thoughts caught up. The comfort she felt here was too easy to fall into.

Trey followed Stuart down the hallway. She stood up from the floor and walked over to the windows. The sun was making its bow in a kaleido-scope of red, orange and pink shafts of light. The water in the bay rippled with the colored reflections. Boats were still coming in, all headed toward the harbor. The mountains were dark in the fading light. Trey's yard was mostly protected from view, but the road was visible in one corner, along with a neigh-bor's house to one side. She started to turn away when her eyes caught sight of a car in the neighbor's drive. Though she couldn't say for sure, the car looked like the one she saw earlier at the grocery store.

Emma's heart started racing and that familiar cold anxiety dropped over her. She moved away from the windows, aware the living room was basically on display. She frantically looked around to find the light switches, immediately turning them off. Waiting in the darkened kitchen, muted sounds filtered from the hallway—water running, Stuart's footsteps padding across the carpet, Trey's voice saying good night, and then a door shutting softly.

Her breathing was shallow. Trey came into the living room a puzzled look crossing his face when he found her huddled against the counter in the kitchen. "Emma?" he asked, walking slowly toward her. He started to reach for the light switch.

"No! Keep the lights off," Emma said, shaking her head.

Trey's steps faltered and his hand froze. "What's going on?" he asked sharply.

"I'm afraid Greg might be out there. I saw a car over in your neighbor's drive. It's just like the one I saw at the grocery store," she whispered, her voice hoarse. Her heart hammered in her chest, and she couldn't slow her breath down. She wrapped her arms tightly around her waist.

Trey moved quickly, walking over to the windows. "The gray sedan in the drive?" he asked.

Emma nodded, her throat tight.

Trey looked for a long moment and stepped away from the window. He walked slowly toward her, his hands in his pockets. Stopping in front of her, he reached up and curled his palm around her shoulder, sliding it down in a warm caress. His small gesture eased her anxiety, but only the slightest bit. Her breath hitched. Hot tears pressed at the back of her eyes.

"Emma, I know you're scared. But I'm pretty sure that's our neighbors' car. Do you mind if give them a call to confirm?"

"But it looks just like the car I saw today! Are you sure?"

Trey held her eyes, his gaze steady and reassuring. "All I know is they have a car like that. If you don't mind me calling over, we can find out for sure."

"Okay, then call. I just don't want them to think you're weird for asking."

Trey shrugged, entirely unconcerned. "I'll tell them I heard the cops were looking for a similar car. That'll be enough."

Moments later, he was slipping his phone back in his pocket. "It's their car. Can we turn a few lights on now?" he asked softly.

Emma took a shaky breath and nodded. "I'm sorry. I overreacted." She was finally able to relax her arms. Her jaw was clenched, along with every muscle in her body. Fight, flight, or freeze—the mantra in therapy for what humans did when confronted with a threat, real or imagined. In her case, she froze.

Trey seemed to sense she needed a few minutes. He quietly moved about, turning on a few lamps rather than the overhead lights. Returning to the kitchen, he put the last of the dishes in the dishwasher before pulling a bottle of red wine out of the wine rack under the counter, along with two wineglasses. Glancing at her, he lifted an eyebrow in question. At her nod, he filled both glasses before gesturing for her to follow him into the living room.

Emma sat down on the couch with a sigh. She felt silly now. It was as if the three years she'd worked so hard to get control of her fears and move on from Greg had never happened. A mere week of learning he was here, and she was a bundle of nerves and questioning everything she saw.

Trey wordlessly handed her the glass of wine, and she took a welcome swallow. She needed something to blunt the ragged edges of her fear. She started to say something and stopped, unsure how to explain or what she even wanted to explain.

Trey was seated close to her and shifted a little closer, his warmth a balm to her nerves. He slipped an arm over her shoulders. "No need to think this to death. You have every reason to worry about seeing a car like that. I'm glad you said something. If you weren't worried, it would scare me. I won't pretend this week has been easy. I hate that you haven't been staying with me, but I'm more relieved than I can say that you're not staying by yourself at your house."

He rubbed the back of her neck, slowly massaging it. The coil of tension inside of her began to ease. She took a sip of wine and glanced at him. He was staring out the window, his expression inscrutable. He turned to her, his eyes meeting hers—intense and probing. Her eyes skittered away, her breath hitching. The rational part of herself—the one she tended to rely on, particularly after the fiasco of her marriage—told her she needed to get a grip, what was happening with Trey was too much, too intense, and too fast, that Greg showing up should remind her of how foolish she'd been to even think she could have something good, and letting her fantasies get the best of her was revealing what a farce they were. But her heart beat its soft wings against her fears. *You don't have to believe that. Maybe, just maybe you can have something with Trey.* Her defensive mind sneered. Emma shook her head sharply and took a gulp of wine.

Trey's hand slowly stilled. His voice broke through the quiet. "So are we gonna talk about how long you need to insist on having space? Because I don't agree. I'm doing my best, but it's not easy."

Her throat tightened. Anxiety bloomed in her chest. She didn't know how to explain, or if it made any sense, even to her. Forcing herself to take a breath, she took another few gulps of wine, the wine starting to dull the fear clamped over her. Trey's presence was everything she wanted and everything she'd convinced herself she could never have. He was strong, sure, intelligent, caring, protective and sexy as hell. On top of all that, he was an amazing single father. And being near him set her nerves alight—shivery sparks skittering, her belly fluttering, and wet heat building.

Emma finally looked over and met his eyes, tumbling into the warm brown. "I don't know. I don't really want space, it just seems like I should. I hate that Greg showed up like this. I want to deal with it myself and not drag you into it." Her words were soft in the quiet room. Restless, she looked away and out the windows. The sun had fallen lower, a curved crescent peeking above the mountains. The sky was deep red and orange fading into dark. The harbor lights cast across the water, the rippling waves visible in the reflected light. A half-moon sat low in the sky, its rise measured by the pace of the sun's fall. So precise, as the tides were.

She felt the lift of Trey's breath and looked back at

him. His eyes were intent, focused on her. When he spoke, his voice was low and firm. "But you don't have to deal with it by yourself. Whether you like it or not, no matter whether it happened too fast, *we* have something and what happens to you matters to me. A lot." He paused and appeared to be considering his words. "I get why you want to deal with Greg yourself. You went through hell to get out of that relationship and stand on your own. But you don't have to be alone anymore. Let me be there for you." His eyes broke away from hers and he shifted abruptly, raking his hands through his hair. He looked out the window again, elbows resting on his knees. His profile, the strong, clean lines of his face, was etched in the shadows. A glimmer of sadness lingered in his eyes when he finally turned back to her.

Emma stopped thinking and let her heart lead her for once. Though it terrified her, she simply didn't have it in her tonight, at this juncture, to fight what she wanted. Setting her wineglass on the coffee table, she spoke his name.

Trey turned, his eyes zeroing in on hers. She didn't look away and slowly stood, coming to stand directly in front of him. With deliberation, she leaned forward and cupped his face in his hands. Tracing his lips with one finger, she fell into the blur of passion that hovered around them.

He muttered an imprecation and swiftly tugged her forward. Her knees collapsed, and she straddled him. Holding her gaze, his palms slid under her blouse and up her back, strong and warm, blazing a path of heat that suffused her body. With subtle pressure, he pressed her forward until she could feel his breath against her lips. "You're not alone," he said, his voice husked with passion.

And then he kissed her, his lips strong, sure and oh-so-thorough. His tongue traced her lips, urging her mouth open before delving in. The fear and anxiety she'd been trying so hard to hold at bay dissolved in the fiery passion between them. Emma became frantic and fumbled with the buttons of his shirt. Trey gentled his kiss and leaned back, his eyes boring into hers—the current between them leapt, her heart stuttered and raced. The sheer depth of yearning in his gaze took her breath away. He slowly slid his palms down her back, bringing one up to cradle her cheek, his thumb brushing away a tear she hadn't noticed.

Straddling him, she felt the heat of his shaft against pressing against her own desire. Her hips moved of their own accord, spikes of sharp pleasure following each minute motion. He stilled her hips with a hand.

"Not rushing this," he said, his voice soft.

He slid his palm down her cheek, skating down the side of her neck, his thumb caressing the beat of her pulse before landing just above where her blouse buttoned. In the haze of her passion, she couldn't break away from his gaze, nor could she focus. With deliberation, he began unbuttoning her blouse. One button at a time, pausing to drop moist kisses as each inch of her skin was revealed. Her desire climbed in increments as he slowly opened her blouse. Feverish and restless, she arched into each kiss, desperate for more. When he finally pushed her blouse off of her shoulders, she sighed in relief. She moved to tug at his shirt and he stopped her.

"Not yet."

Emma whimpered, undulating her hips against the length of his cock. A flash of satisfaction darted through her when he momentarily grabbed her hips and held her hard and fast against him, grinding into her. His breath came in short bursts before he reined himself in. Her nipples ached, straining against the lace cups covering them. Trey turned his attention to them, laving one and then the other through the silky lace. Moving with deliberation, his hands slid around to unhook her bra and toss it away. He sighed in satisfaction when he held both breasts in his hands, cupping them, toying with her nipples, smiling devilishly when she pleaded with him. The silver in his hair caught in the dim light when he leaned forward to nip, suck, lick and tease.

Burning need suffused her. She arched against him, sensation rippling through her. When she moved to unbutton his shirt, he didn't stop her this time. His chest, taut muscles dusted with dark hair, was delectable. His breath hissed through his teeth when she softly licked, kissed and nipped him. The roughened skin of his palms struck sparks on her skin as he slid them up her back again, this time pulling her close, skin to skin. They spiraled into a blur of need—kissing madly, tongues tangling, breathing into and through each other. She ground against him, so wet with desire she could hardly stand the feel of his arousal, so desperate for release that she began to peak, straining against him.

Trey abruptly broke their kiss and pushed her up. Their remaining clothes were torn off, scattered on the floor. He turned her quickly. She fell to her knees on the couch, his hands sliding to cup her bottom, the caress rough and unbearably arousing.

"Trey..."

"Yes?" her voice was husky with desire.

"Please..." she gasped.

He slid two fingers inside her cleft, slippery with her need. Her hands clenched against the back of the couch, her hips pushing into his hand. His slid his fingers in and out, slow and then fast. He brought his other hand around front to tease her clit. She came in a noisy burst. And yet...it wasn't enough. She wanted more, wanted him to fill her.

He slowly removed his hands, sliding them to curl around her hips, the evidence of her desire dragged in wet trails on her skin.

"Emma...can't wait anymore," he bit out. He moved away briefly. She heard the tear of foil and then he rolled a condom on.

His hands returned, one curled around her hip while the other slid up the center of her spine, caressing its curve. The tip of his cock teased her entrance. She whimpered, dripping with want. Just as she thought she couldn't take it anymore, he surged into her channel, driving deep. He established an alternating rhythm—pulling all the way out in excruciating slow motion and driving forward quickly.

She careened into the blaze that surrounded them. The warmth of his palm pressing into the arch of her spine anchored her in the tumult of sensation. She gradually climbed again, her yearning for release building with each stroke. He slid a hand around and at the touch of his thumb against her clit, she shattered, her hips convulsing against him, pulsing around his shaft. His control finally broke and his hips drummed into hers. A final thrust and he called her name, finding his own release.

Nothing but the sound of their breath was left. Trey curled his arms around her waist from behind and slowly tipped them sideways. They fell into a spooned position on the couch. Emma lay still in the quiet, adrift in the aftermath of sensation. He stroked her hair away from her face, placing soft kisses on the back of her neck.

CHAPTER 14

"So what's the update from Darren?" Trey asked Jared.

Jared glanced up from where he stood on the boat. "Hey, don't I get a hello first?"

Trey rolled his eyes and shrugged. "Hello. What's the update from Darren?"

Jared chuckled and wiped his face with his sleeve. Trey had come out to meet him at the harbor. Jared had said he'd be here most of the day doing repairs and cleaning on the fishing boats he owned with his brothers. The sky was bright and clear today, the sun high in the sky. It was an unusually warm summer day in Diamond Creek with little to no breeze giving the sun a chance to create some heat. Trey looked out beyond the harbor into Kachemak Bay. Mount Augustine sat quiet and dark in the distance, void even of the clouds that often lingered around its peak. An eagle screeched nearby. Trey turned to see the eagle launch from its perch on a dock piling and swoop to the water, diving in a splash and coming up with a salmon in its talons. Just beyond the docks, a pair of loons floated in the water.

Trey turned back to Jared who sat down on one of the benches by the boat railing. He tugged his work gloves off and tossed them on the boat deck.

Resting his elbows on the railing, Jared leaned back and eyed Trey with a speculative gleam. "Far as I can tell, you've fallen and *hard* for Emma."

Trey experienced a flash of irritation. He didn't want to explain how or why Emma meant so much to him, but he was terrified Greg's intrusion would ruin what they had. He zoned in on Jared's refusal to answer his question. "Not denying it. But you're not answering my question."

Jared gave him a long look before nodding. "Talked to Darren this morning after you called. No luck confirming Greg's still in town. But now they have Emma's phone records, they've catalogued the calls and they all go back to two different cell numbers—one is listed under Greg's name. The other one surprised me. It's his wife's number. He remarried about six months after his divorce from Emma was finalized."

"You're kidding me," Trey said flatly.

"Exactly what I said," Jared replied. "Darren assured me it's true. When they traced the number and confirmed it belonged to a woman named Barbara Neals, they pulled her public records and found the marriage certificate. So Greg seems to be even more of an asshole than we thought. But you know guys like that, it doesn't matter that he's moved on. He doesn't want Emma to. Probably still can't believe she actually left him."

"Damn. I wonder if his wife knows he's been doing

this all along. And does she know he showed up in Diamond Creek?" Trey wondered aloud.

Jared shrugged. "Hell if I know, but Darren's contacted the local police for the town in Connecticut where they live. They've agreed to go check in with her and find out what she knows. So Greg may not have kept her up to date, but she's about to be."

"Hmm. That oughta be an interesting conversation. I have to let Emma know."

"You think so? I wasn't sure if we should just wait until Darren has info from the Connecticut police," Jared said.

Trey shook his head. "Much as there's a part of me that wants to sit on this because just saying the guy's name stresses her out, I can't. She's not pushing me away. I don't want to make that happen again by withholding anything from her. She needs to feel in control of this as much as she can."

Jared nodded. "Makes sense. Why don't you call Darren to see if he has any more news and then fill her in?"

"Will do," Trey said. He glanced at his watch. "Did you need help with anything before I go?"

Jared shook his head. "Nah, man. Thought I could use your help with carrying some of this gear, but Nathan's headed down in a bit and it makes more sense to load it in his truck, seeing as we store it at his house."

Back in his car, Trey called Risa.

"What's up?" Risa said in greeting.

"Wondering if you'd mind coming to stay for a week or so?"

"Don't you think I might get in the way of time

you could be spending with Emma?" Risa questioned in reply, her tone teasing.

"Better yet, I think it would be good to have you around to help out with Stuart," Trey said before quickly filling her in on what was going on with Greg. "I finally persuaded Emma to stop avoiding me, but her sticking point is that she doesn't want this to affect Stuart. If you're around, you can help with Stuart and I can stay with her at her place."

Risa quickly agreed and said she'd be there tonight. She brushed off his thanks. Trey didn't know what he would have done without Risa sometimes. Yet again, she was stepping up to help, this time for a woman she barely knew. Risa had a huge heart. Though she'd been busy encouraging him to move on from Helen's death, she dismissed him whenever he asked if she was seeing anyone. It would drive her near batty, but Trey figured she was due for a little prodding herself sometime soon.

With Risa on the way, Trey called his assistant at the office to let her know he'd be in tomorrow. He left Emma a quick message to call when she could and headed over to meet Darren.

Darren didn't have any more to add than what Jared had already told him. He seemed bemused that Trey was checking with him, in addition to Jared. "Should I set up a phone tree to make sure everyone has an update the second I have anything new?" Darren asked wryly.

When Trey started to nod, Darren burst out laughing. "Look, we're not doing a phone tree here. I haven't even had a chance to call Emma with Jared breathing down my neck because she's family for him, and now I've got you on my tail too. I gather you've got something going on with Emma, and you're worried about her. But these things take time. Unless we get lucky and spot this guy, we're just gonna have to wait. For the rest, I'm moving as fast as I can. The Connecticut cops said they'd swing by the house where Greg and his wife live today and call me once they have something to tell me. In the meantime, not much else I can do."

Trey kept himself in check. He wanted to shake Darren even though he knew damn well Darren was doing everything he could. He couldn't help himself and had to ask if they had cops on duty round the clock. As with much of Alaska, that was no guarantee.

"Oh yeah, it's summer. We're staffed 24/7 all summer. Everyone's gotten a copy of Greg's picture, and we're on alert for the car Emma saw. I promise I'll call Emma as soon as I have any more news."

Restless to do something other than wait, Trey swung into Misty Mountain Café to pick up baked goods for Risa and Stuart, along with something to surprise Emma with for breakfast tomorrow. Walking in, he spied Susie at a corner table. She appeared to be focused on work, typing rapidly on her laptop. While he waited in line, he saw Jared exit the restroom and head straight for Susie's table. Jared paused beside the table and said something. Susie's head lifted sharply. Trey's curiosity piqued when Susie glared at Jared and returned to her typing. In a rare moment, Jared appeared uncertain, shifting on his feet and glancing around the café. Noticing Trey, Jared waved him over. Trey gestured to the line and nodded. He couldn't help but wonder what was going on with those two.

Strong coffee in hand, along with two loaves of

fresh bread and a box of Risa's favorite savories, Trey threaded through the scattered tables.

"Hey there, seems we're on the same wavelength today," he commented to Jared.

Jared nodded. He'd seated himself across from Susie who paused in her typing to look up at Trey's arrival. Tension rankled in the air between Jared and Susie. Restless to do something other than worry about Emma, Trey accepted Susie's invitation to sit down.

"Have a seat. I'd love to have you join *me*," Susie said in a stilted bubbly voice before throwing another glare in Jared's direction.

Trey glanced to Jared who rolled his eyes. After only a few minutes with Susie, he recalled that Emma had described her as 'forceful'. He wasn't sure that even captured what she was though he had to acknowledge she was protective as hell of Emma, which he counted as a good thing. Jared was mostly quiet, though he bit back laughter repeatedly.

"So Jared swears you're a good guy. For the most part, I trust Jared's judgment…"

Jared interrupted her. "For the most part? Seriously? Do I get any credit?"

Susie glared at him, a flush creeping up her neck. "I just gave you some credit! It was a turn of phrase. I didn't actually mean there are times when I don't trust your judgment. For God's sake, don't be so critical."

Jared shook his head and waved for her to continue.

Susie gave Jared a pointed look before turning her focus back to Trey. "So Jared swears you're a good guy. I just want to make sure you know that if you do *anything* to hurt Emma, I'll make you regret it," she said emphatically, keeping her brown eyes trained on him.

Trey avoided looking away and considered his words before he spoke. "I thought we already went over this, but I'm glad to know how important Emma is to you. Because she means a lot to me. I don't have any intention of hurting her," he said simply.

Susie's eyes softened, a twinkle entering them. "Good. That's what I thought. Just making sure. Now what's the news on Greg?"

Jared started to respond when Trey looked toward the parking lot and saw Greg step out of the gray sedan Emma had described. He whipped his phone out to call Darren.

Susie started to ask what was going on, and Trey pointed to Greg while he waited for Darren to answer. She went to get up from the table, and Jared laid a hand on her arm. "Susie, don't run out there. Let's get Darren on his way at least."

After Darren confirmed he was headed right over, Trey put his phone away and started to walk toward the door only to stop when Jared latched onto his arm and stopped him mid-stride. Trey shook his arm, but Jared held firm.

"Come on, man, let me go," Trey said.

Jared gave him a hard look. "It's better for Susie or me to follow him. He knows who you are. Seeing you might end with him taking off again." Jared looked to Susie. "Now that we know Darren's on the way, let's head over. But you can't run over and make it obvious."

Susie huffed, but nodded tightly.

Trey bit back his words. He knew Jared was right,

but he didn't like it. Not one bit. "Just don't let him out of your sight," he said flatly, directing his words to Jared.

Jared stood with a nod. "Not planning on it. Why don't you have a seat and keep an eye on Susie's laptop?"

It took most of Trey's restraint to not follow Jared and Susie out to the parking lot. He waited and watched as Greg strolled across the parking lot and went into a drugstore in the small cluster of stores across from Misty Mountain. He shook his head when he saw Jared grab Susie's arm, not once, but twice to slow her down. She was all but running. After the second grab, Jared tugged her hand into his and held on. Tense as he was about waiting to see if they'd get Greg, Trey couldn't stop his laugh when he saw Susie look up with a glare at Jared who didn't even bother looking back.

Moments later, a police cruiser pulled up. Trey looked around, hoping to find someone familiar to take over his duty as watchdog for Susie's laptop. Seeing no familiar faces, he grabbed her shoulder bag and stuffed the laptop and her papers in it. Slinging it over his shoulder, he headed out to the parking lot. The next few minutes rolled by while Trey waited with Darren who sent his partner, Charlie Brooks, into the drugstore. Moments later, Jared, Susie and Charlie came back out of the drugstore.

Susie was flushed and looked furious. She threw her hands up when they reached the police cruiser. "He's nowhere to be found! We even had them check the restrooms."

Jared nodded tightly. "Nada."

"What the hell?" Trey asked, the anger he'd been keeping in check flashing.

Jared shook his head. "Swear to you, as soon as we stepped inside, I thought I saw him going down one of the aisles, went to follow him and that was the last we saw."

Charlie, an unassuming, young-looking cop with close-cropped brown hair and blue eyes, spoke up. "The manager's best guess is that he disappeared out the back entrance. Not used much, but there is another parking lot back there that connects to the street on the other side. The manager said the rental car company uses it for storage. My guess is he planned to switch cars all along. Manager said she'd pull the tapes from the only surveillance camera they have back there, but she doesn't know if it covers the whole lot."

Darren looked as tense as Trey felt. "Not good. Get back in there and get those tapes," he said to Charlie.

Charlie nodded. "Already on it. She said she'd email the files in a few minutes. You wanna head to the station, so I can pick up my car and head back out?"

Darren nodded tightly and glanced between Jared and Trey. "Would have been easy if he hadn't planned to switch cars. Now we don't even know what car we're looking for. We can narrow it down though even if we can't see it on the surveillance tapes. I'll call over to the car rental place and find out what cars they had stored in that lot."

"Okay if I call Emma and give her an update?" Trey asked. At Darren's quick nod, he turned away.

After Darren and Charlie left, Trey followed Jared and Susie back into Misty Mountain when he realized he'd forgotten his bag of baked goods. Tension drummed through him as he drove away a few minutes later.

* * *

EMMA RACED THROUGH HER NOTES, the keyboard clicking rapidly under her fingertips. It had been another busy day so far with two emergency evaluations squeezed into her already full schedule. There was a soft tap on her open door. She glanced up to find Stella waiting there, looking uncertain.

"Hey there, is it me or are you early?" Emma asked, hitting save and quickly closing her laptop. With a quick push, she wheeled away from her desk and stood.

Stella shrugged. "I'm early, but I called and Gale said she could fit me in earlier."

Gale was the efficient receptionist for Kachemak Bay Counseling. She usually gave Emma a heads up on schedule changes, but Emma had been at full-speed today and had yet to check her messages or email. Emma sat down in the chair opposite the couch where Stella preferred to sit and waved Stella over. "No problem. Grab some tea if you want it," she said, gesturing to the small table where she kept tea and an electric water kettle.

Stella helped herself to a cup of tea and settled across from Emma with a small smile.

"Nice color there," Emma said, gesturing to the bright purple streaks Stella had added to her hair.

Stella grinned. "Thanks. I got purple all over the bathroom sink this time. Janie made me scrub it with baking soda. I never knew baking soda could be used for anything other than baking," Stella said admiringly.

Emma laughed. "Baking soda's handy stuff. I'm surprised you've never dyed the sink before as often as you dye your hair."

"I know, right? I knocked the bottle over this time."

Emma waited, wondering when Stella planned to mention why she wanted to come early. Stella stuck to her regular time like a burr to clothing.

After a few moments of quiet, Stella piped up. "I had to reschedule because the home study lady is coming over this afternoon. Janie told me that if it was important to me, I'd call you to reschedule myself."

"Well, I appreciate that you called to reschedule. Janie usually calls."

Stella sighed elaborately. "I know. She's on this thing now where I need to start making calls for myself."

Emma chuckled. "That's the kind of thing grown ups do."

Stella rolled her eyes, but she was grinning. This was a shift for her. When she'd started seeing Emma for therapy, Stella wore a semi-permanent scowl and complained vociferously at any expectations Janie had. According to Janie, that had been an improvement since Stella had first been placed in her care.

Emma shifted gears. "So the home study lady is coming over—how are you feeling?"

Stella started twirling her hair with one hand. She shrugged. "Seems like a lot of work when I already live with Janie. I mean, how come they have to do a home study for the adoption when Janie already has to live like the perfect life to be my foster mom?"

Emma nodded. "I'm thinking you've already heard this explanation from your worker, right?"

Stella sighed. "Yeah, but it's still stupid."

"I can see your point. But how are you feeling about going through the process for Janie to adopt you?" Emma asked bluntly. Emma was ecstatic to learn Stella hadn't backed out of this yet, but she kept that to herself.

Stella set her mug of tea on the coffee table and tucked her feet under her. "I guess it's kinda like, now that I decided to go ahead, let's just do it. I know I thought it was stupid to get adopted because I'm sixteen, but I can't imagine being without Janie. I mean, I had my mom before, but she wasn't a mom like Janie. I feel bad saying that, but my mom...she was so out of it. Janie's like I thought moms were supposed to be. I still think it's kinda weird, but now we started, I'm ready to be done. I can't imagine calling Janie anything other than Janie though."

Stella said all of this matter-of-factly, which didn't surprise Emma. She'd witnessed enough people experience attitude shifts, she'd learned it happened when people were ready. And once it happened, they'd already done the processing they needed, whether internal or external. Emma cheered internally, so happy to see Stella move through this. Stella had been through far more than her share already, so getting the chance she had with Janie was a stroke of luck not many teens in her situation got. Emma kept her face calm, but seeing Stella make it through to the other side of this one issue was so moving she had to keep her emotions in check.

"I'm guessing Janie doesn't expect you to call her anything other than Janie."

Stella nodded absently, appearing to have mentally moved on. The hair twirling continued. Emma's cell phone vibrated in her pocket. Without looking, she slipped her hand in her pocket and hit the button to ignore the call.

"So I need your opinion," Stella blurted out, a blush washing over her porcelain cheeks.

"About what?" Emma asked.

"You know the guy that's in the recital?"

"The one who had you upset because he was friends with the kid who tried to get you in trouble last year?" At Stella's nod, Emma continued. "Parker, right?"

Stella nodded again, blushing furiously at this point. Emma felt a pang of sympathy for Stella. Her creamy complexion and dark hair made her blushes stand out. Emma waited to see what came next.

Stella shifted around on the couch before finally speaking. When she finally spoke, her voice was soft. "Parker's really nice to me. And I kinda like him. And it makes me nervous. I mean, is he being nice to me so he can try to make fun of me later? What if he does something like what Byron did?"

Emma chose her words carefully when she spoke, knowing Stella tended to be skittish when she opened up. "Well, for starters, I understand why you'd be leery of Parker. There's no easy way to answer the questions you have unless you ask him. And honestly, he probably wouldn't fess up. But if you were to do that, it would put him on notice. Or you can do what all of us have to do. Be who you are, be genuine and hope for the best."

Stella sighed. "I know. I don't even know what he knows about what Byron did."

"While it was a big deal to you, and he probably heard about it, he may not have known as much as you think. From what Janie and you told me, Byron is the only one who put anything in your locker. Seeing as it was all recorded, I'm thinking it was just him. Plus, just because you saw Parker hanging around with Byron sometimes doesn't mean they're close. We can come to all kinds of conclusions without knowing everything."

Emma's phone vibrated again. She again hit the button to ignore the call. She almost never had to worry about her phone at work because anyone who would call her knew she didn't take calls except during breaks.

"I'm more interested to hear you 'kinda like' Parker," Emma said.

If it was even possible, Stella blushed a deeper shade of red. "He's just...nice and he talks to me about music. And not the cool kind of music, but stuff Mrs. Cooper's been teaching me, like jazz and some other things. He asked me if I could come over and practice with him? I guess his mom has a piano, so we'd be able to practice together for the recital."

"And what did you say?"

Stella shifted restlessly again, twirling her hair rapidly. "I told him I had to ask Janie. Then he asked who Janie was and I got all embarrassed and couldn't say."

Emma's phone vibrated yet again. Yet again, she ignored it. "What do you think about checking with Janie to see if you can go over and letting him know at the next practice?"

Stella sighed and covered her face with her hands. "Oh my god. You know Janie will say she has to call his mom first and I'll just die."

Emma smiled ruefully when Stella lifted her face again. "Most moms call other parents to check in. Parker probably knows that. And you might feel like you're going to die, but I can promise it won't kill you for Janie to call his mom."

"Seriously?" Stella asked with disbelief.

Emma nodded. "Seriously. But back to my question, how about that?"

Stella sighed. "I guess it's the only way I'm gonna even get to go over, so I have no choice."

"I'm thinking without Janie's go ahead, you won't be going over. Your homework for this week is to at least ask Janie about it."

"Homework!" Stella said, throwing her hands up.

Emma chuckled, just as her phone vibrated. Again.

Stella gave her a quizzical look. "Maybe you should get that. Before you give me that song and dance about how my time with you shouldn't involve interruptions, this is the one and only time I've ever heard your phone during a session and it's buzzed like five times now. If you don't call whoever it is back, I'll do it for you," Stella said forcefully.

Emma had been trying to keep her anxiety at bay, but Stella had a point. "Okay, give me a sec. I'll be right back."

Stepping out of her office, she checked her phone. With relief, she noticed it wasn't a dreaded 'Private' call, but Trey. That brought anxiety though because he was scrupulously respectful of her time when she was at work.

Emma strode quickly down the hall and stepped

into the kitchen area to call. With Stella in her office, she needed some privacy.

"Emma," Trey said as soon as he answered. "Sorry to keep calling, but it's important."

Her gut shifted into gear, sensing without knowing that she didn't want to hear whatever Trey had to say. "What is it?"

"We saw Greg in the parking lot at Misty Mountain, but he slipped out the back of the drugstore. We think he switched cars," Trey said, getting right to the point.

Emma's heart raced and dread washed through her. She was instantly weary and wired at once. She knew Trey was still talking, but she didn't absorb any of his words. Long moments passed as her mind spun. She'd been so stupidly proud of herself for managing to leave and divorce Greg. It had been all too easy. She should have known he was just biding his time and would make her regret it. She remembered that last night in their apartment when he'd pounded on the door so hard she thought it would break. Every muscle in her body had been bundled with tension—as always. She'd thought herself so lucky to get through that night without a few more bruises. He'd been so clever to only hit her in places that weren't obvious— her stomach, kicking her in the thighs, but never touching her face. She'd been ready to deal with a few hits and wait him out until he left. He always bolted for a drink afterwards. But she'd gotten lucky that night and should have known her luck wouldn't hold.

Trey's voice finally broke through her awareness again. "Emma! Are you with me?"

She took a shaky breath and leaned against the

wall. "Yeah. I'm here. I didn't hear much of what you said. I just..." her voice broke, tears choking her, "I don't know what to do."

Trey voice came through the phone, calm and clear. "I'm coming to get you. Risa's headed down to stay for a while to help with Stuart. I can stay with you at your place, or you can come to mine. Whatever you're more comfortable with."

Emma heard herself telling him okay and explaining she needed some time to finish up her appointment. Before she hung up, Trey spoke again. "Emma, you are not alone. Just know that. I'll be with you."

"Okay," she said softly. When she ended the call, she walked over to the windows. Kachemak Bay and the mountains were visible through the trees. The water glittered in the bright sun, the mountains deep green from the spruce lining their flanks. The view she found so peaceful felt just as much of a farce as she did. The beautiful day belied the fact that Greg was nearby and now she didn't even know what he drove. She abruptly turned away and wiped her tears. She had to pull herself together to finish up her session with Stella.

When she walked back into her office, Stella was playing a game on her phone. Stella looked up. "Are you okay?"

Emma nodded, keeping her game face on. If there was one thing she'd learned when she was with Greg, it was how to hide whatever she felt behind a smooth, polite façade.

Stella wasn't fooled. "You're totally not okay. I know you won't tell me about it because you're all professional and stuff. So I'll just give you some of your own advice: it's okay to be human."

Tears pressed against her eyelids, but Emma held them back. Stella's smart-alecky kindness was almost too much.

Stella stood to go. "Before I go, thought you might want to know that I already did my homework."

Emma wasn't too focused, but that caught her attention. "What?"

Stella blushed again, but she was grinning. "I texted Janie to ask about going to Parker's to practice. She already texted me back and said she'll check with his mom and let me know. So there," Stella declared. She came over to Emma and patted her shoulder. "I'll see you next week, k?"

"You got it," Emma replied. Just as Stella started to walk down the hall, she called out. "Good job on that homework, Stella."

CHAPTER 15

*L*ater that evening, Emma sat in Trey's living room with Risa. Trey was putting Stuart to bed. The plan was for them to head over to her place for the night. She'd had misgivings about that all afternoon though she didn't know how to explain it to Trey.

Risa brushed her hair out of her eyes and gave Emma an assessing look. "I know we don't know each other too well, but I'm no dummy. You're giving off a pretty skittish vibe."

Emma eyed Risa, trying to gauge what to say. Too worn and on edge to do anything else, she answered honestly. "I don't know if now is such a good time for me to be involved with Trey. That's all."

"My gut tells me Trey and Stuart mean something to you and you're only freaking out about it because of Greg showing up. Am I right?" Risa asked.

Emma nodded with a sigh. Her nerves had been on high idle all afternoon. She'd forgotten how it had felt to have Greg in her life. And he wasn't even in her life the way he used to be. Just to know he was nearby kept her constantly alert, which was exhausting. She shrugged. "I don't know what to do. Trey's all about how this doesn't matter, but it does to me."

Risa nodded slowly. "Maybe you should just accept there's only so much you can do about Greg and stop worrying so much about the rest of it. I *can* tell you this: Trey could care less about your history with Greg, except for the fact that he's worried about you right now. Trey can focus on making sure you're okay and you don't need to worry about Stuart."

Logically what Risa said made sense, Emma just needed to get her emotions in check. All the growth she thought she'd made felt like a mirage. Inside, she was thrown right back to where she'd been when she was with Greg. Doubting herself, doubting her ability to make good decisions, not quite believing anyone good could want her. Much as she wanted to stand on her own and face this without flinching, she desperately wanted to lean on Trey. After talking with him this afternoon and then Darren, she was trying to adjust to learning that Greg was remarried and puzzling over why he was still focused on her. She couldn't quite make sense of it, but knowing he was married and *still* called her and came out here made her uneasy in a way she hadn't been before. She'd hoped against hope the phone records would show that her worries were unfounded and the calls had all been random telemarketers.

Trey returned to the living room with a small duffel bag in hand. He wore faded jeans and a navy t-shirt that clung to his muscled chest. He pierced her with a glance. Just a second, and she felt like he saw right through her. His eyes conveyed strength and understanding. Without a word, he eased her anxiety, and she believed maybe it would be okay.

"So we're outta here, Risa. If you decide not to drop Stuart off at daycare tomorrow, don't forget to call and let them know. Otherwise, I'll call you tomorrow to check in," Trey said.

Risa stood. "You got it. I'm not sure what I'm doing yet. A friend from Anchorage will be down fishing tomorrow. Maybe Stuart and I will join him. I'll let you know." She looked to Emma. "Worry as little as possible. Between Trey, the police and your friends, it can only take so long to flush Greg out."

Emma stood and nodded. "I'll do my best. Thanks for being so understanding."

Risa came over and hugged her quickly. "Absolutely. Now get out of here."

* * *

THE HOUSE WAS quiet and still. The tiny home that had been such a haven for her in the time she'd been in Diamond Creek felt shadowy and had lost its comfort. Sula had remained at Trey's after Stuart pleaded for her to stay. It had been over a week since Emma had been home at all. She quickly showed Trey around and then returned to the kitchen to get him a beer and a glass of wine for herself.

She jumped when Trey said her name. "You startled me!"

"Didn't mean to," he replied. He took a swig of beer from the bottle she handed over. He eyed her speculatively, his gaze thoughtful and tinged with that ever-present heat between them.

"I can tell you're worrying," he said, getting right

to the point. "It's a waiting game right now. In the meantime, you're not going to be alone, so try not to worry so much."

Emma took a breath and rolled her neck, trying to work the tension out. "I know. It doesn't make it any easier. How am I going to get to work tomorrow? I wasn't thinking when you picked me up."

"I'll drop you off and then I'll pick you up later," he said matter-of-factly.

Emma didn't know why precisely, but that rankled her. "That's ridiculous. I don't need a babysitter."

Trey eyed her warily, but held firm. "No one said you needed a babysitter. But it's not a good idea for you to go anywhere alone. Not until Greg is out of here. And before you go blaming me for that, any one of your friends would say the same thing and you know it."

Emma pushed away from where she was leaned on the counter and began to pace. "You have to understand why I need to deal with this myself. I got myself into that marriage, got myself out of it, and I'll get out of this too. It's been a long time coming."

He didn't reply, but simply watched her pace. His patience irritated her.

"Why don't you say something?" she asked, throwing her hands up.

He leaned against the counter and took another swallow of beer. "How many times do you want us to go over this? I've told you, I understand how you feel, and I really do. But you've got it in your head this has to be a problem for us, and it doesn't. The main reason I asked Risa to come down this week was so I could stay with you here, and you wouldn't have to worry about Stuart getting affected by this. Not that I agree with you on that, but Risa visits often enough it's not out of the ordinary. And it's not safe for you to be alone. Not right now."

She stalked over to him, hands on hips, a tide of anger rising inside. Just as she opened her mouth, she heard the sound of a car pull into the drive and whirled around to look out the windows. Dusk had fallen, but it wasn't dark yet. She could just make out the shape of an unfamiliar sedan. Trey came to her side and slid his arm around her waist. Her anger dissolved, replaced by a cold knot of fear in her stomach.

She watched a man exit the car and walk toward the house. "Oh my god. It's Greg."

"Go upstairs," Trey said firmly, his voice brooking no argument.

Emma was torn. She wanted to flee upstairs but didn't want to leave Trey's side. Greg walked toward the house in that subtle swagger of his that had started out charming and become sickening for her.

"Emma..." Trey repeated, his tone edged with warning.

She knew why Trey wanted her to be out of the way and part of her wanted to flee. But she also knew she had to face this, as frightening as it was. "Trey, listen. Greg is determined to have his say with me. You're here, so he's not going to do anything stupid," Emma said, trying to make her voice sound confident when inside she was quaking.

Trey whipped his phone out and called Darren, saying only three words. "Greg. Emma's house." He ended the call and turned to her. "If you're not going upstairs, help me keep him here long enough for the cops to get here. Whatever you do, our goal is to buy time."

Greg came up the stairs and simply walked through the front door, arrogant as ever. Emma took a long look at the man she'd been stupid enough to fall for. He was dressed in jeans and a t-shirt. He shook his light brown hair out of his face. His hair was longer than she remembered, unkempt and sloppy. He closed the door quietly behind him and leaned against the wall beside the door, tucking his hands in his pockets. He looked at her with those flat, cold eyes, flicking them quickly between her and Trey.

Greg gave a cold laugh and shook his head. "Shoulda known your boyfriend wouldn't leave your side. Don't care though. Just came here to make sure you know the deal."

Trey's arm tightened subtly around her waist. His body emanated tension, coiled tight as a spring. The air crackled. Emma could sense Trey calculating. Her voice was frozen.

"So what's the deal then?" Trey finally asked, his voice laced with controlled fury.

"I'm not here to talk to you," Greg retorted.

Emma's voice finally broke free. "Well he's here and he's not going anywhere. Anything you have to say to me, you'll say to him!"

Greg laughed again. "Wow, so you do his bidding too? You always were that kinda girl. One of the reasons I wanted to marry you in the first place."

Fierce anger flashed through her. "He's nothing like you. Nothing. I want him here. That's the only reason he's here. What the hell do you want with me?"

Greg pushed away from the wall and walked right

up to her. "To make sure you know you can't just pretend like I don't exist."

Trey moved in a flash, grabbing Greg's shirt and shoving him back against the wall. "Get the hell out of here. If I see you anywhere near Emma again, you'll regret it. And before you go thinking you can keep slinking around town, this is a small place. You can only hide for so long."

Greg tried to break free of Trey's grip, but Trey only pushed him harder against the wall. Emma wasn't sure what Greg expected, but it didn't appear to be this. He was used to finding easy marks and had probably counted on her being home alone.

"Fuckin' let go of me!"

"No," Trey replied, his voice thrumming with fury.

Greg wrestled against Trey, trying to throw a punch. Emma raced between them.

"Emma, don't!" Trey shouted.

She heard Greg's bitter laugh as she fell against him. Sharp pain exploded when he threw an elbow into the side of her head. She stumbled. Greg grabbed her hair and started dragging her to the door. She fell out of the way when she heard a crack. Her mind went blank and her vision hazy, panic choking her. She scrambled up to see Trey grab Greg by the shirt again and pull back to drive his fist into Greg's face. Blood spurted from Greg's nose. Greg tried to keep his balance, but fell. Just as Trey lifted him by the shirt again, Darren and another cop barreled into the house.

"He fuckin' hit me!" Greg exclaimed.

Darren's partner, who introduced himself as Officer Charlie Brooks, moved with efficiency, rolling Greg over and cuffing him while asking questions calmly. Darren pulled Trey and Emma aside. Once he confirmed what he already knew, that Emma had in no way invited Greg into her home, he directed Charlie to escort Greg to the patrol car. Greg left, protesting loudly that he was being wrongly arrested.

Trey came to her side, carefully sifting through her hair. "Are you okay?" he asked softly. "He got you with that elbow."

Emma glanced up to meet his eyes, his rich brown gaze dark with concern. "I'm okay..." She paused when Darren came over.

Darren shook his head. "Looks like you took a hit," he gestured to Trey's cheek, which was bruising as they spoke, "and it looks like you landed one on Greg there. You hurt, Emma?"

Emma shook her head rapidly, focused only on Trey. She reached a hand up to his face. "Did he hurt you?"

Trey shook his head firmly. "Just a graze. Nothing to worry about," he paused and tugged Emma close, his hand rubbing up and down her back in a soothing and rhythmic caress. He addressed Darren. "He grabbed Emma and started dragging her out of here."

Darren nodded. "I'll need a statement from both of you."

Emma straightened. "There's not going to be a problem because Trey hit Greg, right? None of this would have happened if it wasn't for Greg."

Trey shook his head. "Emma, don't worry. There's nothing to hide here. He tried to hurt you and I stopped him. We both threw punches. My only concern is because of all that, no charges will stick for him."

Darren nodded. "Already worrying about that.

Here's my thinking though. We offer a deal where the charges will be dropped as long as he agrees to leave town. Emma can file the paperwork on the phone harassment and get a restraining order now that he showed up here. That should be enough to keep him away."

Trey mulled it over and glanced to Emma, his eyes sweeping over her, dark with concern. "I think that'll work. What do you think though?"

Emma still couldn't think too clearly, but any plan that involved getting Greg out of town made sense. "I just want him gone, and I don't want you to have to worry about getting in trouble."

Darren shook his head. "Trey's not gonna face any trouble. He's got a pretty simple self-defense argument. This is your house and you didn't want Greg here."

Emma glanced at Trey again, her heart clenching at the sight of the bruising on his cheek. She nodded. "Okay. You two know how these things work." She glanced over at Darren. "Promise me you'll call me as soon as you know what's going to happen."

After Darren left, Emma insisted on checking on Trey's hand and the bruising on his cheek. He waved her away when she tried to get him to put ice on it. "Emma, it was quick and he barely connected. All the blood on my hand is from his bloody nose," Trey said as he rinsed his hand off in the sink.

Emma backed away, tears abruptly welling. Adrenaline pumped through her from the encounter with Greg. Three years away didn't change the flash of panic that held her in a vice grip her the second he got anywhere near. Knowing that he'd tried to hurt Trey terrified her, though Trey appeared unfazed.

Having Greg touch her was sickening. She felt dirty. She turned away, staring out the front windows, tears blurring the view of trees. She felt Trey come up behind her and set his hands on her shoulders. His hands slowly slid down her arms. She started to shake, the numbing effects of adrenaline starting to wear off.

She closed her eyes tightly, trying to shut out the sight of Greg going after Trey and to block out the panic that froze her when he grabbed her hair. She tried to swallow the tears and shove the fear down, but a sob burst out. Burying her face in her hands, sobs tumbled out, tears streaking down her cheeks. Trey turned her in his arms to face him. He didn't try to pry her hands away, just allowed her to cry and slowly pulled her close. She burrowed against his chest, his steady strength a balm to the fear that threatened to overwhelm her. Seeing Greg, having him in her home, watching him try to hurt Trey, and feeling his hands on her...*that* was so much worse than the cold, tired anxiety she'd lived with toward the end of her marriage because she'd been worn down then. Resigned. Having sought to free herself only to have him resurrect the fear she'd trained herself to bury, it was horrifying and demoralizing.

Trey's hands traveled up and down her back in slow sweeps, the warmth slowly seeping into her soul. Her sobs quieted, the knot of fear in her chest loosened, and she finally lifted her face. He glanced down, eyes intent, focused and concerned.

"I need a shower," she blurted out.

Trey tilted his head marginally and reached up to brush her hair out of her eyes, his hand sifting through her hair, gently untangling it. "You okay?"

She nodded. "I should be asking you that, not the other way around."

He gave the barest shake of his head. "No you shouldn't. He made your life a living hell." He gave her a long look, his velvety brown gaze piercing her heart. Her pulse started to race again, the touch of his gaze doing what it always did—sparking the current that arced between them. "Let's get you in the shower," he said gruffly.

* * *

HOT WATER SLUICED over Emma and steam curled around her, easing her tension. Moments later, Trey stepped into the shower behind her. Soap ran in rivulets down her body as she rinsed shampoo out of her hair. He quickly soaped himself and ducked under the steaming water, his hands coming up to follow the water as it flowed over her scalp and down her back.

Emma's emotions were taut—the fear that had crashed through her lingered and mingled with a rush of desire for Trey. Her emotions sought a target and he was it. On the heels of that came a surge of...*love*. She shied away from defining the feeling. The tightrope she needed to walk inside to accept it was too dizzying just now. She looked up at him through the mist.

This man who she'd thought so tidy and uptight at first was anything but. His muscled chest and arms gleamed and flexed in the steamy heat as his hands caressed her back. The bruising on his face had settled to a soft purple. His sharp, angled features with the contrast of his full, lush lips brought a hitch to her breath. His eyes ensnared hers. She cupped his cheek and dragged her hand down the side of his neck into a wet stroke across his chest. He sucked his breath in rapidly. Yearning snaked between them. In a flash, his lips met hers in a scalding kiss. All restraint dissolved in the steam. He *claimed* her mouth, boldly tracing her lips with his tongue, delving inside with deep strokes. Desire suffused her, her body molten with heat as liquid inside as the water that fell around them. She lost all sense of time and space as she tumbled headlong into the swirl of craving.

His hands roamed over her body, curling around her bottom, sliding into the cleft between and caressing back up to cup her breasts. He laved one nipple and then the other, the water mingling with the warmth of his lips. Her nipples peaked to an ache, bereft when his lips moved away, traveling down her abdomen in a meandering path. He pressed her back against the shower wall. Kneeling in front of her, his eyes locked with hers. Mesmerized, she couldn't look away as he leaned forward and licked into the center of her, pushing her thighs apart.

"Trey..." she choked out, her hips arching against his mouth as his fingers followed his lips, teasing apart her slick folds. Long moments passed in a mindless haze as he alternated with his tongue and fingers stroking deeply. Her brought her closer and closer to the brink, each time pulling back just when she was close to release. When she thought she could stand no more, he swiftly stood, lifting one of her legs high to hook under his arm.

"Emma."

She opened her eyes to find his mere inches away. He shifted subtly, more fully lifting her, spreading her opening with his fingers.

"Is this okay?" he asked in a whisper.

"'Sss...okay." Her words slurred with feverish want.

Her eyes started to fall closed when he spoke again. "Look at me." That warm command of his. Her eyes heavy with desire, she opened them again and kept them trained on his. Vulnerable, exposed and open, she was caught in the web he wove around them. The sheer want in his eyes, laced with something much deeper, undid her. In one deep stroke, he surged into her slick heat.

He'd brought her so close already that the feel of his thick length filling her tipped her over the edge into a wrenching orgasm. He stroked in and out as she pulsed around him. The intensity of her release let loose the gates on her emotions and she cried out, tears falling down her cheeks. Had anyone asked, she couldn't have said if they were tears of relief, joy or more—simply an expression of the immense release she felt.

One arm holding her leg up, Trey brought his free hand to cradle her cheek, his thumb brushing across the tears mingling with the hot water that fell around them. She couldn't look away, entranced by the feeling held in his eyes. He slowed his strokes on pace with her orgasm only to start the build up again. One orgasm led into another—a tide that washed in and out in waves. He finally drove deep with a guttural cry, the pulses of his climax coalescing with hers.

Trey's forehead fell against hers. Their breath slowed in unison. He pressed a lingering kiss to her lips. They slowly untangled. Emma could barely stand, melted inside and out. After they toweled each other, they fell into her bed. She rested her head against his shoulder, her hand idly stroking his chest, a leg thrown across his. He softly ran a hand through her hair, his palm sliding in a warm path down her back, coming to rest at the small arch just above her bottom.

Soft quiet fell around them. An owl called outside. No words passed between them. Comfort stole over her, a comfort she couldn't *ever* remember feeling. The last thought that passed through her mind was one of surprise and wonder before she fell into a deep sleep.

CHAPTER 16

Trey glanced up from his desk when his assistant, Lucy, rapped sharply on his door and stepped inside. She quickly strode to the chair in front of his desk, sitting down and placing a newspaper on his desk.

"What's this about?" he asked.

Lucy pursed her lips and gave a pointed glance at the paper. Ascertaining that he was expected to read whatever she set out, Trey picked it up and saw she'd folded it open to the police blotter section of the paper. He didn't need to read far to find the brief description of Greg's arrest, complete with his name listed as the caller.

He set the paper down and looked across the desk at Lucy. Lucy arched a brow. "Well?" she asked.

"Well what?" he countered.

Lucy glared at him. "I'm wondering why the hell you didn't bother to mention you're dating someone! Don't even try to pretend like you're not." She threw her hands up, her bracelet catching on the bright red silk scarf she wore. Lucy was relentlessly practical for the most part. She wore basic black slacks with a fitted cream-colored blouse. But she always added a dash of color, revealing her playful side. Today it was her scarf paired with dangly silver earrings and matching bracelets. Her close-cropped white hair allowed the colors to stand out.

Trey was flummoxed. Though Lucy had been his assistant for years and he considered her a friend, personal talk between them was minimal. She'd worked with him in his law practice in Anchorage. She was steady, caring and efficient. Before Helen died, they had Lucy and her husband over for dinner once or twice a year and exchanged gifts for the family at the holidays. Trey had managed to keep up with the gifts since Helen died, but he hadn't quite managed the dinners. Lucy had been a rock for him after Helen died, simply because she didn't change how she interacted with him. She didn't tiptoe around and just carried on as if she expected him to do the same.

Lucy cleared her throat.

Trey met her eyes and smiled ruefully. "I suppose I didn't mention that."

"Oh there's no supposing. You definitely did not mention it," Lucy said firmly. "I don't usually stick my nose in your life, but that's because there was never any reason. Helen was lovely. You've been an amazing father to Stuart since she died. With Risa's help, you seemed to have gotten through all that. But," she wagged her finger at him, "don't you go thinking you can just start dating someone without letting me know. Howard and I think of you as family. I don't want anyone to take advantage of you, and Stuart needs someone around who's good for him as much as you. So who is she?" Lucy leaned back in her chair and folded her arms.

Trey chuckled and eyed Lucy. Assessing that he wasn't going to get out of this one, he offered a quick summary of how he'd met Emma.

Lucy lifted her brows when he finished his brief description.

"What? I just told you who she is."

"You told me what I could find out if I bothered to look her up online. How about telling me what it is about this woman who you've clearly fallen for? Is she going to take good care of your heart and of Stuart's? Let me tell you something. After Helen died, I worried about you—a lot. Then you seemed to be okay. But honestly, I figured you'd stay single. You've been so..." Lucy paused and waved her hand, "...I don't know, so closed off and serious. Like you just couldn't be bothered. Nothing wrong with that. I figure any of us are lucky if we have one good marriage. You had one with Helen. But this Emma, all I have to do is look in your eyes when you say her name and it's plain as day you love her. I'm not worried about the little mention in the police blotter except for the fact that I'm worried about what kind of trouble this Emma may have brought into your life."

Trey held quiet for a moment, absorbing what Lucy said. He'd admitted to himself that Emma meant *a lot*. But he hadn't allowed himself to think the word 'love' when it came to her. That was something he wondered if others did when they lost someone they loved—simply stopped considering the idea it might happen again. Just thinking about Emma flushed him

—the depth of feelings she elicited went far beyond the physical though the spark between them was unlike anything he'd experienced.

Lucy cleared her throat again.

Trey brought his focus back to the moment. "Right, my turn. Emma is amazing with Stuart. You don't need to worry about her taking good care of his heart, or mine, for that matter. As for what you're worried about...Emma's ex was violent. In case you didn't catch that little detail from the police report. Am I happy about that? Hell, no. Am I worried about what kind of trouble he might bring? Only as far as it affects Emma. If it'll make you feel better, she was all set to shut me out of her life from the get go because of her history with him. She tried again when we found out he'd showed up in Diamond Creek. Way I see it, the upside to his tracking her down is we can probably get him out of her life for once and for all. Risa came down to stay for the week, so she's with Stuart until I'm confident Emma's ex is long gone."

Lucy pursed her lips thoughtfully and drummed her fingertips on the armrest. After a long silence, she nodded brusquely. "Okay then. I'll try not to worry. Any chance I can meet Emma sometime soon? Howard and I would love to have you two over for dinner."

"Of course you can meet her. With everything going on, I hadn't thought about that. Honestly, things have moved faster than I expected with her, but it doesn't change how I feel. I wasn't trying to hide anything from you. I hope you know that," Trey said.

Lucy smiled softly. "I didn't think you were hiding anything on purpose, more that you've been so to yourself you didn't think about it. And like I said, I haven't been one to pry. How about we talk about dinner after this ex of hers is long gone?"

Trey nodded. "Definitely."

Lucy stood up and turned to leave.

"Lucy?"

She glanced over her shoulder.

"Thank you," he said simply.

Lucy smiled brightly and winked. "Back to work."

TREY TOSSED a duffel bag of gear over the edge of the boat, swiftly tugging it against the dock and stepping in. He'd persuaded Emma there was no reason not to enjoy a day of fishing. He and Stuart had come to the harbor a few minutes ahead of Emma and Risa who'd stopped at Red Truck Coffee on the way. It had been three days since Greg's arrest and he'd been transferred to a pre-trial facility outside of Anchorage. According to Darren, Greg was resisting the plea agreement offered to him, though his attorney was trying to talk some sense into him. The District Attorney took a heavier tact than he'd considered, slapping Greg with felony charges for breaking and entering, on top of the assault charges. Darren had also updated him that Greg's wife was on her way out to Alaska to bail him out.

Trey put Stuart to work organizing the fishing rods while he checked the engine oil level and made sure they had enough gas for the day. Stuart was a churn of energy and excitement at having his beloved Aunt Risa and Emma with him for the day.

"Hey ho," Risa called out.

Trey glanced over to see Risa and Emma

approaching the boat. Emma's hair was tied in a loose ponytail, wispy curls framing her face. Her stride was long and loose. She laughed at something Risa said. Trey wanted to see her laugh more. She'd been high-strung the last few days, on edge about whatever might happen with Greg. The only time she seemed to relax for more than a passing moment was when they were tangled up in each other. Not that Trey minded a bit, but he didn't like seeing her so tense the rest of the time.

The next few hours passed with moments of quiet alternating with bursts of activity—such was fishing. The weather was close to perfect, sunny with a touch of wind. Once they'd each reached the daily limit for silver salmon, Trey readied the boat to return to the harbor. They'd found a sweet spot near Seldovia, a small community on the opposite side of the bay from Diamond Creek.

"See, Emma," Stuart said, pointing towards the Seldovia boat harbor. "That's where Dad took me for a festival last year." Seldovia held an annual music festival on Summer Solstice, and Trey had brought Stuart over for the day.

Emma was seated beside Stuart on a bench. Stuart was leaned against her, her arm tucked loosely around him. Her dark hair had fallen loose hours ago and hung in waves around her shoulders. Her cheeks were bright from the sun, deepening the blue of her eyes. She listened patiently when Stuart launched into a mini history of Seldovia. He was fascinated with the older Alaskan villages.

Trey took a long look at the mountains before he turned the boat away. This side of Kachemak Bay lay within the mountains he saw every day from

Diamond Creek. The hillsides were lush and dark green in the summer with patches of snow lingering at the peaks. An eagle called in the distance. Stuart's voice quieted. Trey glanced over to see Stuart sound asleep against Emma's side. She gave him a soft smile. Risa was busy putting gear away. Trey started the engine and headed back to Diamond Creek, thinking only that he wanted more days like this with Emma.

* * *

HOURS LATER, he watched Emma drive out of the harbor lot by herself. They'd had not quite an argument, but a quiet battle of wills. Emma insisted it would be okay for her to stop by her house and run a few errands before coming to his house for dinner with Risa and Stuart. Her point was that with Greg in jail at the moment, she didn't need a shadow. Logically, Trey knew it made sense, but he couldn't shake the unease he felt. He'd sensed her tolerance for his concern might be reaching a tipping point, so he'd conceded. He didn't want to unnecessarily mar a good day.

Risa returned to the harbor lot with Stuart after they had gone to the Fish Factory to have the day's catch flash frozen. She pulled up beside his car and rolled down her window. "So you gave her a little breathing room, huh?"

Trey rolled his eyes. "Against my better judgment, but yes."

Risa laughed. "And you'll see her before you know it. So we'll meet you back at the house? Stu's sound asleep here," she said, gesturing to his slumped form.

"You got it. I need to swing by the post office. Need anything from the grocery store?"

Risa shook her head and waved as she drove off. Trey headed to the post office. Noticing his phone battery had died while they were fishing, he plugged it into the charger in his car. His phone began beeping to indicate missed calls. He yanked the car over when he realized he had three missed calls from Darren, and another two from Jared. When Darren didn't answer, he immediately called Jared.

"Where the hell have you been?" Jared demanded as soon as he picked up.

"Fishing. Phone died. What's going on? Darren's not picking up."

"Greg's wife bailed him out today. Since he's out on conditions of release, he has to give the court an address. He provided one here in Diamond Creek, down at one of the rental cabin places," Jared said succinctly.

Trey put his car back in gear and swerved back onto the road, gunning it to try to get to Emma's house before she did. "Dammit, Emma finally talked me into leaving her side! She's going home right now."

"I'll head over there," Jared said. "I'm home and my place is just a few minutes away."

Trey's heart hammered, fear and anger boiled inside—fear for Emma and anger that Greg was so brazen to come right back to Diamond Creek. He almost missed the turn up the hill and swore savagely as his tires spun out when he turned at the last second. He'd forgotten he still had Jared on the line.

"Man, I'll be there in just a few," Jared said.

"What else does Darren know? Any word on Greg's wife?"

"Well, she bailed him out, but he didn't mention anything else. Look, I'm hanging up because I'm on Emma's road now. See you when you get here."

As soon as the call ended, Trey called Emma. She answered immediately. One word from her and Trey knew she wasn't okay.

"Emma, where are you?" he asked, desperately trying to keep his voice level.

She made a choked sound in reply.

"Just tell me where you are," Trey asked.

"In my truck," she replied, her voice small.

Her breathing was rapid and shallow.

"Okay," he said slowly. "Where's your truck?"

"At my house. I decided to come home first and..." her voice broke. "I can't..."

"Emma, it's okay, it's okay. Jared should be there any minute now and I'm not far behind him."

"Greg's here. I don't know if he knows I'm in the truck. I dropped my keys and can't reach them. He's... he's walking around the house...I'm..."

Trey swore silently, furious with himself for not insisting on accompanying Emma, and sick with worry that she was alone. He prayed for Jared to get there in seconds.

He kept Emma on the line as he sped up the hill toward her house. He simply repeated to her that it would be okay though in his gut, he didn't know if it would. Any more harm Greg did to her, even if she was okay in the end, was more damage piled on to the hurt she thought she'd left behind. Trey couldn't stand to see her hurt again. The emotional toll this had already taken on her was too much, more than she should have to bear. Emma screamed and the phone went dead. He called Darren immediately, barking out that Greg was at Emma's house.

He swerved onto Emma's road and down her driveway interminable moments later. A cloud of dust swirled behind him when he came to a halt. Jared's truck was in the drive, the door left open. Both of the doors on Emma's truck were open and her purse was spilled on the ground. What Trey assumed to be Greg's rental car was parked toward the end of the drive. A woman he surmised to be Greg's wife sat in the passenger seat, staring straight ahead. She didn't even turn to look at him when he stepped out.

Trey sprinted to the house. Yanking the door open, he found the house empty. He paused long enough to hear sounds coming from the backyard and immediately raced to the back. He ran out the back-door onto the deck to find Greg holding Emma, his forearm wrapped around her neck, waving a gun wildly. Jared was a few feet away, frozen in place, his eyes locked onto Greg. Though Trey didn't doubt for a second that Jared could easily dispatch Greg in a fight, Greg had a gun and Jared didn't.

Neither of them looked his way when he came out. He searched out Emma's eyes.

Her eyes were bright with a wild edge of fear. The side of her forehead was red and swelling. Trey had to swallow his fury and stay focused. He moved cautiously, watching and waiting.

Greg finally turned to look at him. "Oh, so it's your savior boy, here. What do you think you're gonna do now?" Greg sneered at Trey.

Trey took measured steps to the opposite side of Greg from Jared. "The police are on the way. How about you just let Emma go?" Trey asked calmly, calculating the best way to break Greg's grip on Emma. "Looks like your wife is here with you. You're already in enough trouble as it is. Why make it worse?"

"Because she," Greg tightened his hold around Emma's neck, "doesn't get to just leave me. I told her she'd pay and now she's paying. Don't do anything stupid because I have no problem hurting her."

"Yeah, we know that asshole. We know all about guys like you. Gotta beat women up because you don't feel like a man unless you do," Jared said, baiting him.

Greg's face reddened. Trey heard tires on gravel and figured Darren had arrived. Greg started to say something to Jared, his eyes shifting away. Trey made his move, swiftly slamming his fist into the arm that Greg held around Emma. Greg's grip broke loose, and he swore as he attempted to keep his hold on Emma. Emma scrambled away. Trey threw him to the ground as soon as Emma was freed.

The gun tumbled from Greg's hands as they fell. Greg tried to reach for the gun, but Jared grabbed it before he got his hands on it. Greg didn't give up the fight just yet though, grappling with Trey and managing to land one punch on his shoulder before Trey slammed him hard and pinned him to the ground. Darren came around the corner of the house with Charlie on his heels.

* * *

EMMA CLAMBERED TO HER FEET, panic pounding through her. She lunged toward Trey and Greg who were scuffling on the ground. A hand closed over her arm, and she tried to break away when she heard Jared's voice, low and clear.

"Easy, Emma. I've got Greg's gun, and Trey's got him," Jared said, his hold on her arm firm. "You're okay."

Darren and Charlie came running into the backyard. Between Jared's words and their presence, the ferocity of her fear began to ease. The next half hour passed in a jumble. Trey came to her, turning her to face him. His eyes skated over her face, a light touch on her forehead where she'd collided with the truck door when Greg dragged her out. "Did he do this?" Trey asked, his hand gently cradling her face, his eyes dark with concern.

She shook her head rapidly. "No, no. I ran into the door when…"

Trey swore softly and began to swing away, only to stop when he saw that Charlie and Darren were taking care of Greg. Trey turned back and pulled her close, wrapping her in his arms. His nearness eased her panic, her chest loosened, and she was able to breathe fully.

"I'm okay," she mumbled into his shoulder. "Are you okay? I couldn't tell…"

Trey leaned back to look at her. A tear slid down her cheek. He brushed it away with his thumb. "I'm fine. I'm just glad you are. You have no idea what went through my head when you screamed and hung up."

Emma took a shaky breath and started to reply only to pause when she heard Jared clearing his throat audibly.

Trey glanced over his shoulder. "Yeah?"

Jared gestured in the direction of Darren who was

radioing in to the station with an update while Charlie cuffed Greg and walked him to the cruiser. "Think he needs to check in with us. Can you handle that now?"

Trey nodded, shifting to Emma's side while keeping an arm sung around her shoulders. They followed Darren and Jared to the front of the house.

Darren took statements, including one from Greg's wife, Barbara. Emma was shocked to realize that she had been there all along. Barbara stood beside the rental car staring at the ground. She was tall and slender with light brown hair and brown eyes. She stood with her shoulders curved forward, as if she wanted to curl inside herself and hide.

Emma walked over to her while Darren was talking with Trey and Jared. "Hi," she said simply.

Barbara looked up, her eyes guarded. "Hi. I, uh...I didn't know Greg was going to do this. He just said he had to pick something up from you. He made it seem like you two were still friends after your divorce. I guess I should have known better." Her voice held a bitter edge.

Emma remained quiet, recognizing that the woman who stood before her was yet another woman who ended up in a relationship with a violent, controlling man. And just as she had, along so many others, this woman stumbled along just trying to survive, never quite sure what was true and what the safest choice was. It felt like every step, every choice was a random roll of the dice with a prayer each time that the die didn't land on something that led to an explosion.

Emma put a hand on Barbara's shoulder. "It's okay.

I get it. Have you thought about what you're going to do now?"

Barbara shrugged, a sharp laugh following. "When he called me about coming to bail him out, he said he'd had a few too many beers and got pulled over driving back to his hotel. I had no idea it had anything to do with you. He pretended like this whole trip was a fishing thing and you just happened to live out here. I kind of wondered, but honestly, him going on vacation without me meant I didn't have to worry about him. And now? I don't know what to do. I won't be bailing him out again. I have a plane ticket home. I'll see if I can change it and leave sooner."

Emma thought of so many things she wanted to say, but she stayed focused only on one. "If you need any help, I'll help. I managed to divorce him, so I'm sure you can too if that's what you want."

Barbara looked at her carefully. "Why would you help me?"

"Because I know what it's like to be where you are," Emma said simply.

CHAPTER 17

*E*mma came awake slowly. The first threads of light were seeping through the shades. Trey's arm was thrown across her, his palm warm against her side where it rested just below her breast. Her mind rolled back to yesterday. After the police left, Darren called later to report that Greg was being held on three charges of aggravated assault with a deadly weapon with no option to be released before trial due to his blatant violation of the conditions of his earlier release. Emma hadn't wanted to stay at her own house, mostly because she couldn't settle down there. It was as if Greg's presence in the house and yard had tainted it. Trey brought her to his house after a quick call to Risa, so she could prepare Stuart for the fact that both Emma and Trey sported a few bruises.

It was so…comforting…to just *be* with Trey, Stuart and Risa. After dinner, she'd gone to bed early, emotionally and physically exhausted from the afternoon. She'd fallen asleep to the soft rumble of Trey's voice as he put Stuart to bed across the hall. Now, she lay still in the early light of morning to the feel of Trey spooned behind her, the heat of his erection pressing against her bottom through the thin cotton of her panties. Desire curled like smoke around her. She shifted her hips against him. His soft chuckle against her neck stoked her.

"Ignore it. Just being near you seems to have that effect," he whispered.

"I don't want to ignore it," she replied softly.

"Emma...after everything you went through, you don't need me acting like a randy teenager. Let me just hold you."

She rotated swiftly in his arms, shifting up to tear her t-shirt off, kick her panties away and straddle him. "No," she declared, pushing him back and shoving his boxers out of the way. She paused to look at him in the dim light. His chest rose and fell in a swift breath. Without waiting, she leaned forward and drew her tongue in a long stroke up his cock.

His breath hissed through his teeth. "Dear God, Emma..." he choked out.

She took him in her mouth, savoring his thickness, bringing him fully inside. His hips flexed against her as she drew back up his length, maintaining suction. She dallied and toyed with him, alternating with licks, strokes and suction. Trey abruptly sat and tugged her up over him. "I need you *now*," he ground out, holding her hips poised just above the tip of his cock.

She was soaked with desire when he surged into her. She thrust her hips down to settle on his shaft, holding still for a long moment, relishing his fullness. Yearning whipsawed through her when she rose up, she clenched around him, unable to control the pulses that started to build. His head arched back in release once she began to ripple around him. She fell forward, collapsing onto him, tremors coursing through her.

He shifted to tuck her to his side, brushing her hair out of her eyes. Emotions rocketed through her colliding with the aftermath of the passion that shimmered between them. She didn't realize she was crying until she felt his hand brushing her tears away.

"You okay?" he asked, his voice low in the gray light of morning.

She thought for a moment and realized she was probably more okay than she'd been in a long, long time. It was just so much to hold. At her subtle nod, Trey shifted again, leaning up to kiss her softly.

EMMA TOOK a sip of tea and waited. Stella sat across from her, twirling her hair, which was damp from the rain pouring down outside. After watching the sunrise with Trey and being treated to a home-cooked breakfast by Risa, Emma had watched clouds scuttle in while Trey drove her to work. The beautiful morning shifted to gray and rainy. The rain had yet to let up since then. Though Trey had attempted to persuade her not to go to work today, claiming she could use the rest, Emma knew she'd feel better if she stuck with her routine. Though the encounter with Greg yesterday had been nerve-rattling and terrifying, she felt a strange sense of relief. Greg had finally upped the ante enough to face real consequences. She craved a sense of normalcy and simply wanted to go to work without the ever-present worry about Greg. Though the situation had only escalated recently, he had finally tipped the scales by materializing her fears. When Emma had insisted she needed to go to work, Trey had merely given her a long look and then nodded firmly when he met the insistence in her eyes.

As usual, Stella had the last appointment for the day. She let the bedraggled lock of hair loose and lifted her eyes to meet Emma's. "So you might want to know I've practiced at Parker's house twice now."

"Oh?"

Stella nodded. A blush crept up her neck, staining her creamy cheeks. "I might have to admit he's a decent guy," she said sheepishly.

Emma schooled her face into a bland expression. For Stella to admit any change of heart about anyone was huge. "It can be hard to know what to think of people until you spend some time with them," Emma said carefully.

Stella shrugged and reached for her tea, holding the warm mug in her hands. "I haven't gotten the nerve to ask him about what happened with Byron last year, but I don't think he had anything to do with it. He's just...nice. His mom's really nice too. She makes snacks when I go over. I practice on her piano while he plays the drums."

The simple experience of being invited to a boy's home after school was something Emma knew Stella had thought was too much to hope for. Whatever came of it, the fact that Stella could relax her well-honed defenses enough to even consider Parker might be something other than a complete jerk was a stepping stone for her.

"I'm glad you decided to try," Emma replied with a small nod.

"Try?" Stella asked, tilting her head.

"Try spending time with someone who you weren't so sure about. That's not easy for anyone."

Stella nodded and looked out the window. "So the home study worker says she's gonna approve Janie to adopt me."

"We kind of expected that, right?"

Stella nodded, turning to look back at Emma, her eyes uncertain. "She says once she has the paperwork done, my worker can schedule my adoption hearing right away."

"And what do you think about that?"

Stella looked back out the window, her shoulders rising and falling with a deep breath. When she turned back, her eyes were clear. "I guess I thought I'd be all freaked about it, but...I'm not. That's kinda weird for me. I remembered what you said once."

"What's that?"

"You said I could decide not to worry about something. I thought you were stupid then, but now it makes sense. Like I was all weird about getting adopted for a while. But I'm with Janie, and I don't want to be anywhere else. And she's more like a mom to me than my own mom ever was. So when we decided to go through with this, I kept waiting for the freak show inside to start and it just hasn't. So I decided it's okay not to worry."

Emma wanted to reach over and hug her. She was so pleased to see Stella's progress. Since she couldn't do that, she smiled and lifted her mug of tea in a faux toast. "Whatever works for you."

Stella grinned, lifting her own mug in return before taking a gulp of tea. "So will I graduate from therapy when I get adopted?"

Emma shrugged. "That's up to you. We all have

issues to learn from and revisit. You might decide you don't want or need therapy and stop. Then life might happen, and you decide you could use it again. I don't set the rules on that."

Stella nodded and gave Emma a hard look. "What happened to your forehead?" she asked abruptly.

Emma had made it through the entire day thus far without anyone commenting on the bruising on her forehead. She'd been careful to keep her bangs over it. She should have known Stella would notice.

"My forehead met my truck door," Emma replied. It was the truth minus the fact that it had happened because Greg had introduced her to it.

Stella scrutinized her and then shrugged. "Just want to make sure you're okay and all."

Emma nodded and smiled ruefully. "I'm okay. And I'm glad you asked."

The conversation moved on, and Stella left not long after. Emma sat in the quiet for a few minutes after she finished up her notes. She glanced out to the parking lot and saw her sister's truck pulling into the lot. Hannah was picking her up since she didn't have her truck today. Emma dashed through the rain and quickly climbed inside. Hannah glanced over, her eyes landing on the bruise on her forehead.

"You okay?" Hannah asked.

Emma had already filled Hannah in on yesterday's events, but figured she'd get more questions. "You're seeing the worst of it. How are you?"

Hannah chuckled. "Okay, so we're moving on. I'm fine. I told Susie and Tess we'd meet them for an early dinner at Sally's. Hope that's okay," she said as she turned onto the road.

"Of course it's okay. Seems like we usually end up at Sally's when it's raining."

Later on, Emma sat in a booth with Hannah, Susie, and Tess listening to Susie complain about her latest spat with Jared, which had something to do with spreadsheets. Her tirade ended with, "...and then he goes and does something really awesome like rush up to your house the minute Trey called him yesterday. And thank God he was there." Susie paused for a breath, swiped a wayward curl out of her eyes and looked at Emma. "I ran into Trey's sister at the store today. She told me all about what happened. I'm just glad you're okay and that asshole ex of yours is finally where he needs to be. So now that you can no longer use Greg's shenanigans as an excuse, are you going to admit Trey is amazing and stop acting like you can't have a relationship right now?"

Tess choked on her sandwich, and Hannah chuckled. As usual, Susie got right to the point. Emma flushed. She'd been holding her feelings for Trey at bay for weeks now. But yesterday and this morning had made it harder for her to hide from what her heart knew—that she wanted Trey more than anyone she'd ever wanted and the only word for what lay between them was...*love*.

"Yoohoo," Susie said, waving at Emma from across the table.

Emma face was hot. "Maybe it hasn't been obvious, but I haven't been trying to avoid Trey the last week or so. And even if you won't admit it, I think I was right to worry. It was just luck Greg didn't really hurt Trey. And it wasn't exactly good he ended up throwing a punch at Greg. Knowing Greg the way I do, I'm relieved he didn't find a way to insist on having Trey charged."

Susie rolled her eyes. "Seriously? Even if Darren hadn't been briefed on your history with Greg, he wouldn't have fallen for some dumb story like that. Trey's the good guy."

"Okay, okay, okay. I was just worried. That's all. But I can promise you this, I'm not making any excuses to avoid Trey now. Good enough for you?" Emma asked, arching an eyebrow at Susie.

Tess laughed. "Well, it's good enough for me. Unlike Susie, I know these things take time. I'm glad you're okay," she said, her voice softening as she reached over to squeeze Emma's hand.

Susie nodded firmly. "Good enough for me. By the way, Risa thinks you're perfect for Trey. I don't know her too well, but she's in town pretty often. She's protective of her older brother, so if you've got her on your side, you're in the clear."

Hannah shook her head. "Dear God, Susie. You never cease to amaze me with your information gathering skills." Hannah shifted her gaze to Emma. "And I second Tess. I'm just damn glad your okay. We've all been worried and tried to keep a lid on it, but the last few weeks haven't been easy. Jared stopped over last night and filled us in. Things could have been much worse, so I'm glad everyone's okay." She looped her arm over Emma's shoulder and gave her a squeeze.

Tears welled in Emma's eyes. The relief at no longer dragging her past behind her like a hidden weight was huge. That combined with the knowledge that she had friends and family like this elicited a wash of gratitude. "Thanks y'all. I don't know what I would have done without you." She took a deep breath, the press of tears subsiding.

"There's that southern in you," Susie said with a smile before waving the waitress over. "I'm buying us another round."

* * *

As Hannah swung the truck into Emma's drive, Emma burst out laughing to see Trey and Stuart waiting on the small front porch.

"I should have guessed he'd be here. I told him he didn't need to worry now, but he can't seem to help himself," Emma said.

Hannah shrugged and turned the truck off. "That's not such a bad thing."

Emma glanced over at her sister who looked so similar to her it was unsettling sometimes. She wondered if it would have felt differently if they'd known each other their entire lives, but that was a question she'd never be able to answer. Hannah's eyes were a mirror for her own, just a slightly darker shade of blue.

"It's not a bad thing at all. I got irritated with Trey for wanting to basically shadow me ever since we knew Greg was around. But now it doesn't bother me," Emma said, her mind rubbing the stone of that thought.

A small smile played at the corners of Hannah's mouth before she burst out laughing.

"What's so funny?"

Hannah swallowed her laughter and leaned her head back against the headrest. "Susie's right. You got it bad for Trey."

Emma glanced up at Trey and Stuart. Stuart waved, his smile wide. She returned the wave. "Even though I hate admitting Susie's right, Trey's pretty amazing. I haven't really had a chance to think about much this last week or so. I keep trying to be rational and that part of me is worried this is moving too fast. But the rest of me has other ideas," she said wryly.

Hannah rolled her head to the side, her eyes meeting Emma's. "So don't fight it. All evidence points to the fact that Trey's a keeper. I may not be as nosy as Susie and always plotting everyone else's relationships, but my gut tells me this is a good one."

Emma nodded. "My gut tells me the same thing. If only I could shut my brain up. Have you met Stuart?"

Hannah shook her head with a smile and climbed out of the truck. Stuart ran up and hugged Emma's legs. "Emma! Are you staying over again tonight? Dad says he doesn't know."

Trey shook his head. "Stuart, what did I just say?"

Stuart looked up at his father, a tuft of hair sticking straight up. "You said it's not polite to ask things like that. But I want to know," he said, his voice trailing off.

Emma brushed her hand through his hair. "How about you give me a few minutes and then I can come over? If that's okay with your dad." She met Trey's eyes and saw an answering heat flare to life.

A long moment passed before Emma became aware she and Trey were staring at each other. Flustered, she looked away, her eyes colliding with Hannah's. Hannah grinned and knelt down beside Stuart, holding her hand out.

"You must be Stuart. I've seen you before, but I'm

not sure we actually met. I'm Hannah, Emma's sister. It's very nice to meet you," Hannah said.

Stuart released Emma's legs and shook Hannah's hand. "I'm Stuart. You must be nice if you're Emma's sister," he said with a grin.

"And if you like Emma, then you're one smart boy," Hannah replied in turn.

* * *

HOURS LATER, Emma fell to Trey's side and rested her head on his shoulder, her breath coming in gusts against his skin. His skin glistened in the lamplight. She tried to catch her breath, the aftermath of her last orgasm still rippling through her body. Trey chuckled, turning his head and softly kissing her, his lips lingering just long enough for twinges of desire to rear again. Though she didn't know how that could be possible. After an early dinner, Risa had swept Stuart out the door for a 'pajama party' with one of her local friends. She'd given Emma a quick hug, whispering in her ear that she'd better take advantage of her alone time with Trey. Mere seconds after the sound of Risa's car faded, Trey had tugged Emma close for a kiss—the start of a maelstrom of passion that held peaks and valleys of intensity. Trey had brought her to the edge and over again and again, until she was limp and sated.

His chest rose and fell in a shuddering breath. "I think you've finally done it." His voice was raspy.

"Done what?"

"Completely worn me out."

Emma lifted her head and then dropped it against

the pillow. "I wore you out? And here I thought it was the other way around," she said, wryly.

The mattress beneath them jiggled in tune with Trey's laugh. "Let's just say it was mutual."

His laugh slowed and he shifted to his side, his eyes inches from hers. A single lamp lit the room with a muted glow. His eyes were almost black in this light. He stroked her tangled hair away from her face, his hand coming to rest against her cheek. Her heart sped and her belly fluttered at the intensity of feeling held in his eyes. He started to speak and then paused.

Closing his eyes, he took a slow breath. Opening them, he cleared his throat. "So...we haven't had much time to talk lately. I thought about this a lot since yesterday and decided I don't want to wait for the sake of waiting. To get right to the point: I love you."

A wave of emotion crested inside, a tear slipped out of the corner of her eyes. No words came. His brow creased, his thumb brushed the tear away. "I didn't want to wait to tell you how I felt, but I didn't want to upset you either."

Emma shook her head rapidly, and drew in a fortifying gulp of air. "You didn't upset me. I just...ah... wasn't prepared for you to say that. I know we had the talk about how I didn't want to rush, and I was worried about the whole thing with Greg, but everything has happened so fast, I haven't even had a chance to think. If I shut my brain off, all I know is...I love you. It's just that I never really let myself think that was an option for me after my first marriage. And then I met you and everything went sideways, and I'm still not sure I'm what you want because..."

Trey put a finger over her lips. "Slow down and

don't even go where you're guessing what I want. I know what I want and that's *you*. And it's not just the great sex, though don't get me wrong, that is one hell of a bonus. It's just...you. The mess with Greg was a good thing. It was on simmer ever since you left him. Now it's boiled over and we'll clean up the mess. All it did was show me how much you meant to me and to Stuart. When I realized Greg was at your house yesterday and you were there alone, I thought I was going to lose my mind. I knew then it wasn't worth dancing this dance where I didn't let you know how I felt. I won't rush you. We can take all the time you need, but I wanted you to know exactly where I stood. And that's right by your side. I don't plan on going anywhere. As far as I'm concerned, as soon as you're ready, let's make it official. Stuart's all but decided he's going to ask you to marry me if I don't do it soon enough, so you better be ready," Trey finished with a chuckle.

Another tear slipped out, and she wiped it away. Her mind, such a creature of habit, started to say the things it usually said—*this is too fast, you were never meant to have something like this, it must be a fluke, no one would ever love you like that*—and Emma shook the thoughts away and listened to her heart. Her heart flung itself skyward, arms wide open, calling out for her to notice that someone amazing was right in front of her, someone she wanted with all of her heart.

Her eyes locked with his. "It's okay. You're not rushing me. I want to be right here...with you. And if Stuart wants to ask on your behalf, that's just fine," she said, a soft smile blooming through the blur of her tears.

CHAPTER 18

rey walked down the dock at Otter Cove Harbor. He was picking up Stuart's favorite fishing rod for a day of fishing with a school friend. After grabbing the rod and tucking it away in its carrier, he paused on the boat deck to look out over the bay. Gulls swooped and called, and a few eagles were perched on pilings. A raft of otters floated near the harbor entrance. It was early evening, and boats were starting to stream into the harbor from the bay. As it was late summer, there was a bite to the evening air. A salty breeze gusted through the harbor. Mount Augustine was clustered with clouds around its peak. The volcano's flanks were scattered with light that angled through the clouds, glittering it with a golden hue.

Trey had persuaded Emma to meet him for dinner at the Boathouse Café. Not that meeting him signified much since they spent almost every night together lately. With Stuart off for an overnight with friends and a day of fishing tomorrow, Trey planned to capitalize on some private time with Emma. As he headed back up the dock, he heard his name and turned to see Jared and his brothers waving from their guide boat. He detoured to the adjacent dock.

"Hey guys, what's up?"

"Not much. Just finished up another run today and saw you," Jared replied as he quickly tugged a cooler to the side and handed it over to Nathan who stood on the dock.

Nathan grinned. "Notice who gets to do the heavy lifting," he said sardonically.

Jared checked the mooring lines and hopped off the boat. "As if you're the only one," he replied with a roll of his eyes.

Luke appeared from the boat cabin and stepped onto the dock, nodding at Trey. "Is he trying to act like he does all the hard work again?" Luke asked, his question directed to Trey.

Trey held a hand up. "Hey, no need to get me in the middle. Innocent bystander here."

Nathan winked. "Just having fun getting my big brothers riled up." He caught Trey's eyes. "So Tess tells me Susie is about ready to hammer down your door. Thought you might want to know, advance warning and all that."

Trey was puzzled. "Huh? Why does Susie want to hammer down my door and what's Tess go to do with it?"

His questions were met with collective chuckles. Luke lifted an eyebrow. "You seem to have not quite caught on that Susie likes to take charge when it comes to her friend's love lives. Don't get me wrong, it worked in my favor. But you should be prepared in case you have a chance encounter with her. She was over at our place the other night for dinner and told Hannah that you had a month or else."

"A month?" Trey asked.

This time, Jared lifted an eyebrow. "A month to declare yourself. That's what Susie calls it," Jared said with a roll of his eyes.

"Declare myself?" Trey was starting to feel like an idiot with his questions. He was met with a group laugh.

Nathan stopped laughing first. "That would mean Susie thinks you need to be officially shacked up with Emma."

Jared piped in. "To clarify, she said that it's stupid Emma's at your place all the time anyway, and she's wasting money on a rental. You two should stop dilly-dallying – her words, not mine – and move in together. She also thinks you should get married, but she's not going to force it," Jared said, his eyes dead serious for a solid moment before he burst out laughing at the look on Trey's face.

Luke and Nathan shook their heads in unison. "You obviously haven't spent enough time with Susie," Luke said. "How about you come over for dinner one night? Hannah and I can host everyone. You can see Susie in action. Don't get the wrong idea now. Susie is the best kind of friend. She's just...opinionated."

Jared met Trey's eyes. "That's one way to put it."

"I think Emma said Susie was forceful," Trey said, recalling the way Emma had described her once.

"That about says it. Guess you just didn't realize she would be so forceful about your love life," Jared said with a chuckle.

Trey considered pointing out Jared was the one who needed to worry, but all he had were heavy-duty suspicions about Jared and Susie, so he kept it to himself for now. He shrugged. "Fine by me. I'd like nothing more than to have Emma move in. I've been waiting for the right time to move things along, so knowing I only have a month by Susie's timeline is helpful. I love a deadline," Trey said, half-joking and serious at the same time. He glanced over at Luke. "As for dinner, name the time and I'll be there. Okay if I bring Stuart or should I plan on finding a babysitter?"

"Great. I'll check with Hannah and let you know. And the babysitting, either way. John's easy going."

Trey nodded, and talk shifted to fishing as they walked to the parking lot together. Trey drove home to help Stuart get ready for his overnight.

EMMA STOOD on the beach looking out over the bay. She and Trey had finished dinner at the Boatyard Café. The sunset had drawn her to suggest a walk. When she'd first moved to Diamond Creek, she'd walked on the beach every day she could even when the weather was on the rough side. She loved the ocean and the mountains. A walk on the beach here meant the best of both. Those solitary walks had been cleansing for her—the bracing winds, salty gusts and the constant flux of life grounded her and anchored her in the reality that she'd managed to walk away from a destructive marriage. So much had happened since then. She couldn't have imagined she would find Trey and fall in love with him, or that he would insist on standing by her side when the ghosts of her past reared to life. On the other side of that now, the sense of freedom from the haunts of that past was immense.

She gulped in the crisp ocean air, relief and exhilaration washing through her.

The sun was well on its way to dropping behind the mountains. The mountainsides were shadowed. Arcs of light reached skyward behind them. A crescent moon rose in the background, a perfect curled sliver standing out against the rose and gold. Trey had paused to gently place a starfish back in the water. When the tide rolled in, starfish came with it in all their starred and colorful glory. But when the tide went out, some starfish were left behind on the sand and often died because they needed the ocean water, even if only a small puddle. Emma had been oblivious to this fact when she first moved here and cringed to think of how many hapless starfish she'd walked by. Once Hannah had pointed this out, she'd taken to carefully relocating the stragglers when she found them. Trey had the same habit, which he said he'd developed as a boy. She glanced down to see him gingerly release the starfish into the water where it lapped against the sand.

He rinsed his hands in the water and gave them a quick shake. Without a word, they began walking again. The sounds of late evening on the Alaskan coastline swirled around them—waves rolling softly in and out, the call of a loon who rested near the shore riding the soft rhythm of the water, the beat of a raven's wings against the air, and the sudden sound of water breaking as a pair of seals surfaced. They watched Emma and Trey for a quiet moment, their sleek heads holding still above the water. Another moment passed and they dove in unison back under the water, nothing but a swirl left behind.

Trey reached for her hand. She savored the

strength in his warm grip. The wind started to pick up, gusts coming in bursts off the water.

"Should we head back?" he asked.

Emma turned toward him, the wind blowing her hair across her face as she did. With a laugh, she nodded, brushing her hair out of the way only to have it blow wild again. When they reached the parking lot and climbed into Trey's car, the car was a refuge from the wind that had continued to pick up on their short walk back. Emma ran her hands through her hair, swiftly untangling it.

She looked over to find Trey watching her, his eyes intent. Without a word, he closed the space between them, his lips landing softly on hers. Before she could form a thought, she was ruled by sensation, tugged into the tides of desire that were in flux between them.

Long moments later, he gentled the kiss and pulled a fraction away. "Just had to do that," he whispered, his lips moving against hers.

A slow smile curved her lips, his following until they both laughed. Trey shifted away. He nodded toward the bay when he looked up to start the car. The sun had made its bow, leaving only streaks of fading red and gold above the mountains. The crescent moon was bright now, rising higher in the sky. The water shot glinted sparks in the colored reflections.

They drove home—she was beginning to think of Trey's house as home—and tumbled into bed. Emma fell into a deep sleep. She woke sometime during the night, in the dark, to feel Trey's hands skating over her body—a warm caress on her bottom, a palming of her breast, the roughened skin of his palms scattering a trail of heat. Desire shimmered around them, enveloping her in its spell. They made sleepy love in the quiet of the dark. When Trey slid into her core, she sighed in relief. He held still for a moment. Her channel pulsed around his thickness. A slow draw out and surge back in, and she shattered, careening into an intense orgasm that rippled through her. He captured her cries in a deep kiss, convulsing inside her. Gentling his kiss, he slowly shifted to her side. She fell back into sleep, held skin to skin by him.

* * *

EMMA CAME AWAKE, savoring the warmth from the sun splashed across the bed. The shower was running. Before she could summon the energy to roll out of bed, the shower stopped and Trey came out, a towel wrapped around his waist. She took a moment to enjoy the view. His muscled chest and abdomen rippled as he tugged his shorts on and toweled his hair dry. He chuckled when he found her ogling him. She shrugged and winked as he turned away.

"Want breakfast?" he asked, leaning against the doorframe.

A long look in those chocolate brown eyes and she'd have said yes to anything.

"Definitely. Want me to cook?"

"I got it. How about an omelet?"

"Perfect," she replied before tossing the covers back and heading for the shower.

After she showered, Emma walked into the living room and kitchen area to find a fresh pot of coffee with a mug waiting beside it. Trey was nowhere to be found. She immediately went to get her coffee only to find a folded note inside the mug. *Go outside.* Curiosity prodded her, but she filled her coffee first. Trey had come to know her well. She didn't do much of anything in the morning before she had coffee. A few sips of coffee, and she walked out the kitchen door. The deck was warm under her bare feet, the sun high and bright in the sky.

A bouquet of wildflowers, mostly fireweed and daisies, sat in a vase between two table settings at the small round wooden table on the deck. A small box sat beside the wildflowers with a folded note with an arrow pointing to the box. Unfolding the note, she found a small message from Stuart in his careful scrawl. *I like you. So does my Dad and Tootsie.* A smile bloomed in her heart. She reached for the small box and opened it carefully, her heart beating rapidly. Inside was another note, this one from Trey. *If you want to keep waiting, that's okay. But I wanted you to know just how much you mean to me. Stuart has quite a bit to say about this, so I let him tell you the most important part for him. When you're ready, you can wear this. In the meantime, keep it somewhere safe. I chose the stone because it makes me think of your eyes.*

Inside the unassuming white box lay a beautiful silver ring with a sapphire. Tears tumbled forth, surprising her. She carefully lifted the ring out of the box and held it in her hand. Once it was warm, she slipped it on her finger where it settled in a perfect fit. She heard the door and looked up to find Trey coming out from the kitchen, carrying a warming pan with two omelets in it. His gaze landed on her hand and shifted immediately to her eyes. That current, always between them, quivered with the intensity of his gaze.

"It's beautiful," she said, smiling through the blur of her tears.

Trey set the warming pan on the table and turned to face her. "We can still wait. However long you need. I've been thinking a lot, and I don't want to waste time without you knowing exactly how important you are to me."

Emma shook her head. "We don't have to wait. All that..." she lifted her hand in a small wave, "... worrying about the right time is over for me. Let's just let this be what we already know it is."

Trey pulled her close and rested his forehead against hers. "Okay then. I love you."

She giggled, undone with emotion. "Good thing because I love you too."

Trey pulled away, keeping one of her hands in his, his thumb rubbing across the ring. "So how long do I have to wait before you stop making me run back and forth to your house?" he said with a sly smile.

EPILOGUE

*E*mma leaned down by the garden bed. "Oh wow, Stuart! That cabbage looks well on its way to being record size." The cabbage in question was gigantic by any measure. But it would have steep competition. The last three record size cabbages came from Alaska, the most recent weighing in at one hundred and thirty-eight pounds. Stuart had spent most of last winter reading about gardening and became determined to try to grow a record size cabbage. Emma eyed the giant cabbage, a far cry from those usually found in the grocery store, and glanced down at Stuart who was rubbing the cabbage with his small hands.

He grinned up at her. "Cabbie has a few more weeks before the fair, so she'll be even bigger by then!"

Trey's chuckle followed Stuart's words. Emma turned to find Trey walking to the small garden from the house. He'd returned from a day of flying. His salted black hair was windblown, and his eyes stood out against his tanned skin. He looked delicious in his worn, fitted jeans and the faded black t-shirt that clung to his chest. It was late summer and just about a year since she'd moved in with Trey and Stuart. When she thought back to the fact she'd once thought she should stay out of Trey's life, she couldn't ever believe it had crossed her mind. She hadn't looked back since the day she unpacked her boxes.

Though she stopped hemming and hawing about being with Trey, she'd turned into a raving lunatic when it came to planning her wedding this past spring. Probably because her first wedding didn't hold good memories for her. Tess, who was a fundraiser *not* a wedding planner, gamely stepped in and took over after a girl's night out when it became obvious Emma was careening toward becoming a caricature of the crazed bride. Tess meticulously organized the wedding and enlisted Hannah, Susie and Risa to keep Emma sane during the process.

The wedding had been perfect. They'd married on Trey's boat, anchored in Kachemak Bay, as close as Trey could guess to where they'd first kissed. Seeing as Trey's boat could only hold six occupants legally, they had been surrounded by three other boats that held family and friends. Only she, Trey, Stuart and the pastor had been on Trey's boat. She'd removed her life jacket during the brief ceremony, her wedding dress ruffling in the soft breeze.

Trey knelt down beside Stuart's beloved cabbage, gave it a pat and Stuart a hug before standing to drop a kiss on her cheek. He carried the scent of the ocean and a tang of spruce on him.

"So do we have fresh halibut for dinner?" Emma asked as they turned to walk inside, hands loosely clasped. Stuart lingered by his cabbage until Trey called over his shoulder for him to come inside.

"You have options for dinner: halibut or king salmon. Ran into Jared who had a cooler full and handed a few over. It's on the small size for a king, but king salmon doesn't get any better."

"How about halibut and king salmon for dinner?" she parried.

Trey chuckled and swatted her bottom when they walked through the screen door into the kitchen. Hours later, she lounged on the couch, her legs thrown across Trey's lap while she read a book and he watched the news. He flicked the television off and glanced over. She set her book down while his palm slid up her thigh, lighting a trail of sparks in its wake. The passion between them had only multiplied in the past year. He took her breath away just about every day. Yet again, she lost herself in the heat of his gaze. His palm crested over her abdomen and paused. "You haven't mentioned how your appointment went today," he said, an eyebrow lifted.

Emma giggled. "We agreed we wouldn't talk about it in front of Stuart yet, so I was waiting." She paused and took a breath, a wash of emotion cresting inside. "It's not like I didn't already know, but it's not just a fluke on the pregnancy test. I'm pregnant. She thinks I'm about six weeks along."

Trey tugged her close for a searing kiss. When he pulled away, he rested his forehead against hers and sighed. She closed her eyes and took a breath. A life she'd written off was happening.

Thank you for reading Love Unbroken - I hope you loved Trey & Emma's story!

For more steamy, small town romance, Susie & Jared's story is next in Love Untamed. For years, the spark between Susie & Jared has been on slow burn. When it finally ignites, passion and emotions explode. An epic enemies to lovers romance, don't miss Jared's story!

For more swoony & sassy romance…

This Crazy Love kicks off the Swoon Series - small town southern romance with enough heat to melt you! Jackson & Shay's story is epic - swoon-worthy & intensely emotional. Jackson just happens to be Shay's brother's best friend. He's also *seriously* easy on the eyes. Shay has a past, the kind of past she would most definitely like to forget. Past or not, Jackson is about to rock her world. Don't miss their story! Free on all retailers!

Burn For Me is a second chance romance for the ages. Sexy firefighters? Check. Rugged men? Check. Wrapped up together? Check. Brave the fire in this hot, small-town romance. Amelia & Cade were high school sweethearts & then it all fell apart. When they cross paths again, it's epic - don't miss Cade's story! Free on all retailers!

For more small town romance, take a visit to Last Frontier Lodge in Diamond Creek. A sexy, alpha SEAL meets his match with a brainy heroine in Take Me Home. Marley is all brains & Gage is all brawn.

Sparks fly when their worlds collide. Don't miss Gage
& Marley's story!
Free on all retailers!

If sports romance lights your spark, check out The
Play. Liam is a British footballer who falls for Olivia,
his doctor. A twist of forbidden heats up this swoon-
worthy & laugh-out-loud romance. Don't miss Liam
& Olivia's story.
Free on all retailers!

Sign up for my newsletter, so you can receive
information about upcoming new releases & receive a
FREE copy of one of my books: http://jhcroixauthor.
com/subscribe/

FIND MY BOOKS

Thank you for reading Love Unbroken! I hope you enjoyed the story. If so, you can help other readers find my books in a variety of ways.

1) Write a review!

2) Sign up for my newsletter, so you can receive information about upcoming new releases & receive a FREE copy of one of my books: http://jhcroixauthor.com/subscribe/

3) Like and follow my Amazon Author page at https://amazon.com/author/jhcroix

4) Follow me on Bookbub at https://www.bookbub.com/authors/j-h-croix

5) Follow me on Twitter at https://twitter.com/JHCroix

6) Like my Facebook page at https://www.facebook.com/jhcroix

* * *

Visit my store to purchase ebooks & fun swag!

J.H. Croix Shop

Diamond Creek Alaska Novels
When Love Comes
Follow Love
Love Unbroken
Love Untamed
Tumble Into Love
Christmas Nights
Last Frontier Lodge Novels
Take Me Home
Love at Last
Just This Once
Falling Fast
Stay With Me
When We Fall
Hold Me Close
Crazy For You
Just Us
Fireweed Harbor Series
When We Meet - free prequel!
Make You Mine
Dare To Fall - due out June 2023!
Be The One - due out October 2023!
Light My Fire Series
Wild With You
Hold Me Now
Only Ever Us
Fall For Me
Keep Me Close
With Every Breath
All It Takes
Take Me Now - due out August 2023!
Dare With Me Series

Crash Into You
Evers & Afters
Come To Me
Back To Us
Take Me There
After We Fall
Swoon Series
This Crazy Love
Wait For Me
Break My Fall
Truly Madly Mine
Still Go Crazy
If We Dare
Steal My Heart
Into The Fire Series
Burn For Me
Slow Burn
Burn So Bad
Hot Mess
Burn So Good
Sweet Fire
Play With Fire
Melt With You
Burn For You
Crash & Burn
That Snowy Night
Brit Boys Sports Romance
The Play
Big Win
Out Of Bounds
Play Me
Naughty Wish

RESOURCES

*L*ove Unbroken is a love story above all, but its heroine, Emma, only finds her happy ending after escaping a marriage that involved domestic violence. Domestic violence is a social problem of massive proportions. It is estimated that approximately 20 people per minute experience physical abuse by an intimate partner in the United States, which translates to more than 10 million victims per year (National Coalition Against Domestic Violence, 2015). It is devastating and has life-long effects for victims, families and children touched by it. If you or anyone you know has experienced domestic violence (emotional, physical, psychological), there are resources for help.

THE NATIONAL DOMESTIC VIOLENCE HOTLINE: http://www.thehotline.org
1-800-799-SAFE (7233)

. . .

NATIONAL COALITION AGAINST DOMESTIC VIOLENCE: http://www.ncadv.org

DOMESTICSHELTERS.ORG: https://www.domesticshelters.org

NATIONAL DATING ABUSE HOTLINE (for teens and youth): http://www.loveisrespect.org
1-866-331-9474

NATIONAL CHILD ABUSE HOTLINE/CHILDHELP: www.childhelp.org
1-800-4-A-CHILD (1-800-422-4453)

NATIONAL SEXUAL ASSAULT HOTLINE: www.rainn.org
1-800-656-4673 (HOPE)

NATIONAL CENTER for Victims of Crime: www.victimsofcrime.org
1-202-467-8700

ACKNOWLEDGMENTS

A toast to my husband – you stole my heart, you make me laugh every day, *and* you are still my biggest cheerleader. My mother graciously provides me with free tech support, and she's as skilled and much nicer than anyone professional I could find. Humble thanks to Laura Kingsley who edited this story with grace and honesty.

My readers...wow. Thank you for such fabulous support! Writing the Diamond Creek Novels lets me revisit Alaska in my mind, a place I love dearly. To that wild and wonderful place – much gratitude for its simple existence and the amazing friends I found there.

xoxo

J.H. Croix

ABOUT THE AUTHOR

USA Today Bestselling Author J.H. Croix lives in a small town in Maine with her husband and two spoiled dogs. Croix writes contemporary romance with sassy women and alpha men who aren't afraid to show some emotion. Her love for quirky small-towns and the characters that inhabit them shines through in her writing. Take a walk on the wild side of romance with her bestselling novels!

Places you can find me:
jhcroixauthor.com
jhcroix@jhcroix.com

facebook.com/jhcroix
instagram.com/jhcroix
bookbub.com/authors/j-h-croix